A NOVEL

DANIEL JAKACIC

ISBN: 978-1-953865-75-5 (Paperback)
ISBN: 978-1-953865-76-2 (eBook)
Library of Congress Control Number: 2024907379

This is a work of fiction. Although its form is, or may be similar to, that of an autobiography, it is not one. Related matters, including space and time, have been rearranged to suit the convenience of the book, and with the exception of public figures, any resemblance to persons living or dead is coincidental. The opinions expressed are those of the characters and should not be confused with those of the author. Any references to historical events, real people, or real places are used fictitiously. All characters, incidents, and dialogue are drawn from the author's imagination and are not to be construed as real.

Books Fluent
New Orleans, Louisiana

To my mother,
and all those running toward something better

ACKNOWLEDGMENTS

Thank you, my dear Mum, for all your support. I love you more than words can ever convey. No amount of thanks will ever express the depth of my gratitude to you. Thanks, Dad, for all your help. We still need and love you. Someday, we'll all be together again. Until then, rest in peace. Thanks to all those whose assistance made this novel possible. In particular, I would like to thank Emily Colin for editing the manuscript and for providing the description on the cover. I would also like to thank Eric Labacz for the cover design and Hannah Robertson, Publishing Director at Books Fluent, along with her team, for managing publication of the book. Thanks to Hannah Gaskamp for the interior design. Finally, I'd also like to thank you for reading.

LIVING WITH COMMUNISM

Hiding in the back of the van hurtling toward the checkpoint, I tried to calm myself. *Mum will have woken up long ago and realized I've gone.* My heart ached. *She'll be sick with worry, crying, inconsolable. Dad, Val, and Lina will be doing their best to calm her.* Under the tarp, alone in the darkness, I sobbed and tried to imagine life without ever again seeing my family, the farm, and everything and everyone I'd ever loved. *God, please give me strength.*

I recalled Dad's advice, "Stay focused. Remember the times we went across before and act the same."

I'd loved and been loved and had done what I thought was right, the way my parents had taught me. Neither prison nor death could ever take that away from me. I wasn't sure who I'd be on the other side, but there was no time for doubt and no telling the driver I wanted to go back. In minutes, I'd either be free, in shackles, or dead by a border guard's bullet. In spite of all the help, I figured my chances weren't good. After the driver let me out, if I could make it to the checkpoint on my bicycle without Dragon's men spotting me, at least I'd have a chance. Palms pressed together tightly, I prayed for the best, for God's mercy, and to take me quick, if it came to that. I'd heard the stories but tried not to think about what they'd do to me if they caught me alive.

Even with my pass, I was terrified. I'd have been insane not to be, but I was also excited at the closeness of freedom. Others without paperwork had attempted to cross along what they thought was some deserted track. Some made it, but they didn't have the same enemies I had. I kept praying. *Please, God, don't let me make a mistake!*

More than anything, I was exhausted, sick of keeping quiet and always looking over my shoulder. I found some solace. Nobody could ever rob me of who I was. I reminded myself of why I was escaping and how grateful I'd be to make it. Could I ever forgive myself for the pain I'd caused Mum? The prospect of life and liberty on the other side was a kind of joy I knew existed but had rarely experienced.

After the war, possibly the autumn of 1946, my weary nine-year-old heart came to know pure joy for the first time. It's tough recalling exactly when the triumphs of peace and Dad returning from war—alive and in one wonderful piece—resurrected my childhood. But more importantly, it happened. Dad's return wiped away all the relentless fear and havoc that had hung over my older sister Lina, Mum, and me, like some enormous boulder constantly teetering on the edge of a towering cliff. The joy was short-lived. Years later, following that joy would lead me to lose everything I'd worked so hard for. Fascists during the war, Communists after, different goons, same idea: lie, take over, steal everything, kill anyone in the way. When there's nothing left to steal, make a war somewhere and repeat the process.

When the Italian Fascists took Dad, I felt completely naked and exposed, we all did, but Mum somehow kept us going, along with what was left of our farm. Could anything beat the happiness and gratitude in '46 of putting all that behind us? Maybe that was the best time in my life. Back then, dreaming of success was the farthest thing from my mind. Life on our little farm was freedom and all the world

I could ever want.

One of my favorite things was rambling through the forest with Spartacus, our Labrador. Finding a quiet bit of woodland, I'd lie on a pristine and fragrant bed of maple leaves or pine needles. Through swaying branches, the wind gently whistled its hypnotic tune as birds sung a happy chorus. Bright shafts of sunlight made the leaves sparkle in the swirling breeze. Lying against me, his tail happily flapping, Spartacus would bury his warm, moist nose into my side, constantly sniffing for attention while I'd hum the melody to whatever silly song I'd made up. Singing folk and religious songs was something Lina and I did for fun, never anything we took seriously. Happiness was simple and weightless, yet so intense it brought tears to my eyes, eyes weary from too many horrors. Knowing we'd made it filled me with light. All the dark fear was gone, at least so I'd thought.

The most joyful part of those times was having Dad back. Somehow even our prized bull, our beloved Aristotle, a gentle and noble behemoth, had come through unscathed, along with a ragtag assortment of other farm critters. Occasional nightmares and unwelcome memories still sometimes intruded during the day. It was hard comprehending hidden flows of emotion that followed their own logic.

In '48, Lina and I jumped at the news we'd be getting a brother. That more than anything helped place in time what was otherwise a timeless interlude for me, between the Fascists leaving in '44 and the Communists choking the life out of everything by the mid-50s. Mum was certain the baby would be a boy. She'd even picked out a name, Val. I instantly loved the name and marveled at her certitude but didn't for a moment question it.

Whatever our challenges, it was wonderful growing up knowing my family loved me. It gave me a sense of certainty and solidity about who I was, even from a young age. I don't think my parents ever consciously tried to cultivate it; it was just there. It was a joy that burned inside like a gentle but inextinguishable flame. That pure love was the greatest gift I'd ever been given. It gave me something warm and sure to hold on to.

After the war, Lina and I couldn't wait for the future to arrive. We'd lay awake at night dreaming about it out loud. Before bed, we'd pray for Mum and Dad, our farm, our health, togetherness, and a brighter future. God had different plans.

There'd been talk in our village, Zana, that the Communist government was hunting subversives, but we didn't know what it meant. Gossip grew that the secret police were collecting information about everyone. Rumors circulated about harassment, arrests, torture, even murders. Some said officials deliberately targeted innocent people to leave no doubt. There were no boundaries.

Communist propaganda encouraged people to report anyone criticizing the government, even family members. Religion was banned. All were to be reborn into a new faith, an insane brew they called reductivist empiricism, just a fancy way of saying God didn't exist. To us Catholics, Communists were deluded lunatics dancing merrily to Satan's tune. To urbane Communists, we were ignorant country folk needing re-education. Their way of admitting they were impatient for our demise. Curiously, they still wanted us to see them as charming and enlightened. Their newspapers promised prosperity and protection, even from atomic fireballs. Nobody believed it. We knew the Japanese had been vaporized and melted, dripping discarded flesh, not even fit for maggots.

Despite our loathing of Communism, we respected Tito, the national leader and genuine war hero who stood up to Stalin. It was Tito who kept us from falling into the Soviet abyss, and we were grateful for that much. Many countries fully behind the iron curtain had it worse than us. From our perspective, Tito was a strong but terribly fearsome father. There was definitely no utopia for us in the regime's vision of independence from East and West. For those who didn't stand to gain from all the lies, theft, and false promises, there was little to show for all the suffering, except perhaps bitter survival. We didn't know whether all the stories we heard were true, but the message was clear enough— the regime wasn't squeamish about doing whatever it took to keep power. As Catholic Slovenians with family ties to Italy and Austria, we were not well placed to prosper in this new larger country, Yugoslavia. Communist propagandists pretending to be journalists were constantly talking up threats from the East and West. Mostly, they'd bang on about enemies within. Naturally, this included Catholics.

Communists did more than write in newspapers. They'd dragged priests out of churches during Mass and if they failed to renounce God, they'd shoot them on the spot. The warm body bleeding out, the executioners would give a sermon on the evils of religion, decree Church festivals, ceremonies, and gatherings banned, and warn about what could happen to those who didn't leave the Church. Many brave priests continued holding Mass in people's houses. These tiny congregations were often infiltrated by informers. Beatings, arrests, torture, and murders followed. Sometimes the informer was the priest himself. Eventually, an uneasy truce prevailed. The price of faith was living with discrimination.

As might be expected, absorbing everyone into some miasmic Communist blob created resentment. Those not on the take didn't much like subsidizing lavish lifestyles for countless local petty despots. Oppressive taxation without liberty, privacy, a say, or prospects was a good recipe for unrest. As long as technology and informers couldn't read our minds, we could always dream of better days. Anger, resentment, and hope thrived.

I never spent much time in formal schooling, but I think my siblings and I received quite an education. These days, I sometimes wonder if the reverse is true. I'm not sure if learning ever ends, but it's the personal and immediate part of learning that made me want to write. Having said that, no one should intentionally rely on anything here as accurate or truthful. I grew up with stories. Some were about Yugoslavia. Some may have ended up here, as fiction. Maybe some people can lay out stories in one unbroken, even stream of immutable truth. Not me. If you're looking for propaganda, you need not look far. Radio. Television. Perhaps even history books. If you're looking for the truth, God help you. God help us all. Maybe the burden of searching and occasionally sharing should be meaning and truth enough?

I scarcely ever dreamed of writing anything more than reminder notes to self. Not that reminders aren't important, especially now that I'm old. To me, writing feels like rocks poking up above the frothy surface of a fast-flowing river, slippery islands jutting out above the white fury of life's present concerns. Before I go, I'd like to linger on those rocks to get a better sense of life's fast-flowing river, but the rocks are slippery, and there's so much swirling around demanding attention that it's not always possible to linger. Perhaps committing something, such as it is, to paper is a way of helping me navigate the river.

In my youth, if the news of Val's impending arrival was one of the happiest memories, losing Aristotle was one of the worst. I thought I might not be able to bear it. With our farm still struggling to recover from the war, Dad announced he'd decided to sell Aristotle. I immediately knew Aristotle would not be long for this world and pleaded with Dad not to do it. It was one of the only times in my life I ever shouted at Mum or Dad. I was ashamed of myself, but I didn't know what to do. The tears poured out of me until I couldn't stand it. I ran out of the kitchen, to the end of the hall, and collapsed onto the floor in the corner. Lina came to console me. I tried telling her it was all right, but I could hardly speak through my sobbing. It was not all right.

I ran to the barn to find Aristotle. He was standing in his favorite spot, looking at me with his big black eyes glistening in the lamplight. He nodded, like he knew something was up. I carefully hung the lamp and tried hugging his massive neck. I tried to be strong, but I couldn't stop crying. Aristotle, gentle and stoic as ever, let out a couple of bellowing breaths. I wanted to stay with him all night. Eventually, Mum came, rubbed my back, kissed me on the top of my head, and told me to come inside.

The next day, Mum, Lina, Spartacus, and I walked next to Aristotle as Dad led him up the road to a house on the other side of Zana. Nobody said a word. I felt so ashamed and scared for Aristotle. At the house, a man exchanged a few words with Dad and gave him some money—Aristotle was no longer part of our family. I did my best to keep it together and gave Aristotle one last hug. As we walked away from the house, I cried and turned to look at Aristotle one last time. He was looking straight at me. He raised his majestic head and let out a loud and long bellowing cry, the kind I'd never heard from him before, as if he knew we wouldn't see each other again. I shook and sobbed all the way home. We'd sold a member of our family. I couldn't stop crying for days. I couldn't even bear to look at Aristotle's favorite part of the barn for weeks.

One day, I saw Dad standing in Aristotle's spot in the barn, his head bowed, shoulders hunched over. Putting my hand on his shoulder, Dad turned away. He'd been crying. It wasn't something he did often.

I took off my boots and socks. "Look, Dad, don't you remember?" I pointed at my toes.

"What are you talking about?" he said.

The big toe on my right foot was a little smaller than my other one because while still young, Aristotle had accidentally stepped on it with a hind hoof.

Dad nodded. "You screamed in agony."

"I thought he'd clean chopped it off!" I said. "But my toe was still there, bright red and throbbing. Mum came running, asking what was going on, and I accused Aristotle of being clumsy while I'd been cleaning his space."

"After inspecting your toe, Mum chided you, saying Aristotle had always been interested in you since you were a baby," Dad said.

I reached up and wiped the tears from his cheeks.

The only reason I still had that toe was because Aristotle had immediately rebalanced himself so as to not crush it. If anyone had been clumsy, it'd been me. There was a lot more to Aristotle than I'd thought. Growing up around him, I think he knew I loved him. We all did. Aristotle probably understood more than I'll ever realize.

Aristotle taught me letting go of family was impossible; I could only keep loving them and live with the pain of separation. It was a lesson that came in handy when, not long after Aristotle passed, we lost another member of the family. A big fancy car—Communist flags on the front flapping furiously as it sped through Zana—ran over Spartacus. Between Mum, Dad, Lina, and me, there were too many tears to count. For weeks, I'd cry every time I passed an old collar hanging near the door. I could hardly bear to look at it. Eventually, Dad took it away. But that made me cry even more. At least we could give Spartacus a decent burial.

CHAPTER 1

FIELDS OF GREEN AND GOLD

The midday sun roasted everything as I swung my scythe hard. I'd worked a good clip from sunup, and my muscles screamed with fatigue. I chose not to mind. There was quiet pleasure in guiding each stroke, neatly felling pocket after pocket of wheat. My mind focused, my breathing deep and steady, my body kept its familiar rhythm. I rode the rhythm through the fatigue like many times before. The possibility of singing at the harvest festival, White Sunday, reminded me how eager I was to perform again. Best not get distracted with a sharp blade in hand. *First work, then play at singing!* I gently refocused. *Watch out for snakes, and whatever you do, don't bend the blade on a rock or you'll never make it.* I kept my mind quiet, and my body became one with the tool. Sometimes, the wheat sang to me. Sometimes, I'd sing back. Eventually, the urge for water got the better of me. I eased up, and the blade came to rest lightly, my aching hands releasing their grip. Break time.

I joined Val under the shade of the old almond tree on the edge of our wheat field, our favorite resting spot at this field for many a year. He was pretending to read his schoolbook.

"You're sweating like a pig, Anja," jibed Val as I wiped my brow.

"If you study hard and finish high school, maybe one day you won't have to," I replied.

"Schoolbooks are boring. There's always some crap about Communism. I'd rather learn about farming."

"You should finish your book anyway. Wouldn't you like to be the first in our family to finish high school?"

Val shrugged and handed me a flagon of water, invitingly cool to the touch.

"Every year, you get quicker and quicker. Lina's a couple of years older than you, and you're faster than her now. Even Dad can't keep up anymore. When are you going to teach me?"

"I'm not that much faster. Age, strength, and technique all matter differently for different people, I guess. I'll teach you when you get straight As," I joked, putting the flagon to my lips.

Val kicked at the dirt, making me laugh.

"I'll teach you. But seriously, you have to get straight As, not just a few. Otherwise, forget it."

Val buried himself in his book. Looking out over the expanse of wheat in which Dad, Mum, and Lina continued to work, I admired how steadfastly they labored. Next to that was another similarly sized field of rich clover that also belonged to us. I gave Val a pat on the back.

"I don't blame you for wanting to be a farmer. It looks beautiful in the light, doesn't it?" I asked, pointing at the shimmering waves of gold and emerald swaying gently in the breeze. Looking over the fields, Val smiled. He was truly our father's son.

Our fields of wheat and clover, nestled in thick forest, were a forty-minute walk from home. There was no one else around, yet everywhere was music. It was in the breeze in nearby trees, in the woodlarks chirping, the cicadas rattling, and the scythes cutting. Harvesting was brutal but glorious work. There just wasn't any better feeling than all of us working together as one.

Lina joined Val and me under the almond tree. I handed her the flagon.

"We're making good progress," I happily observed.

"Yes, you're leading the way as usual," she replied, breathlessly wiping her lips. Lina and I broke into exasperated laughter at how drained we both looked. Mum and Dad walked slowly toward us.

"Val, please take another flagon to them," I said.

Val, glad to have something to do other than clutch his schoolbook, swept up another flagon and took off like a jackrabbit.

Dad patted Val on the back, put an arm around him, and passed the flagon he'd delivered to Mum. All of us reunited under the almond tree, Val wasted no time parking our scythes in a neat row and got busy sharpening blades. It was a task he performed with unusual care and skill for someone of his tender years. Val, helpful, sharp, athletic, even handsome, not that I'd ever have told him! I felt sorry for him. No matter how good his grades, the Communist Party would never let a Catholic Slovenian boy like him have a job that was worthy of him. It was a good thing farming was among the most noble of things. It was a good thing he dreamed of nothing else.

"It's good we'll finish in a few days," said Mum, red-faced and huffing.

"A bumper crop. But it couldn't get much more mature without spoiling," observed Dad.

Harvesting was a race against time. The last few years we'd been winning. It was just as well, because I couldn't stand the thought of the endless work of weeding throughout the growing season going to waste. Apart from the satisfaction of finishing, the prospect of enjoying a few days' rest before White Sunday were strong incentives to get it done.

"Dad, are we going to finish in time for White Sunday?" asked Val, on cue.

White Sunday had been going on for eons. People from all over the district came and put as much effort into having fun as they did into farm work. For Lina and me, it was a chance to sing with proper musicians. The eagerness of people to sing along and their raucous applause tasted better than a big dollop of fresh cream. I knew we were on track to make White Sunday. But Dad's response wasn't inspiring.

"We'll go. I think it's going to be different this year. Government people are running it, so a lot of farmers we know aren't going," said

Dad. Lina and I exchanged disappointed looks. *There goes our opportunity to perform.*

"But Dad, what's a harvest festival without farmers?" exclaimed Val.

"In that case, there's no need for us to go," declared Mum, in a disinterested tone. Dad had other ideas.

"We'll still go. I want to see a fellow about getting a permit to sell produce over the border. Trieste isn't far and it sucks in everything the region can throw at it," said Dad.

Mum and Lina were unimpressed. But Val's face lit up at the unrealistic expectation he'd be part of some exciting Italian adventure.

I couldn't blame Mum and Lina for not liking Dad's plan. Cross-border selling was ever riskier because of the increasing bribes it took to get the permits. The profits made staying under the radar of corrupt officials that much harder. Slovenian farmers were meant to stay poor and invisible, not show signs of ambitious capitalist tendencies.

"Let's have something to eat," said Mum in frustration. Her face was as red as beetroot.

We all helped Mum unpack our spread of sauerkraut soup, potato and sausage salad, salami, prosciutto, mortadella, boiled eggs, pecorino, tomatoes, olives, and roasted peppers, along with my favorite crusty, fluffy bread. It was perfect for ripping and dipping into a nice bit of olive oil, washed down with homemade wine, coffee, and kamilica caj. As a final lunch treat, Mum reached into a basket and, as if by magic, pulled out a bowl of roasted chestnuts and baked apples. Dad passed on dessert, instead opting for his special harvest lunchtime dessert of a raw egg. Val, as much as he admired Dad, could never quite manage to hide his disgust as he watched Dad prick a tiny hole at each end and then suck out the contents. Refueled and rested, we packed up and headed back out to the field.

"Remember those grades," I said, pointing at the schoolbook as we left Val under the almond tree.

CHAPTER 2
HAYRIDE

Come White Sunday, I woke up well before dawn. No singing and no butterflies this year, but the wood and the well were still calling. The full moon seeping in through the windows lit my way as I crept downstairs, floorboards creaking underfoot. Draping a coat over my nightie and goose bumps, I headed for the barn. Our cows, massive sentinels in the dark, huffed and puffed their good-morning greeting.

"Good morning, it's only me," I whispered, as a couple of the gentle behemoths moved their hay about. The chickens were a bunch of easily-disturbed individuals, so I took care not to startle anyone. Aristotle's old spot was still empty. None were interested in taking it. *Oh, Aristotle, I miss you so much. It's just not the same without you.* Wooden buckets and yoke in hand, I quietly loaded up kindling and a few logs. I did my best not to scream as a mouse, more terrified than I, scurried away. After stoking the kitchen woodstove, I hurried to the well. Warming my hands against the kitchen stove, I heard the muffled sound of arguing upstairs. *No butterflies there either, I suppose. I know who's going to win that argument, not that it's going to make any difference. Better get more water.*

I could have sat in the bath all morning, but Lina poked her head in. "Is the water still warm?"

We didn't take baths every day; there wasn't time. Daily washes were out of a bucket of cold water. Face, armpits, privates, and feet. The only beauty routine was going to bed early.

Lina poured in another bucket of hot water and undressed. I was barely out as she got in.

"I don't hear any more shouting," I remarked. Lina giggled.

"We're still going," came her sanguine response.

"No surprise there. I'm curious to see what it's like even though I'm sure it'll be crap," I ventured.

"I agree. Pity we won't be singing," said Lina.

"After so many years on that stage, I don't even want to think about it. I'm going to miss it. Anyway, who'd want to sing for Communists?" I said, drying off.

Freshened up, I floated into the kitchen to find Mum had already milked the cows and was boiling milk. Two pots of coffee were on the go, one super-strength for Dad. She also had bread baking and polenta and porridge simmering. The aromas of milk, bread, and coffee swirling around brought a smile to my face and made my tummy rumble. I hugged Mum extra tight and gave her big kisses on both cheeks.

"Good morning, my wonderful Mum. I'll get more water so you and Dad can have a good scrub," I said, without mentioning their shouting. Before I could move, she firmly but gently pushed me toward a chair. I wedged my hands under my thighs with delight as she went back and forth between the stove and the table, putting a coffeepot, bread, and a pot of boiled milk on the table in front of me.

"Eat," she commanded, running a hand lovingly over the top of my head.

"Thank you, Ma," I said gratefully. *Thank you, dear God, for this food I'm about to receive and for my lovely Mum who looks after us so well.*

Pouring steaming coffee into a wide bowl was to pour myself a bowl of pure bliss. My whole chest filled with the energizing aroma. In went lots of boiled milk. The crusty bread, still beautifully warm, tore easily. Ripping a generous piece filled my flaring nostrils with the smell of intense satisfaction. I could have inhaled the whole loaf. *Oh, how I love bread!*

Dipping the bread into the silky strong brew, I hummed with anticipation. Dribbles of coffee ran down my chin as the hot, coffee-soaked bread hit my tongue. Mum tipped more freshly baked bread onto the table and put two apples in front me. She knew the green apples from the trees growing wild in the courtyard were a favorite.

Before long, Lina, Val, and Dad came in. Mum poured Dad some coffee out of his special little pot. It was more like shiny, slick mud than actual liquid. As Mum poured, Dad impatiently rubbed his clean-shaven face. He added a touch of milk and carefully swirled the dirty mess around a few times. Lifting the sludge to his lips, he enthusiastically slurped at the grittiness. Soon after, I knew he'd announce he was going for a smoke, and sure enough. . .

"I'm going outside for a smoke, woman," he said, in a mock snarl.

"Be quick about it then, man," Mum said, in mock sheepishness.

Dad took his tobacco and pipe from the pantry where he kept his stash and winked at me as he headed outside. After breakfast, we washed dishes and put on our nicest clothes, the ones we only wore to church or special occasions. Lina, Val, and I were resplendent in our clean and freshly pressed clothes, all the promise of youth, lovingly nourished. Crisp white linen shirts. Black linen skirts with hems just past the knee. Scarfs to cover our heads and cream-colored short socks in black, low-heeled, leather shoes on our feet.

Dad and Val both looked smart in their white linen shirts, black linen suits, black leather shoes all shined up, and hunting caps.

"Mum, thanks to your needlework we look lovely," I said.

"Yes, indeed we do. Nobody makes clothes as good as you," agreed Dad heartily, enveloping Mum in a hug, at which point we all piled in. Mum was perturbed but also flattered we were making a fuss over her.

"If we're going, let's get this over with," said Mum, still unhappy we were going at all.

Dad wasn't given to false praise. Mum was the best seamstress I'd ever seen. Anything from her hands always fit better, was flattering, and was of finer workmanship than anything I ever tried on in a store. She scrimped and saved to buy the best, longest-lasting material available, linen or hemp. She cut patterns and sewed by hand or with a foot-powered sewing machine she guarded with her life. What couldn't be sewed, like socks and jumpers, she knitted. I'd watched her like a hawk make all these marvels from as early as I could remember. As soon as I could, I became her eager apprentice.

"I don't make shoes and hats. Fix, yes, but make, no," said Mum.

"Not many can buy material, let alone shoes and hats. After the war, too many people had nothing but rags on their feet and not much else for their modesty. Without good clothes, many didn't make it a single winter," I observed.

Dad chimed in, "Anja, at eighteen years of age, you might feel all grown up, but to me it feels like it was just yesterday when you were but a child who'd turned eleven. We sold a cow to buy you your first pair of proper shoes. Before then, you wore your slippers everywhere or borrowed an oversized pair of shoes from Lina, Mum, or me."

"Yes! What a special day. We went to Sezana. You bought me the best pair we could find. They were a bit oversized, but I could have walked to the moon and back, especially as I grew into them." Going to school in slippers, in the snow, was better than wrapping my feet in rags like many other kids did, but it still wasn't much fun. Coming into this world not that long before the war, I don't remember there being much room for childhood, at eleven or any other age. The sights, sounds, and smells of death and destruction in war were all frequent visitors. Kids grew up pretty quick. Even when I was younger, I could see the war in other kids' faces, just as I knew they could see it in mine.

"I didn't mind spending the money because I knew how well you'd look after them and how well Mum would be able to repair them," said Dad.

"I lost count of how many times Mum was able to re-sole those shoes until they finally fell apart," I replied. *Those first pair of shoes were my first crush.*

"Are we going to talk about shoes all day, or are we going to White Sunday?" asked Mum, at which point we all drowned her in another group hug. *She pretends to be annoyed, but I see how her eyes sparkle. It just makes me want to hug her even more tightly.*

It would take a good hour to get to White Sunday in Sezana by oxcart. While Mum checked that all the windows and doors to the house were bolted shut, Dad hitched up the cart.

Mum and Dad sat up front while the rest of us sat on some hay bales in back. Warmish sun overhead, cicadas making their soothing racket, and a mild breeze in our faces, it was a pleasant ride. Dad pulled Mum toward him; she readily slid over and put an arm around him.

Any previous year, we would have expected to see other families on the road heading for White Sunday, but not this year.

"Are they going to let the two of you sing this year?" asked Val.

"I doubt it," I replied.

"It's their loss," said Dad.

"We're not the right kind of people," said Lina.

"What do you mean?" asked Val.

"We're not Communists, that's why," said Mum.

"But that doesn't make any sense. It's a harvest festival without farmers, and now it's a festival without singing. Why did we bother getting dressed up?" asked Val.

"Exactly!" said Mum.

"The people running the country have some funny ideas, Val," answered Dad.

"I thought the war was supposed to fix all that," observed Val.

"I'm not sure if wars fix anything, at least not for people like us," said Dad.

"Dad, you hardly ever talk about the war. Why is that?" asked Val.

"Not talking about the war is good," interjected Mum.

"It's all right, Val. I understand your curiosity. As you know, I wasn't fighting. After the prison camp, I was traveling with soldiers and nursing the wounded," said Dad.

"But. . ." said Val, wanting more.

"Val, I have a war story for you," I said, enticing Val's curiosity away from Dad.

Val looked at me suspiciously. "But you were only a little girl," he said.

"Yes, but this story has lots of soldiers in it," I said. Val was unconvinced.

"We hadn't heard from Dad in a long time. Most of the farm had gone to seed and most of the livestock had been slaughtered. The only reason Aristotle survived was because Mum hid him in the forest. There wasn't much fat on our bones, but thanks to Mum, we scraped by," I said.

"Sounds awful, but where are the soldiers?" asked Val.

"The partisans that came through Zana were exhausted, smelly, dirty, and always looking for anything they could take. One day, they told us the Germans were retreating, and the Americans and the English were not far away. Lina and I screeched with delight. For a little while, we even forgot how hungry we were," I said.

"I'm not enjoying this story," said Val, making Lina laugh.

"Stay with me. A week later, old Diana from up the road went around screaming all of Italy, Slovenia, and Croatia were liberated. Mum took Lina and I to the square. People were smiling, tears in their eyes, hugging and kissing. Some kissed the ground. Some prayed. Others laughed, danced, and congratulated each other. Some huddled, their drained faces watching divot-riddled walls with empty eyes," I said, catching Val's interest.

"Yes, I heard about those walls," said Val. Mum shook her head. She didn't want me feeding Val's curiosity about those walls.

"The next morning before sunrise, Mum woke us up and told us to get dressed. We, and many others, walked all the way to Sezana, over four hours. We ate breakfast—stale bread and water. We were lucky to pick some wild, under-ripe apples on the way. But we were so happy, our feet hardly touched the ground. I kept hoping Dad could come home," I said.

"Was Dad in Sezana?" asked Val.

"No. As we got closer, it got crowded. In Sezana, people from all over the region had gathered. We wormed our way onto Main Street to the edge of the footpath. Everyone was pitifully emaciated. Many wore little more than torn rags. But everyone was smiling, talking, and laughing. A priest and some helpers handed out little partisan, British, and American flags from a big sack. Someone played a piano accordion. The loud roar of cheering from down the road drowned it out. The cheering and piano accordion got louder and louder until everyone around us started cheering and waving their little flags. Lina and I squealed and excitedly squeezed Mum's hands," I said.

"Then the soldiers marched past," said Val.

"Sort of. The man with the piano accordion appeared. Behind him came rows of men marching loosely—partisans. Some hobbled, bloody bandages tied around their bodies, sheer determination carrying them strongly. Others were so broken, they had to be carried, their patched-up clothing worn ragged. Those who could, proudly wore assorted guns and belts dotted with ammunition. Some looked grim, others stoic, some blank, but mostly they were smiling," I said.

"Did people cheer?" asked Val.

"Many gasped. Some covered their faces. Others put their hands to their cheeks and cried. Some went to them, kissing cheeks and hugging them," I said.

"Wow, the partisans were pretty cool," said Val.

"When they came to our house, Mum always freely gave whatever she could. But they'd often turn everything upside down, demanding more food or alcohol or anything else they thought they could have. We were lucky to survive. If Mum didn't hide livestock and food in the forest, I'm sure we'd have lost everything and starved," I said.

"So you didn't like them much," said Val.

"They were fighting Nazis, and we were very grateful for that. In Sezana, we cheered happily as they limped past. Then the Americans swaggered up, marching in neat rows behind their stars and stripes," I said.

"Did people at least give them a cheer?" asked Val impatiently.

"No, the crowd absolutely erupted. Onlookers cried, yelled, and screamed. People clapped and hugged those around them, and flags waved wildly. The sound was wonderful. It was so deafening it vibrated right inside my chest. For a few minutes, I had to block my ears. Flowers were thrown, raining down on the rows of marching Americans. Many smiling Americans handed out tins of food and blankets, even lollies and chocolates. Many cried with delight at receiving those gifts.

"No sooner had I uncovered my ears than the ground rumbled under my feet, intense vibrations running up my legs, through my entire body. My teeth chattered as revving engines drew closer. Jeeps drove past with older men, officers in the back, waving casually. These were followed by a big iron monster of a tank with grinning soldiers sitting on top and some big trucks towing cannons, and then another tank rumbled through. Lina and I couldn't stop smiling, jumping up and down, and screeching at the tops of our voices," I said.

"I wish I could see those machines," said Val, no longer skeptical or interested in pressing Dad for a story.

"Behind the Americans came others Mum told us were British. Over the cheering and frantic flag-waving, I was gripped by a weird sound I'd never heard before. It was so whimsical yet so stirring. I strained to see where it might be coming from. A large man immediately caught my eye. He was blowing into a pipe sticking out of a big bulging sack he carried under one arm. Lina and I looked at each another astonished, and we laughed out loud because not only was he blowing into a bag, but he was also wearing a dress! We'd never seen a man wearing a dress before, at least none apart from some of the clowns at White Sunday," I said.

"You're expecting me to believe British soldiers go to war wearing dresses. Come on, don't crap in my ear," said Val.

"I kid you not. This fellow kept squeezing the bag under this arm with his elbow as he blew into it. There were many other pipes hanging off the bag, which also looked very strange. Behind the soldier with the big noisy bag under his arm came others, but Lina and I couldn't stop laughing because they also wore dresses! We couldn't help but immediately like them. I tugged at Mum and shouted, asking why they wore dresses," I said.

"It's a Scotland thing," said Mum.

"At the time, Lina and I thought this was so amazing and fun, we started dancing about, clapping, and cheering along with the strange music. We may have gotten a bit carried away because out of the blue, to our shock and horror, one of the Scottish soldiers headed directly for us. The sight of this dress-wearing giant striding our way made us immediately stop dancing, hide behind Mum, and cling to her legs for dear life. We peered out from behind Mum's legs to see that the giant now stood in front of Mum, talking to her. He held a stack of three flat-looking boxes with what looked like material hanging off the top of the boxes."

"What did he say? Could he speak Slovenian?" asked Val.

"I couldn't hear what he was saying over the crowd," I said.

"Mum?" asked Val.

"It was a bit of a blur, Val. I couldn't really hear much either. I just nodded and smiled as respectfully as I could," she replied.

"Suddenly, the dress-wearing giant knelt down in front of us. Mum put her hands on us, but we still trembled. We sneaked peeks at him from behind Mum's legs. He looked a scary but friendly giant. Bright blue eyes, just like ours. His smile was so gentle, and his eyes held us with such softness. I relaxed and even let go of Mum. Together, Lina and I came out to face him. He smiled even more and spoke to us," I said.

"Did he say anything about fighting?" asked Val.

"Most things I couldn't hear over the noise, let alone understand. In my heart, I somehow felt he was a good man, and I wondered if he had any children. I noticed the bloody nicks and scratches on his face. They were like the ones Dad sometimes got when he shaved, except these looked bigger and deeper and were in places where Dad wouldn't shave."

"Did you say anything?"

"I didn't know what to do. Lina and I beamed bright smiles back at him like a couple of little lighthouses, which made him chuckle. The giant handed Lina and I a box each with a bit of folded material. The boxes felt almost as big as we were. Mum nodded. Lina and I carefully put the gifts on the ground and hugged the giant as best we could. We kissed him on each of his scratched, stubbly cheeks. I can still feel his big hand gently patting me on my back. I think we made him very happy. I thought he must be so wonderful to come help us," I said.

"Isn't it amazing? Who knows what would have happened if they hadn't come," opined Lina.

"I shudder to think. The giant got up and handed Mum the remaining box. She hugged him and gave him a kiss on each cheek. Just as suddenly as he'd come over, he was off. Our meeting seemed all too brief. But I know I'll remember every single bit of it, along with the rest of what I saw, heard, and felt that day for the rest of my life," I said.

"I wonder where he is now," said Val.

"That's an interesting question, Val," I said, glad he'd gotten past asking about fighting. "We'll never know his name or even whether he survived. It would be so nice to see him again, to give him another hug and say thank you."

"Just hearing about that day again gives me goose bumps," said Lina.

"Yeah, me too. I'll always love those men and what they did for us. Everyone there that day I'm sure felt the same way; it was in their faces," I said.

"What was in the boxes?" asked Val.

"Treasure!" exclaimed Mum.

"No, seriously, what was in the boxes?"

"Actually, we were more interested in the cloth. They were spare dresses from the soldiers. We felt so special to have been given that material," I said.

"Yes, it was exciting. We clutched at our new dresses and boxes, but the contents of the boxes were still a mystery to us," Lina said.

"I was so happy, I went to scream but hardly anything came out," I said.

"Our voices were gone. We didn't care," said Lina.

"Clutching our gifts, we kept cheering as best we could. More trucks piled past and then in an instant, it was all over. The crowd died down, and people started leaving. Lina and I sat on the sidewalk and opened the boxes, which were filled with lots of little packages. But it was the dresses that brought us no end of fascination," I said.

"Yes, the things in the boxes looked plain next to the dresses," agreed Lina.

"Mum made carrying boxes for hours look easy. Even though our voices were gone, we kept chattering all the way home. Once home, we opened the packets to find vitamin-enriched biscuits, cans of tuna, condensed milk, coffee, sugar, aspirin, matches, butter, powdered milk, powdered eggs, and even cans of vegetables," I said. *Oh, how I hated vegetables.*

"So nothing that exciting," remarked Val.

"We were hungry almost all the time. To us it was exciting, even if vegetables in tins and milk and eggs in a powder was bizarre. At the bottom of the box was a picture of a man wearing jewels. I held up the picture and asked Mum who it was," I said.

"The King of the British Empire, including Scotland. You and Lina took such care holding the picture," said Mum.

"I said how he must be very lovely to send his soldiers to set us free and give us food and their fine cloth," said Lina.

"If they saved the world, why didn't all the countries become friends?" asked Val.

"People will always be grateful. But they'll also remember the old hatreds," said Mum.

"As for governments, they'll forever resent being saved," said Dad.

Val looked confused. "But that doesn't make any sense," he concluded.

"You're beginning to understand," said Dad, confusing Val even more.

"There was no confusion about the bars of chocolate in the boxes that day. But there was some confusion about the packets of hard lollies," I recalled.

"Some went flying as we broke open a packet. We locked onto those colored lollies like hawks. Some broke on the floor and others rolled around. All the colors of the rainbow. We'd never before seen lollies with holes in the middle. We picked up every piece, even the tiniest shards," said Lina.

"You were both obsessed with that candy. But you still asked permission before eating any, such good girls," said Mum.

"And still are, thanks to the way Mum raised you," opined Dad.

"Not a single shard of broken candy was wasted. I kept sucking until my toes curled. But the more I sucked on the sweet hardness, the more yummy juice there was to swallow. I tried to be patient and not bite, but biting through the hardness was half the fun," I recalled fondly.

"We were totally seduced by the rare pleasure of colored sugar," said Lina.

"So hungry, even the canned and powdered food tasted wonderful. The only thing missing was Dad. Mum, I remember how you hung the picture of the King and the little American flags on the wall. We all prayed for God, Jesus, the Holy Ghost, and the Virgin Mary to protect Dad and bring him home safely," I said.

"How come I've never seen the King's picture or that American flag?" asked Val.

"The Communist Party officials that used to inspect people's houses looking for subversive literature took them and gave us a lecture about how they could have us locked up just for possessing suspicious material," said Mum.

Val raised his eyebrows in disbelief. "I suppose they took the Scottish dresses away as well."

"They're kilts," I said, prompting Val to attempt in vain to pronounce the strange word.

"One day, after Mum and Lina went to check the fields, I laid out one kilt, chalked out patterns, and, heart in mouth, I cut. I fed the sewing machine with thread just like Mum. By the time I'd finished, there was a dress each for Lina and me with plenty left over. The mirror told no lies. I could hardly wait for them to see what I'd done," I said.

"I couldn't believe it! You were skipping rope in the courtyard like it was nothing. I had no idea you'd learned so much," said Mum. I flushed with pride.

"I had the best teacher—my Mum. I just hope the nice soldier who gave us the material wouldn't have been offended if he'd known what I'd done," I said.

"You did such a good job. I'm sure he would have been all right with it. I almost screamed when you told me you'd made one for me. Mum clapped, dumbfounded," said Lina.

"Your face lit up. We couldn't get inside quick enough so you could put yours on," I said.

I was so happy to see Lina admiring herself approvingly in the mirror wearing a dress I'd made for her. We hugged and jumped with glee before running outside, bouncing along like a couple of jellybeans. We played chasey around Mum in our new dresses. She protested, but I knew she liked it anyway.

"How long after was it that Dad came home?" asked Val, not keen on dress-talk.

"A couple of weeks later, we began getting letters, more like notes. He wrote he was all right, he loved us, missed us, thought about us all the time. He couldn't tell us much, only that he was working. He told us to be good and to stick together," I said.

"Mum, it must have been a relief," said Val.

"I was furious. I wanted him home. And I could see how frustrated, hurt, and sad Lina and Anja were. Other village men were returning, but not your Dad. After a day or so, I came to my senses and realized I had to be patient, but for Lina and Anja, it was not so easy accepting yet more uncertainty," said Mum.

I wondered whether the notes were really from Dad or whether he was lying to us.

"I knew it! You were doing secret work, weren't you, Dad?" asked

Val. Dad chuckled and gave Val a reassuring pat on the back.

"Val, it was two more years before Dad came home," I said. Val's jaw dropped.

"One day, when I was returning from tending our remaining cows and Aristotle in my favorite tartan dress, Mum came out," I said.

"And I said, 'Come inside, someone important is here,'" said Mum.

"I knew it was Dad," I said. Possibilities opened in my mind like a too-long-dormant flower suddenly blossoming. After so much time, I still felt unprepared.

"You froze," said Mum.

"As I closed the barn door, I couldn't move. My heart pounded. What if he was badly hurt? What if he wasn't my dear old Dad anymore? What if he didn't love—or even like—me anymore?"

"Dad kept on asking for you. I found you in the yard, just standing there. I called you," said Mum.

"I remember the ground crunching under your feet as you came near. I don't know why, I started running. You told me to come inside when I was ready," I said.

We'd seen and experienced things, intense things I could not forget, and I—we—had all been changed. Gigantic swirling waves of emotion kept crashing into me, feelings I thought I wasn't entitled to. I was drowning. Anger he'd been gone when we needed him most. Guilt at knowing I was no longer the little girl he'd left behind. Sorrow at how much he'd missed of our lives and how much we'd missed of his. Angst at how we'd now get along. And relief and happiness he was back.

"I don't understand, how could you keep away? Didn't you want to see Dad?" asked Val.

"Of course I wanted to see Dad," I said.

Part of me wanted to burst into the house to see for myself who he was now. We'd prayed so much for him, so many times and with so much fervor. Living with the memory of how loving and affectionate he was was ending. I had some idea of how the war had changed me, and I was about to find out the reality of what he had become, and it terrified me. Either I'd be even more heartbroken than I'd been living without him, or I'd be so full of joy I wouldn't know what to do.

"Girls make no sense," said Val.

"Sometimes a person just needs to take a minute, Val," said Lina.

"I'd be running inside like a shot!" declared Val.

"Different people do things differently," said Lina.

"Anja did come running to me, didn't you, my darling daughter?" said Dad.

"Yes, I did. It wasn't long before curiosity got the better of me," I said.

Wiping my sweaty palms on my kilt, taking a deep breath, I quietly slipped inside the house. I heard talking, a male voice, unmistakably Dad's voice. Sounds I'd not heard in almost five years. Drinking in the music of him, the enormity of how much I'd missed him welled up in me. Wanting more, in a few steps I found myself standing in full view of my family.

"You'd grown so much. I could scarcely believe it," said Dad.

As soon as I saw him sitting in the lounge room with Mum and Lina, with every fiber of my being I knew it was my darling Dad. The same Dad from before, the man we'd all been waiting for, for so long.

"You looked so smart in uniform. Next to you, more Red Cross aid boxes," I recalled.

As proof Dad was indeed right in front of me sank in, I trembled with happiness. So much so, the intensity of it frightened me. Dad stood up, tall, whole, and strong, smiling. At the sight of him all in one piece, I whimpered with delight.

"Dad told you you looked beautiful and asked you to come to him," said Lina, smiling.

He crouched slightly and extended his arms to me, tears welling up in his eyes. My lungs quivered, filling with air and anticipation. The sound of his voice calling me pierced and tore down all tentativeness. My little body exploded into a full gallop. I bolted toward his outstretched arms.

"I don't think I'd ever seen a girl run as fast. I was frightened you'd hurt yourself. You'd stepped onto a nearby footstool, launching yourself, flying, arms and legs splayed outward, making sure you couldn't miss your target," said Mum.

I sailed past his big hands into his open arms, and my chest crashed happily into his. It was no dream. It was all our prayers made real.

"Hugging Dad that day was the best. His tobacco smell still lingers," I said.

Safe again in his arms, I felt all the yearning for him I'd bottled up so tightly come gushing out. My hands grabbing at the material of his uniform, I pulled him to me as hard as I could. We both shook as our chests heaved out the same tears. We hugged tightly until my muscles ached. We kissed each other on each cheek over and over, his lips and the stubbly wetness of his cheeks once again pressing firmly against mine.

"We laughed and cried at the same time," said Dad.

I couldn't take my eyes off his. They sparkled so brightly. Streams of love continually poured out of them. Dad whispered into my ear, "I'm back now, and I will never leave you." Hearing those words filled my chest to bursting all over again. I wanted to stay in that moment and yet was hungry to get beyond it.

"I remember looking at you that day, feeling so proud of you. I was so impressed by how hard both you and Lina had worked and helped Mum while I was gone," he said.

For the first time since he'd been taken away, I felt whole again. Just having him home again made me think I couldn't have gotten any happier but hearing him tell me that day how proud he was of me took my happiness to a whole other level. From the look on Lina's face, I could tell that she felt the same way too.

"We couldn't stop hugging each other. Eventually, Dad sat in the big chair, his chair, and you sat on the floor between his knees," said Mum, smiling.

I loosely hung my arms over his knees. I didn't want to stop touching him or feel some part of my body resting against his.

"Dad looked so good and healthy, and yet different. I noticed he had perfect teeth! He looked so dapper and handsome," I said.

"You asked me how I'd made my teeth grow back," said Dad, chuckling.

"I was shocked when you pulled them out to show me," I said.

"The Americans sure made me a fine set of teeth. I was amazed at your tartan dress. Mum had told me about your fine handiwork. I can't put into words how good it felt to finally come home to the family I love."

Mum nestled closer to Dad on the bench seat. They swayed together in unison while Dad drove the cart. Such gratitude rose in me in that sunny moment, I felt like crying.

"Val, to answer your earlier curiosity, when I saw soldiers coming to where the fighting was, especially the new ones, they'd often look scared, but some were excited. Being so close to death all the time, some probably had never felt so alive. Whatever they felt at the start, after a while, the fighting would destroy everything and everyone around them. If they survived, mostly only fear was left. Beyond that was only numbness. Once I saw numbness in their eyes, I knew they could never be normal again. How could they be?" asked Dad.

"Is that White Sunday?" asked Mum, pointing to a group of people outside the town hall.

"I suspect so," replied Dad, our cart slowing and coming to a stop.

"It sure doesn't look anything like last year's festival," opined Val.

"Let's have a closer look," said Dad.

CHAPTER 3

THE SPEECH

We avoided the White Sunday crowds gathering in front of Sezana's town hall and eagerly piled into the church next door for the White Sunday service. If Communists had any respect, they'd wait until the service was finished. But being disrespectful was probably their whole point. Father Anton, who'd been giving services for twenty years, was nowhere in sight. A couple of thuggish goons standing up at the back flashed us sly looks as we slid into one of the many empty pews. Some interloper was up front. His robes were untidy; he rushed ritual and mumbled like he was tipsy. In previous years, the church would have been packed, everyone eager to hear one of Father Anton's impassioned sermons sprinkled with personal anecdotes and humor.

"Do you think this one's a real priest?" Dad quizzically whispered to Mum.

"Are you kidding?" answered Mum quietly, the rest of us giggling. "Let's go," she said.

"No, don't move. Keep facing front. There's a couple of government types in back watching us. Just act normal," said Dad.

"What do we do now? Poor Father Anton," said Mum.

"Stay calm. I'm not sure whether they're here to take people or names. I'll say when it's time to leave," said Dad, in a voice so low I could hardly hear it.

Thankfully, the slurring priest skipped most of the service. When the time came for Communion, surprisingly, a couple of people went.

After Communion prayers, the "priest" encouraged parishioners to give generously to the church as the goons walked collection bowls between small pockets of parishioners. As one of the goons leaned over to pass a collection bowl to Dad, his jacket fell open just enough to reveal a pistol in an underarm holster. Nothing was said, and the man quickly closed his jacket. Dad didn't flinch and only put in a couple of ten para coins, instead of the normal notes. The goons quickly disappeared with the collection bowls.

"Okay, quietly and calmly, we're going," whispered Dad, leading us out. "*Psst*, now might be a good time to get out," said Dad very softly to a small group huddled in a pew we passed on the way out. They quickly followed us out and left immediately.

"We're going home right now," said Mum frantically.

"No," said Dad.

"Didn't you see those people were running away?" said Mum.

"Relax. Actually, I think they're walking briskly, not running."

"Don't get cute. Did you not see the gun? Do you know where you are? Do you know where you've brought us?" asked Mum, exasperated.

"Is everyone all right?" asked Dad, turning to Lina, Val, and me.

Lina and I nodded, unsure what to say.

"Who were those guys, Dad?" asked Val.

"Hard to be sure, Val. Probably Communist Party thugs trying to make extra pocket money," answered Dad casually.

"Don't make it sound like it was nothing," said Mum.

"You're right," answered Dad, "but they were only interested in the collection. Them and their fake priest are probably already down the pub."

How could he be so composed? "What do you think happened to Father Anton, Dad?" I asked.

"I have no idea, Anja. Maybe the Communists ordered him to take the day off. I'm not sure who here we could safely ask about something like that."

"What's the world coming to?" I asked.

"I ask myself the same thing, more and more these days. When we get home, we can say a prayer for him. Maybe he'll turn up again," replied Dad.

"Well, we can't stay; we're going home," declared Mum.

"If you want, you can all stay with the cart, but I'm going to talk to my contact," said Dad, as Mum fumed.

"Dad, I want to go with you," implored Val. Lina rolled her eyes.

"You're not going anywhere, young man, except to stay by my side," commanded Mum, terribly deflating Val.

"Actually, I'd like to go as well," I said. Mum looked shocked at my betrayal. "I'm sorry, Mum, but I think Dad is right. It's one thing for them to steal from Catholics in Church, but I don't think they'll act like that in whatever festival they've slapped on top of ours."

I wondered if they'd at least keep any of the music and dancing from previous years.

"If you're going, I'd better go as well to keep you safe, my little sister. I'm sorry too, Mum. It's probably safer in the crowd than with the cart," said Lina.

I was glad, but I bet she was just as curious as I was about what it was going to be like.

"Excellent points, girls," said Dad. But Mum looked hurt and betrayed and wasn't budging.

"Look, I've got to do this for the farm. I'd feel so much better if you came," said Dad, turning the screws on Mum. Crossing her arms, Mum wasn't having a bar of it.

"Okay, that's fine," said Dad. "Lina and Anja, you come with me, but stay in sight. Don't touch anything, and don't talk to any strange people. Val, you wait with Mum in the cart, and if anyone comes close, take off. We'll come back as soon as we can."

"You're not leaving us?" asked Mum, incredulous.

"You'll be fine with Val and the cart. We won't be long," said Dad, leading the way.

We took about three steps before Mum relented and pulled Val along by the arm as she ran to Dad's side. Mum slapped Dad hard on the shoulder before holding onto him tightly. "You weren't seriously going to leave us there, were you?" she asked.

"I was hoping you'd change your mind, is all. Going as a whole family will look so much less conspicuous. And besides, I always feel better when we're together, my love," said Dad, smiling as he gave Mum a kiss and patted Val on the back.

"Poor Father Anton. Who knows what they've done with him," pondered Mum.

Dad led us through the crowd lining the street. There was talk about a march of patriots. We were close to the spot Lina and I had stood to see the march of kilts all those years ago. The air here was thick with promise then; now it smelled stale.

The crowd hushed and everyone turned to face the street.

"Let's wait here for a bit," said Dad.

A chap proudly strode past carrying the national flag, followed by people carrying a huge portrait of Marshal Tito. About a couple dozen veteran partisans, older men and women proudly wearing their medals, walked past. There were even veterans on horseback. People applauded enthusiastically. Dad applauded respectfully, so the rest of us did likewise.

The partisans looked quite regal and polished. The white and ashen horses looked beautiful; their uniformed riders perched majestically. Yet it still left me feeling flat. It was a caricature of the brave but wretched bandits we'd seen during the war. Flashes raced through my mind of beaten-down partisans yelling and swearing at Mum, demanding more food and animals, while turning over cupboards shouting for Rakia. Turning away from my memories, I looked to Mum and Dad for any hint of what they made of the parade. They looked on impassively, not giving away anything. Others cheered approvingly, but all were strangers to me. The march of kilts brought strangers closer together; this one seemed designed to do the opposite.

After the partisans came a large red flag with hammer and sickle insignia being waved about emphatically. Dad didn't clap for that one, so neither did we. Behind the frantic red blur marched teenagers dressed up like farmers in brand new clothes carrying new farm tools.

I elbowed Lina. "They look cute, like city kids who've never worked a day in their lives."

A couple of horse-drawn carts went by, one displaying assorted produce. The other carried more interesting fruit, a band we recognized as Slavko's Players. Lina and I had performed with them at previous White Sundays.

"Do you see what I see?" asked Lina.

"I sure do," I replied, putting a hand up to wave at them.

"Stop that," commanded Mum, as Slavko and several band members waved back.

Even if we weren't singing, at least the music would be good.

A smiling troupe of folk dancers in full traditional dress proudly sauntered past.

"Oh, don't they look wonderful? Much bigger troupe than previous years," opined Lina.

"Actually, they don't look half bad," replied Mum, through squinting eyes.

Actually, they looked magnificent. Very promising. I just hoped the Communists would not be dancing on Father Anton's grave.

Bringing up the rear was a gaggle of folk clowns with their odd hair, dressed in ladies' aprons and ill-fitting, baggy overalls and brightly colored rags. They waved and handed out candy to children.

At the end of the march, we got swept along by the crowd into a field adjacent to the civic hall. In the crowd, we swam through familiar festival smells of beer, bread—I loved that yeasty smell—simmering minestrone soup, spit-roasted pork, and lamb. Through gaps in the crowd, I was dazzled by a row of massive, steaming cooking pots over open wooden fires, rows of display stalls featuring homemade preserves, jams, and pickles, and others with tools, clothing, and leather goods. It was multiples bigger than previous years and must have cost a fortune.

"I hear something nice. Do you recognize that sound, Anja?" asked Lina, as music started blaring over a public address system.

"I'd recognize Slavko's steirische harmonika anywhere," I replied. "The dancers are out. At least the Communists buy good music and dancers with our tax dollars and money stolen from the Church."

"As well as good-smelling food," said Lina.

"The fresh bread has been calling me since we got here," I replied.

"Only the best for the Communists," said Lina.

"They've definitely hijacked White Sunday. Nothing about giving thanks to God and plenty of kitschy stuff to gawk at. No wonder they discouraged Catholics and robbed those of us who came anyway," I said, careful not to speak too loudly.

"Spoken like a true subversive, Anja. Father Anton would be proud," said Lina.

"God, I hope he's all right," I replied.

"It's too upsetting. I don't even want to think about it."

"Shall we at least see if we can get a closer look at the dancing? Who knows if we'll ever come to another one of these White Sundays again."

"Dad seems to have found his contact. I'll let him know we're going to watch the dancing," said Lina.

Dad was immersed in conversation with a man of similar vintage as himself. He looked a professional type. It was bizarre seeing Dad, the knockabout farmer who'd countless times said Communism and Fascism were just about the worst things ever invented, talking with someone who I imagined had to be a Communist and a rather urbane looking one at that. What made it doubly strange was that they looked so comfortable in each other's presence. Such an odd pair. Dad may as well have been talking to someone from outer space. *How does he do that?* Just when I thought I knew all there was to know about Dad, he surprised me.

Mum and Val were enthralled by a display of leather goods. Lina and I sensed the moment for escape had come. We got as close to the makeshift dance floor as we could. The dancers were resplendent, powerful, and poetic, occasionally letting out a wildly delicious *yeeh-haaa*.

"They're flawless; they must be professionals on a Party retainer," said Lina.

"It's both moving and repulsive," I replied.

"And yet I can't look away."

"It's a search for artistic perfection. But are we watching propaganda or people having fun?" I pondered.

"With Communists, even art does national service," replied Lina.

"Whatever it is, it's a world away from the village."

No sooner had we settled into the performance than the music and dancing stopped. We exchanged disappointed glances as dancers were replaced by partisans lining up behind a couple of imposing official types who'd taken center stage. A microphone stand was frantically set up by a couple of men in a hurry to get out of sight as onlookers piled in around the stage.

"I'm looking for a way back," whispered Lina.

"It's too late; leaving might cause a scene," I replied.

"We don't want to draw attention."

"Dad knows where we are. It should be all right," I murmured with forced optimism.

One of the officials stepped up to the microphone, the crowd quiet with expectation. The official surveyed the crowd, making everyone wait.

"Today we celebrate the bountiful harvest the sun- and rain-drenched fields of this fertile land have bestowed upon our comrade farmers and our great nation," he said, each word dripping with hubris that reverberated over the public address system.

You mean, thanks to God who works through Mother Nature and thanks to us peasants who manage to survive despite your suffocating exploitation!

"I proudly present some of the nation's legends, men and women, veterans of the National Liberation Army and Partisan Detachments of Yugoslavia!" he said, lifting his arms toward the veterans. The crowd erupted into rapturous applause, whistling and cheering.

As Lina and I clapped respectfully, gusts sent thick smoke from nearby spit roasts wafting across the stage, the scent of burning flesh enveloping all. Through the smoke, the official waved his hands for the crowd to pipe down.

"The war is not so long ended. We have buried our dead. Much of the world has succumbed to imperialism. But we, your National League of Communists, stand defiant and united with Yugoslavia's Socialist Republics, over whom we govern in your name. We also stand with each of you as part of the international brother and sisterhood of Communism, soon to sweep the globe!" he said, in a crescendo of enthusiasm. The crowd again erupted.

Oh, please! What does your so-called league deliver except misery?

"Your government works to reap a greater harvest. Agile and innovative reforms are reshaping our nation as precious resources are diverted to grow industry and agriculture across the republics. Change is hard and the League understands there is hardship. We are all impatient for better things. Remember comrades, only through sacrifice and perseverance shall we prevail. Remember our National Liberation Army, as commanded by our great father, Marshal Josip Broz Tito. Our sacrifice can never outdo theirs."

Cronyism is what's reshaping our nation. I'd love to know what sacrifices those like you are making, apart from the time it takes to figure new ways of skimming.

"Germans, Italians, Bulgarians, Hungarians—they all presumed to carve up our lands and riches. Tito, leading the army, took the fight to the Nazis, Ustaše, and Chetniks. In the face of overwhelming force, our guerrillas gave surrounding enemies a rousing welcome, ruffling many a gold-braided feather. Even Fascist supermen can learn, as we taught them slowly and painfully in our own good time, much to their chagrin," he said, laughter rippling through the crowd.

Your unholy league of state fanatics sanctifies veterans' legacy and Tito's leadership, perverting both at every turn.

An arm rudely pushed between Lina and me, thrusting a bottle toward the speaker. From the smell of his breath, I figured it must be Rakia. We sheepishly averted our eyes as the speaker took the bottle, raised it in casual salute, and took several gulps.

Nodding his thanks, he wiped his mouth with the back of his hand. "Thank you, comrades. Talk about failing Fascists and our partisans' bravery is hard work, especially when there's so much of both to talk about!" More hearty laughter erupted.

"Their noses bloodied and their occupation faltering, the Nazis sent us their elite counterinsurgency forces. Murderers in uniform, they gleefully swept through villages, turning them upside down, interrogating, torturing, and murdering with rope, knives, bullets, and fire as if it were sport, sowing terror everywhere."

They made a mess of everything, leaving people opened up and spread out, the broken, sick, and infirm thrown onto bonfires, dead or alive. The screams, the smell, and the silence. We kept calm, didn't move, and didn't let them see us cry. We waited, cleaned up, and rested without rest.

"Their objective was to so subdue this land and its people, as to permanently extinguish hope of resistance. At the battles of Užice, Montenegro, Sandžak, Herzegovina, Kozara, Bihać, Neretva, Sutjeska, the Adriatic coast, and western Bosnia, Fascists attempted to corner and obliterate us. Our brave boys and girls fought without rest, with or without strategic advantage. Our warriors overcame every obstacle, sought out the enemy, and engaged it in constant guerrilla action, bloody hand against bloody hand. To our people's eternal credit, they endured impossible brutality, finding ever more ingenious ways of supporting their glorious partisans. Each battle only made us stronger, more committed and determined. Partisans, though hunted, were ever resolute, agile, and persistent. With the love and support of the people at their backs, they moved forward. Even when facing certain death, they shouted, '*SMRT FASIZMU, SVOBODA NARODU!* DEATH TO FASCISM, FREEDOM TO THE PEOPLE!'" yelled the speaker, a fine mist of saliva spraying forcefully from his mouth.

Many in the crowd punched the sky with fists, repeating the declaration in a passionate staccato chorus. The air was combustible; it crackled and tingled against my skin. The hairs on the back of my neck stood on end. Lina looked as petrified as I felt.

"The bond between our people and our partisans proved too strong for the most technologically advanced, most well-equipped, most highly trained fighters the barbaric Fascist horde had to offer. The bond made our National Liberation Army of Yugoslavia one of the most effective anti-Axis forces of the war. This bond still thrives today."

You've squandered that bond on petty thieving.

"Our people and the land itself now bear the scars of war. In time, such scars are worn like jewelry, but we shall wear ours lightly. We bear our invaders no ill will. They grieve for their injured and fallen as we do for ours. As Communists, we believe in the common brotherhood of humanity. We do not lust for the scepter and ball. We do not seek to kneel and kiss any imperial hem. We regard all directly and unassumingly, meeting all squarely on the level, holding ourselves as neither slaves nor superiors," he said, to respectful applause.

It's all good so long as your snout is the first in the trough.

"Dearest comrades, we won the last war, but today we face a bigger one," he declared.

Yeah, the one you wage against your own people.

"This new war rages in every sphere of human endeavor, militaristic, agricultural, industrial, even cultural, and artistic. Each must sacrifice and play their part. Our country is in an industrial revolution and faces new imperialist threats. Give us your support, for all forthcoming policies, so that we can secure, for the sake of our children, our country's future," he said, waving to the side of the stage.

What new policies? You already take whatever you want.

A row of cute children, between about six and eight years old, walked onto the stage holding hands and stood directly in front of the partisans.

They're even using kids in propaganda now?

While we respected veterans, Lina and I discreetly shared a look of horror.

"Comrades, this land breeds a special people, Yugoslav people." The crowd cheered, a broad smile lingering on the speaker's face.

"Others have resisted imperialism. Think on Guatemala's subjugation so capitalists could save a few cents on a cup of coffee. What imperialists practiced in Greece, they perfected in Guatemala and the Congo. Horrors so heinous they eternally damn vain quests to slake the blood lust of slave-driving colonialists. Remember the venal oppression of the Irish. Workers, poets, schoolteachers, parents, even children, slain warriors all. People never at peace are the banquet of those who endlessly exploit."

What about your endless exploitation of us?

"Western capitalists now feed on their own people. Workers are increasingly squeezed as wealth is concentrated. Republics founded on high ideals, dispossession, and slavery, are succumbing to the poison of crony politics, infecting every organ of democracy. Their elites are merely criminal gangs fighting over exploitation privileges, at home and abroad. Those who looted us in war have still not returned our gold. Expropriation and wage slavery can never withstand the antiseptic of true enlightenment, selfless love of one's fellows, and the will to freedom. Comrades, the struggle of many peoples against imperialism is our struggle. It is a joy, not a labor, to hold out the hand of friendship and support those who struggle."

Who can help us struggle against your exploitation privileges?

"Their next targets are you and me. But fear not, from the ruin and ashes of empire, a new world comes. Imperialist inequities form rich seedbeds for a global harvest of productive destruction, bringing forth new shoots of self-determination everywhere. That this will to freedom eventually defeats all everywhere is the essential teaching of history. No empire is immune to truth."

How is it the truth of your own empire-building seems not to bother you?

"We must be ready to meet others emerging from exploitation as our non-aligned independence inspires others. We are truly forging a new path and we must stay strong. The signs are clear: empires are collapsing. Witnessing your legion and fervor, I am confident. United under Communism and Marshall Tito's leadership, our country will succeed."

I wonder if Tito knows how badly his own party is betraying him and the people.

"On behalf of your ruling National Communist League, I thank all members of the Socialist Republic of Slovenia for your attendance and hope you enjoy today's celebrations," he said, finishing to enthusiastic applause.

My goodness, I've never seen it laid on so thick. He certainly put on a show.

I whispered to Lina, "They've really got their own religion now."

"Don't look now, but the high priest of Communism is headed straight for us," said Lina.

I wanted to disappear.

CHAPTER 4
STRANGE HARVEST

As the high priest of propaganda neared, cheering fans behind pushed forward, a few stretching out their hands in the hope they'd shake his. I was surprised by how many women were among the admirers. It was all a bit much, but we were too tightly packed in to get away. Lina and I held on to each other so we wouldn't get toppled over.

"I just wanted to thank you for the Rakia. If that happened every time I spoke, I'd be a drunkard. But I enjoyed it just the same," he said, talking to someone behind Lina and me. We did our best to be invisible, but I stole a glance anyway. He was engaging but held himself upright, polite in welcoming adoration while remaining above it. His wrinkles spoke of long experience, but his posture was strong like someone who'd been rewarded richly for their striving. Behind that polished and aloof smile lay a weighty purpose beyond entertaining speeches. Thankfully, he didn't pay attention to Lina or me.

With the propagandist gone, the war-talk over, and the Communist cheer squad dispersing, Lina and I heaved a sigh of relief. The tension in me drained out, mostly. Adjusting my ruffled clothing after the jostling, I half-expected to see myself standing in a puddle of expelled anxiety.

"There's Dad, still engrossed with his mysterious friend," observed Lina. Without skipping a beat, Dad turned to meet my gaze almost immediately, his eyes asking if everything was all right. I smiled, and he gave me a wink and went back to his conversation. Two minutes ago, we would have run away given half a chance, but now we didn't want to go anywhere. After the speaker had resurrected our bloody memories and we'd seen children used as propaganda props, Slavko's Players and the dancers were bringing the sunshine back.

The throbbing polka and yelping of dancers in full flight quickly attracted a more hedonistic crowd. The relentless beat, masterful dancing, and fabulously bright costumes whirling about lifted me out of myself. I wanted to be on stage, dancing with skillful abandon like they were. Swaying dreamily, I no longer disputed their artistry nor cared if they were sponsored by Communists. I appreciated being immersed in something beautiful. But the nearby slapstick dancing antics of those unable to hold their Rakia kept pulling me away from a wonderful moment. Too many undomesticated drinkers only wanted to join in jubilant shouting.

As nearby drunks graduated from incoherent shouting, wobbly dancing, and chasey to wrestling on the ground and tearing at each other's clothing, Slavko motioned to a well-built official offstage. He looked like a soldier in a suit. They spoke briefly and the official disappeared.

"It looks like the striptease wrestlers are about to get the boot," I said. *Even drunk Communists carry things too far. They just can't help themselves.*

I felt a tap on my shoulder. It was the same suit who'd just been talking to Slavko. I couldn't work out why he was interested in us and not the drunkards. Another suited official appeared, squinting at Lina and me, as if sizing up how much of a fight we could put up. My gut knotted itself into a tight ball, my heart pounding. Lina and I instinctively held hands and I forgot about the drunkards. One of the officials asked Lina for our names. I looked around to see if I could spot Dad, but the crowd was too dense. *Next, he'll be asking to see our nonexistent Communist membership papers.*

Through my dry throat, I tried telling the suited goon we needed to get back to our family, but the words weren't making it out. Interrupting impatiently, he asked us if we could perform a song with the band. Our jaws dropped.

There was no time to call out to Dad. In seconds, we were frog-marched backstage.

"Are we actually doing this?" asked Lina, still in shock.

"Ah, it's looking that way. I'm not sure these people take no for an answer." I liked singing, but not like this.

"Don't worry, Anja, we'll be fine," said Lina, hyperventilating.

"We'll just do one song and get it over with. It's not as if we haven't performed before," I replied, quivering. *Who is she kidding? Who am I kidding?* The dancers, band, and drunken crowd was in front, the goons behind, and no warm-up. We were going to get slaughtered.

Slavko introduced us as a couple of folk gems from the Slovenian heartland. I felt like grabbing Lina by the hand and running away. But there was nowhere to run except center stage. The officials pushed us out to faint applause, wolf whistles, and catcalls. Lina and I exchanged quizzical greetings with Slavko, smiling proudly as if he'd done us a favor instead of having dropped us in it.

We reluctantly adjusted and tapped on the microphone, but it was dead. Lina and I hung out on the stage to swing freely in the barbeque-infused breeze as stagehands frantically fiddled with power cords.

Someone in the crowd yelled that a striptease was in order, precipitating merry laughter and more drunken catcalls. I shrank, my shoulders caved, and my heart began beating so hard I thought it was going to explode. I made the mistake of looking at faces in the crowd. Perhaps it was all the earlier war-talk, but those ghoulish, unfeeling smiles stirred memories of similar smiles I'd seen years ago. Mingling in the crowd were flashes of Germans—Nazis. They were leering, drinking, laughing at us. I knew where I was, but part of me was back in Zana, a little girl again, watching German soldiers laughing and leering at us as they took over our yard and house after having had their fun in the streets and neighboring houses.

The screams still rang in my head. Hang on. . .beneath those screams, I recognized a faint melody. A slow tune, my favorite. What was it doing there? *Slavko is playing the intro; focus!*

Occasional nightmares were still part of my nocturnal routine, but it'd been a long time since I'd felt in danger of being overwhelmed during the day. I was not feeling well. I was not sure what I was feeling. I was not sure I could do this. Part of me was still looking over my shoulder for Nazis. *Will I ever stop looking out for Nazis?*

I reached out for Lina's hand. I focused inward, on breathing. Against my better judgment, I obeyed an urge to look into the crowd again.

No Nazis this time.

I caught one face, a familiar face. Dad's face. He was standing where Lina and I had been moments ago, his eyes locked onto mine. In his steely gaze, he asked me to let him come get us.

My dear Dad, I know you love me, love all of us. You'd go through anything for us.

In an instant, his expression changed. He took a deep breath in, held it, and let it out, slow. Something inside shifted, like my heart was falling into a bed of duck down, so quiet, so soft. My breathing lapped lazily and rhythmically against the shores of relation, with Dad, with Lina, the band, even with the crowd. Dad and Lina felt solid, and the band was present. But the crowd. . .they felt like children lost in an unfamiliar forest looking for a distraction instead of a path.

So this is what it's like not caring what they think.

As the band repeated the intro, my breathing found a way into the melody.

There's a path. Let's walk it together for a while, see where it goes.

Lina sang with me as Slavko poured out the tune.

Oh, it's been too long.

All that pounding fear was turning into beautiful, lyrical pain. I'd found myself.

Lina was feeling it too. It was all right, now.

We smiled, as one. Dad winked. Seeing him happy was all it took. I was free now, free to be me in the melody.

The crowd was quiet, attentive. Like a sweet savage, I tore them open in song. Raking through their hearts, we reached them, even the ones cowering behind booze and bravado, and showed them they could still feel. The past fear only became power. Something deeper opened up, and I gave it everything, letting it all go into the lyrics. . .

"Kako lepo cvetijo te pomladne rože
Pa vendar mi srce umira brez tebe, moji dragi, vas in polja doma
Ko se moje misli obrnejo k tebi, si ti zame edini Edina prijaznost in
moja edina sreča
Ti si edino prijazno mesto. . .moj edini pravi dom"

How beautifully these Spring flowers bloom
Yet my heart is dying without you my loved ones, the village, and
fields of home
When my thoughts turn to you, you to me are the only ones
The only kindness, and my only luck
You are the only kind place. . .my only true home

One song turned into two, two into four, and before Lina and I knew it, we'd been performing for over half an hour. We'd been more than generous. I gave Lina's hand a long squeeze—that had always been our signal. We exited the stage just as abruptly as we'd come on. I didn't care for the applause and was glad Slavko was disappointed we were leaving. But I didn't hold any grudges, smiling and wishing him well as we left. Musicians must play for whomever pays. Even the suited Communist goons applauded us as we left.

It had been quite a day. First the Communists robbed us in our own church, then they expected us to sing for them, which we did, and now they applaud us.

I just about leaped into Dad's arms when we found him.

"Very nice. Don't be surprised if they ask you back next year," remarked Dad.

"If they do, the pleasure of saying no will be all mine," I replied.

"Good for you," said Dad, chuckling.

"Fine performances, but you could have stayed for the applause," said Mum, arriving with Val.

"I didn't feel like it," I replied.

"Neither did I. They were overly insistent we sing," said Lina. A strange man came over brandishing a large bottle of what looked like beer and handed it to me, along with a glass.

"Don't look at me; I didn't buy it," said Dad, shrugging.

"What's this about?" I asked the stranger, who smiled and left.

"He didn't even wait for us to say thank you. Just because they're heathens with no respect, doesn't mean we have to be the same. If there's a next time, stay for the applause."

"Yes, Mum," replied Lina and I in respectful chorus. We all partook, making light work of the beer.

It was nice to wander around the stalls of trinkets as a family, even if we couldn't afford to buy anything. However, it wasn't long before the dancers reappeared on stage. Lina and I could hardly contain our excitement. Dad chuckled. He'd hardly finished telling us to be careful before Lina and I were making a beeline for an empty spot next to the stage.

We'd been there for barely a minute when I felt eyes on me.

"I think those men are looking at you, Anja," said Lina.

"Are you sure?" I replied.

"Yep," said Lina, ominously.

"They look ordinary enough, just having a drink. Whatever, I don't like it." I didn't understand what men got out of ogling. It was repulsive.

"I'm with you on that one," said Lina.

Part of me wanted to run and hide. It sickened me. They appeared to be grown men who should know better. I didn't bother hiding my disgust as they shamelessly looked us up and down.

"Maybe we should go back to Dad?" asked Lina.

"I don't want to let idiots rob us of a good time. I'd like to stay, but only if you're staying with me. If it gets any worse, we should go back."

This year, White Sunday was much bigger and flashier, but it had definitely taken a turn for the worse.

The women dancers looked pretty in their yellow dresses, blue vests, and white shirts. I bet I could have made us a couple of those outfits, if only I could get my hands on the fabric. I particularly liked their dainty shoes, little more than black slippers, not like the heavy work boots I normally wore.

"How nice it must be to create beauty for a living," I said.

"Mmm, especially if it meant dancing with such capable-looking boys," replied Lina.

"Oh, Lina, I'm shocked you'd be so indiscreet," I remarked, feigning offense. "They're definitely handsome and cute in those black knicker-bockers and vests. I like what the white stockings do for their calves."

"Anja, are *you* ogling? You should be ashamed," said Lina, playfully. We shared a deliciously devilish laugh.

"Well, at least we're discreet about it."

"Not discreet enough. The one off to the left is looking at you," said Lina, lightly elbowing me in the ribs.

"Is he really?" I asked, pretending I hadn't noticed. What a study in youthful masculine beauty he was. I tried not to look at him, at least not too often. He looked slightly familiar, but I couldn't place him. He gazed at me for far too long. He was bold but relaxed. I liked it.

"Now he's smiling right at you," said Lina, calling the play as if we were at a football match.

"Okay, I think you might be right," I replied, wishing Lina would stop talking about it but also that she'd keep talking about it. I was desperately trying to remember where I might know him from, and then it came to me.

"We may have seen him at church in Sezana. I think his family has a big farm in the valley. If I'm not mistaken, he has a reputation for being a heartbreaker. Best ignore him, I think," I said, unconvincingly.

His dancing was impressive, effortless, graceful, and strong. His body did its own thing while his smile played with mine, which drove me nuts. His gaze embarrassed me, yet I wanted more of it. No sooner did I try to look away than my eyes were drawn back to him. I stood as elegantly as I could and tried to relax. I wasn't sure it was working; actually, I was positive I looked quite the fool. But his warm gaze and generous smile remained constant. Supremely confident, he made perfection look so easy, yet didn't seem to take himself too seriously. He sure put on an intoxicating display.

In a shocking move, the shameless flirt playfully bounced over to dance right in front of me. Lina and I recoiled at his boldness. I couldn't help but admire how tall he was and how even more beautifully chiseled he looked up close. I laughed at how giddy his nearness made me and cradled my cheeks as hot blood surged to my face.

Okay, now I really want to run and hide, but my feet feel glued to the spot.

Before my head had any more time to explode, he did a kind of dancing flurry, his gaze a touch more serious as his crystal-clear blue eyes penetrated deeply into mine. My stomach flip-flopped. No one had ever made this kind of fuss over me before.

He made me feel like I was the only woman in the world. I was dumbfounded and enthralled and couldn't look away. Even his sweat looked beautiful, glistening and dripping off his taut and elegant features. If my jaw kept dropping, I'd have to prop it up with a stick.

Wave after wave of blush washed over my face, along with the rest of me. I was drowning in embarrassment. My knees weakened. My toes curled, as if clawing all the way through my socks and the soles of my shoes, scratching at the earth for some stability. In that moment, there was none to be had.

I must have been glowing an iridescent red.

I wanted more of his performance, of him, but I just couldn't stand the attention.

"Okay, I've seen enough I think. Let's get out of here," I said, short of breath.

We scurried away. I turned just enough to admire him one last time. He smiled at me again. Daringly, I smiled back.

"We mustn't mention what just happened to anyone, otherwise they'll get the wrong idea," I said.

"Fine by me. But he is quite cute. He's still dancing, and he's still looking at you," said Lina, looking over her shoulder.

"Stop looking!" I said, stealing another glance and a giggle.

Dad was talking with his mystery friend again. They were plotting something big.

Slowly, I gathered the courage to look back at the stage. The dancers were still going, people were still watching, yelping, and clapping, and apart from the sweat on the palms of my hands, it might have seemed like I was never there. Just as I was calming down enough to eavesdrop, Dad's friend tipped his hat at the rest of us and left.

"Did you enjoy the dancing?" asked Dad.

"Yes, it was much better than the lecture," I replied, as innocently as possible.

"We haven't eaten since breakfast. I'm hungry," declared Val.

"Me too, Val. Let's hit the road. We'll eat when we get home. But I'm curious to see what they've got in the way of food this year. We'll take a quick look," said Dad.

We perused what, to me, looked like an open-air animal crematorium-outdoor kitchen. They were selling spit-roasted pork, lamb, fried cevapcici and onion in crusty continental bread rolls, along with a few other basics like minestrone. Apart from the obligatory vino, Rakia, and beer, they even had an assortment of cakes. The smells made my stomach grumble loudly. Luckily, there was no danger of anyone hearing over the din of the crowd.

On nearby chalkboards, there were two price lists: one for Party members and another for non-members. The members' prices were surprisingly affordable while the non-members' prices were an astronomical rip-off. Doing the math, one meal for all of us, including drinks and cake, would have cost about as much as our farm made over an entire month. As we looked over the offerings and wrapped our minds around the expense, Dad nodded politely at the ladies serving behind the counter. Only one acknowledged him, smiling contemptuously. We left speechless, as the sound of them laughing at us rang in my ears.

It was a lot like this morning's church robbery.

"Apart from beautiful singing, what a rubbish festival," said Mum as our cart ambled along the road.

"A bit strange this year, not really catering to our type," said Dad matter-of-factly.

"What's our type, Dad?" asked Val.

"Anyone who is not a card-carrying Communist," said Dad, dryly.

"Unbelievable. They can stick their prices up their asses," said Mum, indignantly.

"Discounts and bribes for Communists, rip-off taxes and extortionist prices for the rest. Welcome to the class-ridden classless utopia," opined Dad.

"Dad, what was all that about Guatemalans, the Irish, and such?" I asked.

Mum interjected, "Maybe he secretly wants to be Irish? If he likes them so much, maybe he should go live there? They might straighten him out. Obviously, no one here can!" she said, with sarcastic venom.

"I wasn't really listening to him, but I think he was talking about empires. He was saying when a new one comes, they make themselves strong by making friends with enemies of the old one. They fight and the winner gets the right to steal from everyone, like the Guatemalans or whoever, I'm not sure," said Dad.

"So according to him, America or England is supposed to be the empire doing the stealing now?" asked Val.

"Something like that. Empires go well for a time. Before long, they become corrupt. Eventually, people revolt. It's never-ending. According to him, now it's the Americans taking over from the English. In Jesus's time, it was the Romans. Romans used to feed Christians to the lions. I think he'd say the current empire is feeding everybody to the bankers," replied Dad.

"But I thought Russia and Germany were the enemy? Didn't

America and England help everyone in the war?" asked Val, confused.

"In the end, they were all fighting Germany, and yes, America and England did help. If it wasn't for them, I doubt any of us would be alive. That guy was trying to say empires fight more for money than they do to help people," said Dad.

"I don't like the sound of that," said Val.

"Do you believe anything of what he was saying, Dad?" I asked.

"He was talking propaganda, so they mix loads of bullshit with some truth and twist the whole lot around. Unfortunately, we are stuck with the Communists, but every empire is far from perfect. Holding together things is an ugly business. How long America stays good and strong for ordinary people I don't know, but the Communists are not keen to let anyone compare for themselves," replied Dad.

His answer wasn't entirely what I think I was hoping for, not that I necessarily even knew what that was, but it felt right, in an uneasy way.

Mum chimed in, "There's no good in it; all politicians, everywhere, liars and cheaters. They've no shame, no respect, and no value, just one lot of gangsters after another. The only reason people join the Communist Party is to get ahead without working. The only reason they go higher is to steal more. Communist, capitalist, socialist, fascist—they talk like they're against one another, but they're not; they all use each other to justify themselves. At bottom, they're all shit," she announced with certitude.

"You have a good point. Money still travels everywhere and wherever it goes, politicians are not far behind, regardless of the era or empire," said Dad.

"Dad, who was that man you were talking to?" I asked, wondering what had consumed him so much in their conversation. The mood changed.

"I don't think you'd know him. He's a Communist Party organizer," said Dad.

Lina and I exchanged glances and raised eyebrows. Mum looked away in disgust.

"So if we aren't Communists and don't like Communism, why would you talk to a Communist Party organizer?" asked Val.

Mum turned to look squarely at Dad, daring Dad to be an honest politician.

"I knew him from before the war. He was a farmer once, much like we've always been. In the war, he became a partisan. After the war, he became a Party official. He might be able to help us with the farm," said Dad. Mum snorted at his politician's answer.

"Help? Us? Since when do Communists help anyone except themselves?" asked Mum.

"He knows people in external affairs and might be able to help us get that permit to sell produce into Italy, make a bit of extra money," said Dad, not convincing anybody he was at all coming clean.

"Permit. Ha!" responded Mum.

There was more to the story than getting his contact to help with a permit, but a twinge in my gut gave me the feeling an argument might be brewing.

"Does this Communist friend of yours have a name, Dad?" I asked, at the risk of re-igniting Mum.

Dad mumbled something about it being better for us not to know the man's name. Instantly, I sensed confirmation there was more to it than Dad was letting on, and that Mum also felt the same way.

Dad furrowed his brow, as if sensing we would not let him leave it at that. Mum huffed in apparent frustration at Dad's feeble attempt to be a closed book. He put on a brave face and promised to tell us more when we got home. That didn't satisfy anyone. It wasn't often anyone in my world spoke respectfully or even remotely positively of Communists. While I knew that being a Communist and being a good person were not necessarily mutually exclusive, it would take me a while to process a member of my own family having anything to do with a Communist, and a Party official at that.

The ride home was one of unpleasant anticipation. I wished my thoughts would wander to singing and dancing, but my agitated mind was having none of it.

CHAPTER 5

LIQUID SURGENCIES

Arriving home, Mum dismounted the cart to unlock the barn door. Dad suggested the rest of us go inside. Sensing something brewing, we watched and waited from the kitchen window for them to emerge from the darkness of the barn.

"They're noisy, but are they ever coming out?" asked Val.

"Hush, I can't quite make out Mum's yelling," I replied.

"She's having a red-hot go all right," observed Lina.

There was no shouting from Dad; it wasn't really his style. When Mum shouted, which was rare, he'd stand his ground, listen carefully, and as if by magic, he'd find a way of making sense out of what they were both saying. He had a knack for calming things. But that didn't stop him from sometimes being backhanded about it.

"Do you remember the time Dad told her yelling was self-indulgent?" I asked.

"I can't remember what the argument was about. But I remember she went nuts after he said it," recalled Lina.

"They always make up afterwards, though," said Val.

Coming out of the barn, Mum stopped cold. As Dad closed the barn door, she looked blank, mouth open. Covering her face, she shook her head. As she began sobbing, she looked around, desperate to regain her composure. We recoiled in horror, sensing we were next.

Glumly, Dad led Mum into the kitchen, her eyes red and puffy. I wanted to hug her, but Dad told us to sit at the table.

Surprisingly, Dad told us we'd be allowed to sell grain and produce into Italy, as long as we paid the taxes and bribes. If you wanted to get anything done, you couldn't do it without paying bribes. Dad's Communist associate even passed on some Italian farmers' markets contacts who would probably spy on us as much as help us.

"Mum and I agree there's something you all should know. But only if you promise not to tell anyone. If what I'm about to tell you was traced back to us, we'd be in serious trouble. Is that clear?" asked Dad.

We nodded, then in solemn chorus replied, "We promise."

"The government is soon going to nationalize farms or parts of farms, which means the government could take some or all of our farm."

What! The farm was everything we had; it was everything we were.

The enormity of the suggestion was beyond our comprehension.

"I know it's a shock, and it's all right to be confused and upset, but we need to start planning and preparing, and that's what I want you to focus on," said Dad.

Mum buried her head in her hands again.

Dad continued, "Land-owning farmers will be invited to surrender all or a part of their holdings to the government for the good of the Communist nation."

Val asked, "When? And what do you mean 'invited'?"

"Don't know when for sure," said Dad.

"Invited means they're stealing," said Mum.

"But how can they steal a farm? It's here, it's ours," said Val.

"It makes no sense, I know," said Dad.

"Farming is all we do. Where will we go? How will we survive?" asked Val.

Reasonable questions to which there were no good answers.

Dad reassuringly put a hand on Val's shoulder. "We'll work it out somehow, together. We must stay calm, focused, and keep putting one foot in front of the other."

I couldn't blame Val for remaining unconvinced, nor could I understand how Dad could be so calm. I wanted to run, find the nearest official, grab them, and ask, "Have you people finally gone completely *insane?*" But for not wanting to undermine the reassurance Dad was giving Val, I might have self-indulgently shouted and pounded the table.

"Dad, how sure are you about this contact of yours?" asked Lina, clinging to hope.

"I certainly wouldn't say anything if I didn't think it was highly likely," said Dad.

The insolence of "inviting" people to give up everything. The idea. The audacity. The injustice. I wanted to scream.

So that was it, generations destroyed at the stroke of a red pen. Without justification, the government was going to blatantly rob farmers and their families of everything they'd worked so hard for. The unfathomable arrogance kept turning itself over and over in my mind. It was theft on an industrial scale. Is this what the partisans fought for? Is this our reward for surviving?

"Once farmers see they might not survive, wouldn't they do something?" I asked.

"Anja's got a point, Dad. Many farmers are veterans; they'll know what to do," said Lina.

"Nobody is going to revolt," came his matter-of-fact reply.

"But why?" Val demanded, rising up and stomping his foot against the floor as hard as he could, a born rebel spoiling for a fight.

"Anger doesn't even begin to describe my feelings. We apply our labor, skill, and tools to grow and sell things people need. Done well, few things are better in life. Communists are jealous of the value families like ours, with God's blessing, create. What Communists can't create for themselves they steal. It's wrong, but they make the laws, and they watch everyone. There's no right to congregate, deliberate, or agitate. Informers are everywhere. They have the information, manpower, and guns to force obedience. People are too busy starving or surviving, with no time or energy for rebellion," said Dad, rubbing Val's back reassuringly as he slumped into his chair.

"If it's that dire, people will see something big must be done," Lina retorted, hope slipping through her fingers the more she strained to hold on to it.

"Unlikely. When people feel trapped, no hope of outside help, most obey authority, even if they sense they're about to be slaughtered. It's what most people do when the only choice is comply or die," said Dad, making the stakes clear.

"Let's fight, Dad. You and I will find others and make hope and then some," declared Val, pounding a righteous fist on the table.

"You'll do nothing of the sort! The only thing you'll find is yourself right by my side, young man, and that's where you will happily stay," decreed Mum.

"I admire your spirit, son. But it's not quite that simple. My contact told me a minority of mid-level Party officials actually lobbied against nationalization after a draft edict was floated. Minority leaders were swiftly ostracized, expelled, or forced to sign requests for their own demotion on the pretext they'd been poor performers."

"But how is that expressing the will of the people like it says in the Communist books?" asked Val.

"In the Communist Party, whenever anyone is asked for an opinion, it's only an opportunity to show obedience. Apparently, dissenters who didn't denounce minority colleagues were immediately listed for surveillance and disruption. Even relatives and friends will be interfered with. The Party will strive to ensure the fate of dissenters is denigration, obscurity, poverty, and an early death. The most vocal have already been disappeared, helped to suicide, died in accidents or from sudden illnesses. Others suffering lesser deaths of demotion will serve as examples. More overt action will await dissenters not in the Party, let alone so-called Slovenian Triestinis like us. Open defiance from our kind would be labeled an insurgency and make us all targets for instant liquidation."

"So what are we going to do, Dad?" asked Lina.

"It's like in the church this morning," answered Dad.

"But Dad, we could leave the church. If we leave the farm, how will we feed ourselves? Where would we live?" asked Val.

"We have to somehow get out of the way of the law," said Dad.

"But how?" asked Lina.

"Just like Val has to study his schoolbooks, even if not everything in them is true, we'll have to wait for the policy to come out and read carefully for anything that can help us. It's not much, but for now that's the best we can do on that front," replied Dad.

"What's a liquid surgency, Dad?" asked Val, furrowing his brow.

"Liquidating an insurgency is what Stalin tried to do to Tito several times after Tito refused to give him loads of free stuff."

"You mean when Stalin sent secret agent assassins?" asked Val.

"Exactly. The secret police were meant to protect the country from assassins; now, they run the country. They bang on endlessly about insurgencies to keep everyone scared and in line," explained Dad, Val soaking up every word.

"Sounds like there's a war going on," opined Val.

"As far as the secret police are concerned, war is permanent."

"Without the farm, are we going to die?" asked Val, saying out loud what we were all wondering.

Such a sweet, innocent boy with so much potential. I was not sure what hurt more, the prospect of losing everything or watching my younger brother come to realize his future was being stolen from him.

"No! Of course not. We'll manage somehow," said Dad, giving Val a hug. How could Dad be so sure? Val hugged Dad, hard. I felt like crying, but I didn't want to cry in front of Val.

Dad noticed how upset I was. As the compassion in his eyes calmed me, it was as if I could see that compassion retreating. A more purposeful part of his soul came forward to make itself visible in his eyes. I felt his gaze go deeper into me.

"Our world is colliding with the big city. Keep faith close. Keep your antenna tuned. Listen to the signal when it comes, even if it's a faint little voice, and respond according to what you feel is best," said Dad.

I had no idea what he meant, but his words addressed something in me, yet also beyond me, as if he were addressing a future version of me.

I wanted to ask, but all too soon, the moment passed.

*

Retiring for the night, I felt the war was again nearby. Lina smiled as I asked if I could climb into her bed. Unsure about the future, at least this time we could face the uncertainty together, as a whole family. Under the covers in the pale moonlight, we held hands.

"The government doesn't care about us. Already so many are struggling to feed themselves. How will people cope with this new thing? How will we cope?" I asked.

"I have no idea. I'm not sure the government thinks we're human. Without farms, farmers won't be able to feed anybody. It's all a bit much," said Lina.

"I'm glad Dad was honest with us," I said.

"That was the only good thing," agreed Lina.

I didn't want to say it, as if that somehow made it more real, but without the farm and with our ethnic and religious background, even if we survived, it might be difficult for us to ever make enough money to own our own homes or aspire to one day having our own families. I wondered if that was the government's plan. We could end up like those people who lived on the roadside, in rags, always dirty, with nothing to eat. Many of them didn't last a single winter. Even the ones who camped in the forest didn't live well or long. As far as the government was concerned, they were all from the undesirable classes and were surplus to requirements. Perhaps Val was right to clamor for a fight.

"Val's ready for war," I said.

"Typical boy, talking big while clinging to Mum's apron strings," replied Lina.

"Mum holds him in check. But all it would take would be one word from Dad, and Val would be raring to go."

"You might be right," responded Lina.

I shared Val's desire for rebellion, but unlike him, I was certain it was unrealistic and didn't want to encourage him in it. I tried distracting myself by reminiscing about happier times.

"I remember how hard Mum had to fight when Val was born. Maybe some of that fight rubbed off?" I wondered.

"His birth was the happiest time and one of the scariest," said Lina.

"Dad hung around in the mornings instead of heading to the fields," I said.

"He didn't do that when either of us came," observed Lina.

"I guess it's different with fathers and boys."

"Sons are prized as laborers, hunters, protectors, providers, and future leaders whereas we girls are prized for our mothering, laboring, and homemaking," said Lina. Dad was a man of his time, but not blindly bound by it. He always made it obvious he loved us equally, and he enjoyed unique relationships with each of us that reflected our individuality.

"Mum's a wonderful provider, protector, and leader," I said.

"She certainly got us through the war," said Lina.

"The morning Val was born, I'd never seen Mum in so much pain, yet she held herself with such dignity," I recalled.

"I hated leaving her alone with the midwife," said Lina.

"The disturbing noises were what got to me," I said.

"At least we could hold on to each other."

"Grunts like rumbling from inside a mountain and screams like she was being torn apart by wild animals," I said.

"We squeezed each other so tight, it hurt. Dad, Auntie, and Uncle just waited patiently," recalled Lina.

"I don't know how they stayed so composed. Sounds came from Mum I didn't realize any human could make," I said.

"I thought the whole house might shake from the noise."

"I was desperate to do something but had no idea what," I recalled.

"Dad told us it would be all right," said Lina.

"It wasn't until I saw you were crying, I realized I was doing the same," I admitted.

"Suddenly, Val's crying filled the air, and we jumped."

"It was wonderful. 'Oh, your son looks perfect!' the midwife shouted," I said.

"Auntie and Uncle smiled. Dad crossed himself and wept."

The fear had been so great it couldn't all be relieved at once, but rather had to come off in stages. The midwife told us we had to be quiet and not excite Mum. Dad, with much reverence, nervously handed over a wad of cash. They told Dad he had an amazing wife. Dad nodded in humble agreement and choked back tears as he whispered, "I know." It was then the nervous tension flowed out of him in a torrent he tried to hold back but couldn't. I'd never seen Dad be so openly emotional with people he didn't know.

Dad invited Auntie and Uncle to come in with us, but they politely declined, saying they would wait until after our newly expanded family had spent this time alone. As we exchanged warm but impatient parting hugs, I mulled over how much suffering Mum had gone through. I wouldn't have been without any of my family for anything, but I couldn't help but wonder whether I'd be able to endure it with as much strength and grace as Mum had shown.

Dad slowly opened the bedroom door, and an all-too-familiar room was suddenly transformed into a sacred place. Mum's face was flushed and glistened brightly as if she'd done a month's farm work in a morning. Yet, she looked so serenely happy and utterly contented. She smiled tenderly, like an angel, looking down at the tightly wrapped bundle she held closely and gently to her chest. The squeak of the bedroom door closing gently broke the silence. Mum lifted her glassy, exhausted eyes that twinkled and shone upon us like the most beautiful stars. As we gazed into Mum's eyes from across the room, loving warmth filled the entire room and radiated through me. Seeing Mum holding the little bundle filled every corner of my heart completely. In that moment, I knew I wanted to be a mum one day, whatever it took.

"Seeing Val's face for the first time, he was the most beautiful and precious thing I'd ever seen," said Lina.

"Wrapped up in his little cocoon. I fell in love instantly. The feeling was so intense, like nothing I'd ever experienced," I recalled.

"I'd never seen Mum look so exhausted, but she couldn't stop smiling."

"Days later, she wrapped Val to her chest and went about like it was nothing."

"It was magical seeing him grow so fast, soaking in everything. He was so cute, everyone who looked at him fell in love instantly," said Lina.

"Who could blame them? Everything about him was wonderful, especially his little hands and feet, and his eyes were totally enchanting. The look of sheer joy and pride in Dad's eyes made me smile. Dad even cut back on his drinking and smoking," I said, letting the sweet memory linger in my mind.

"I'd never thought I'd live to see that day. I sometimes wonder if I'll ever be as good a mum as Mum," pondered Lina.

"Of course you will," I said without hesitation.

"What about you? How do you feel about the prospect of motherhood?"

"Val changed everything, gave everything new meaning. Even dealing with baby poo or hearing how painful it was for Mum giving birth isn't enough to put me off. But after tonight, I'm unsure what God has in store for me, for us."

Rolling over and pretending to sleep, I silently prayed to God for some idea of what I could do to help. I prayed over and over again, until sleep eventually took me.

*

Walking in the moonlit forest, leaves and twigs crunched under my rough work boots. A wolf bayed in the distance, stalking me. Coming upon a staircase, I climbed the uneven, rocky steps. The higher I got, the cleaner and neater they became. I had on fine but well-worn dress shoes. *I must be dreaming.*

Entering a big dark room, I discovered that lots of people were at a party. Apart from shoes, I was naked. Smells of antiseptic and Sulphur wafted over me. Some people were dirty and disheveled while others were clean and fancily dressed. I grabbed at nearby abandoned clothes, well-worn but new to me. Two dirty people sitting nearby were talking about me. Somehow, I knew they were Satanists. They complained I could see them.

Waking in fright, I reached out for Lina, but she was gone. I felt so alone. Seeing I wasn't in my own clothes, I realized I must still be dreaming.

With a jolt, I sat bolt upright. Lina was sound asleep beside me.

Suddenly a thought popped into my head: I could get a job. *Don't be stupid. Who's going to give a Catholic Triestini a job?*

Lying back, I took care not to wake Lina, contemplated my bizarre dream, and wondered if I really could get a job.

CHAPTER 6
GOING TO MARKET

Weeks passed without news of the nationalization. Uncertainty hung in the air like a putrid, inescapable stench none of us wanted to mention. Selling grain and produce into Italian farmers' markets was something we could do more than talk about. Lina did the first few trips with Dad. I think she preferred the farm to crossing to the West. Finally, it came my turn. Trepidation robbed me of a good night's sleep. Nevertheless, I was keen to practice my Italian. Dad was his usual calm self while sensing I was on edge.

"Farmers cross every day. Hold close, I'll tell you what to do."

Sitting next to Dad in the early morning light, our cart loaded to the brim with grain, fruits, and vegetables, the border post loomed. *Beyond butterflies, something isn't right.*

A car waited to cross, a guard talking to the driver. We didn't often see cars, a sign of the modernity and cosmopolitan people my daydreams of Italy promised. Reaching into my pocket, I rubbed my border pass between my fingers. One advantage of living near the border as a primary producer was qualifying for an international trade pass, even if they cost a fortune in taxes and bribes.

"What are you doing?"

"I'm checking my pass is in my pocket."

"Is it there?"

"Yes."

"Slowly take your hand out of your pocket, hands on knees so they can see. Look ahead. If he talks to you, look at him. While we're waiting, think about something else. It'll be all right," said Dad, gently patting my hands.

My heart beat faster. There was that strange feeling again.

Obtaining trade passes meant paying an official in Sezana to process an application. A generous bribe ensured paperwork didn't languish. Paying bribes at each crossing ensured passes remained valid. Without a big enough bribe, a pass would lapse, requiring another fee and bribe to re-apply for the pass. All that only got you as far as the border. Over the border, everybody wanted a piece of you. They knew all it took was one complaint to get you into trouble. The Communists relished using rules to choke anyone preserving contact with relatives or livelihoods on the other side. The iron curtain was more made of money than iron.

I made out three occupants in the small, shiny sedan in front. Two women with big fancy hair, possibly in their late twenties or early thirties, wearing brightly colored tops. The male driver, possibly older, with short, cropped hair and a dark-colored shirt. Rich folks. Not locals. They had to be important to be from further away and still be allowed to cross. Probably connected to the Party. The strange feeling was getting worse.

The driver handed some papers to the guard, who disappeared into the guardhouse. Almost immediately, the woman next to him started waving her arms. They were arguing. Muffled sounds matched the gestures, words too strained to make out. Dad looked on intently.

"Keep calm, stay still and quiet."

Easy to say.

Suddenly the passenger side door of the car flung open. The driver clawed at the slim, elegant young woman getting out in an inelegant hurry, but it was no use. He held his head in dismay. She looked at me briefly. She looked very disturbed. A shiver ran up my spine. The other lady, like a twin of the first, also took leave of her senses and disembarked in a hurry. They had to be city people, far from their natural habitat of cafés in Trieste, Milan, or Rome.

Sickness gathered in my stomach, but I couldn't look away.

Both women ducked under the boom gate with some difficulty on account of their heels and form-fitting dresses. Carrying their heels, they snuck past the guardhouse as if no one would see them and legged it up the road toward Italy. Dad looked blank; he knew this was not ending in a stylish Italian café. Gasping through a slack jaw, I marveled at their hopeless idiocy or brave desperation. The women held hands as they dashed, frantically looking for a way off the road, the barbed wire on each side ensuring there was none for a good stretch.

As the women madly scrambled, the car revved so hard I thought its engine might burst. Launching forward, it crashed into the heavy boom gate, dislodging it but not enough. Pulling himself out, the driver staggered toward the boom gate, desperately jumping over it only to tumble on the other side, the whites of his eyes bulging with dread, like an animal wrestling with death.

I was also sick with dread.

As the man gathered himself upright, two guards burst out of the guardhouse. Dad put his arms around me and tried to cover my eyes. I put my arms around Dad and held on with all my might. *Who's whimpering? It's me. I don't want to look, but I can't not.*

A guard drew his pistol, crouched into a wide stance, and shouted at the man to stop. Two rounds slammed into the man's back. In a couple of steps, he stumbled to the ground. The other guard shouted at the women to stop. They were almost at the end of the barbed wire. If they made it that far, they might veer off the road quickly enough to make the forest. I wanted to cheer them on. Astonishingly, the man who'd just been shot lifted himself up a little and yelled, "Run! Run! Run!"

The guard cradling a rifle casually jogged down the road, knelt on one knee, brought his weapon fully up, aimed, and fired like it was nothing. A portion of long hair on the top of one woman's head flew up, and something flew off. It had to be a piece of her head. There was no stumbling. She dropped, a limp mess of torso and limbs. I recognized that drop.

The women no longer held hands. The man on the ground stopped yelling. Amazingly, he tried crawling toward his female companions. The other woman doubled back and crouched by her friend's side. Cradling her friend, her impulse to comfort was replaced by wild screaming. She shook her friend, but she was no longer there, dead before she'd hit the ground. *I don't want to see this, but something stronger than my churning gut is preventing me from turning away.*

The guard with the pistol ran toward the man he'd shot. The loud thud of the guard's boot striking the man's head and the crack of his skull bouncing off the road were sickening. *Don't vomit, swallow! It's burning the back of my throat.*

The man was quiet now, but was he dead? The guard with the pistol grabbed his victim's collar and dragged the limp body back toward the post. The guard with the rifle nonchalantly jogged toward the screaming woman, rifle up, ready to take two for two.

The woman sobbed and shook, the tension wracking her body seemed to radiate outward with such power that I felt my own muscles twitching involuntarily in sympathy with her. From the profound sorrow smeared all over her face, the poor woman must have known her friend was dead. I wondered if anything good in their world and their dreams of freedom could survive the death of her friend. At least one life taken, at least two others destroyed, and I could only guess how many others irrevocably and horribly transformed. *Why did they ever get out of the car?*

As the guard marched the crying woman back to the guardhouse at gunpoint, her pretty, colorful clothes splattered with blood, the tragedy in her face was complete. In that moment, I knew living was as painful to her, and possibly more so, than facing her friend's death. In becoming disturbed at the constant provocations of Communism, they'd given in to desperation. The guilt would take its time and toll, only get worse, and never leave. I'd seen that pain too many times before. How could anyone live through oppression from the Nazis and then the Communists and not become at least a little disturbed? The pressure was constant and unrelenting, especially for anyone who didn't internalize the oppression and side with the abusers. Could anyone still with some humanity in them see and not feel something of the pain themselves, not feel something of the death and guilt themselves? Maybe that's why I couldn't look away. Perhaps some part of me wanted to make sure I could still feel the pain. And what of the guilt? Were we not all desperate? The only thing more frightening than seeing and feeling was seeing and not feeling. I'd seen that in people too. It was even more frightening, and I didn't want to become that.

If the guards felt anything, they didn't show it. Perhaps to them, it was just another day—a successful day—at the office. They'd probably get a commendation. Maybe that's why they didn't mind Dad and I bearing witness: they wanted us to see the banality of their proficiency. Like these guards, the Germans had wanted us to see their doings. But for some of them, it went beyond proud proficiency. Some, anyone could tell, enjoyed their killing as a sick and depraved sport, an expression of creativity. If not with bullets, then with knives, fire, the butt of their rifles, or even their hands. Shooting was comparatively merciful, and the smells certainly weren't as bad as the other methods they used. At least these border guards were a world away from that. And yet, how depraved had things gotten when shooting was a mercy? This woman running in vain for freedom, killed in front of people that cared about her, and for what? What good could there be in it? Not even five minutes ago, she was full of life; now she was gone, a limp, bloody mess.

To this day, if I close my eyes, I can still see them, still hear their screams and sobbing, added to those of all the others. *How many screams must I hold inside?* I wanted to know who they were, who they were to each other, and how they came to be where they were. Maybe it was better I didn't know.

"Should we turn back?" I asked, suppressed vomit still burning the back of my throat.

"You're doing fine. I'm sorry you had to see that. We keep going," answered Dad with steely resolve.

A third guard emerged from the guardhouse and approached us, one hand resting on the pistol tucked into his belt. "Papers please," he asked, smirking at me as I held onto Dad.

"Where are you headed, why are you crossing, and when are you returning?" he asked as if it were a normal morning.

"We're headed to the farmers' market in Rezillia to sell our produce, returning mid to late afternoon," answered Dad, as the other guards carried the dead woman's body inside.

The guard handed Dad our papers. "Wait until I wave you through."

I was breathing again. I kept holding onto Dad as the guards cleared the car and partially broken boom gate. They casually helped themselves to a large bag of grain and bag of fruit from the back of our cart, after which they waved us across. Dad took up the reins and our oxcart lurched forward. I could feel another set of eyes on us. In the bushes not far away was yet another guard pointing a rifle right at us. He'd been there the whole time. I froze solid. I wanted to tell Dad, but I had no air, no words.

Letting go of Dad, I couldn't help stealing a glance back at the guards, but they weren't paying us any attention.

"Don't look at the spot where that lady fell," said Dad.

I couldn't help it. A pool of thick, almost black, blood was still seeping into the road and a tangled mess, chunks of skull and brains, were strewn nearby. The long hair still attached to some pieces was no longer blonde. We both crossed ourselves and Dad said a prayer for her under his breath as we rode on. Once through the Italian side, I asked Dad to pull over. After I threw up, Dad hugged me, and I cried. He handed me a bottle of water, and we rode for Rezillia.

I hardly spoke for the rest of the trip and let Dad deal with customers. The market was busy but felt empty.

Our produce sold out quickly, meaning it was time to go back. When we passed the spot where the lady had been shot, bits of hair-encrusted flesh, bone fragments, and blood still stained the road. As our cart came up to the post, I did my best to suppress feeling sick. The same guard who'd spoken to us before greeted us cheerfully at the mangled gate.

His manner astonished me.

"Come inside," he said, motioning to Dad.

I trembled and thought I was going to piss myself.

"Keep calm, stay here," murmured Dad.

In horror, I watched him disappear into the guardhouse. Every second he was gone was an eternity. Within moments, he re-emerged. The tension drained out of every muscle in waves.

"What happened? Did he hurt you?" I asked as we rode away.

"More bribes."

"How much?"

"Including the value of what they took on the way out, about thirty-five percent of what we made. He asked to see my papers, repeatedly, until I put enough money into the papers to make it worth his while to stop asking,"

"How could he do that?"

"Ha, he knew exactly how much everything we had was worth. On top of taxes and fees to the farmers' market, our take-home from today's load is about twenty percent."

I was speechless.

On subsequent crossings, Dad knew how much to put in our papers and wasn't required to go into the guardhouse. Greasing the wheels of Communism was expensive. On those trips, Dad taught me how he priced produce, how to display produce, and haggle. I learned about the monetary value of time. But even more important, I came to appreciate how much he cared about giving us the best life he possibly could. It deepened my love for him, and I even came to enjoy those trips but not the paperwork I got to do. My Italian got pretty good. We diversified, selling baby cows and pigs, even the wine we'd been making for ourselves. While the border guards changed frequently, their taste for bribes and our wine remained. The booze side of things got so good, it wasn't long before wine became the only thing we sold.

No matter how many times Dad and I made the trip, I always looked at that spot where the lady had been shot. We always crossed ourselves and said a little prayer as we passed. After some months, I thought I saw her again at the market with her friend as I stacked crates. They looked all right apart from her friend's dress, which looked like it had been torn. *Were they both dead?* Looking away, I shook my head. When I forced myself to look again, they were gone. *I must be daydreaming.* They'd been standing in the crowd, staring at me. I dismissed it but couldn't shake the feeling that came with that stare of hers, like she was trying to tell me something.

The following week, a letter arrived.

CHAPTER 7

SUPPORT YOUR GOVERNMENT

The letter, addressed only to the landowner, gave me a sinking feeling as I carried it from the letterbox.

"You open it," said Dad.

It was a short letter, a notice of nationalization of all farming land across the country. The absurd document instructed farmers to prepare but didn't give enough detail to understand how the scheme was going to work. It contained no acknowledgment it was, in truth, a death warrant for ordinary farming families already suffocating under rampant taxes and corruption. There was nothing to say. We each took turns holding the rudest little piece of paper I'd ever seen. There it was, in black and white. At the stroke of a pen, the state was stealing our future.

"Let's go for a walk," said Dad.

Other families mingled in the street, brandishing their copies, trying to understand, weeping. Some shouted to the heavens. Presumably, informers took note. It was one of the few times I can recall the state ever being thorough about ensuring everyone got information at the same time. I didn't hear any talk about revolt or revolution. But the crushing uncertainty and despair was plain enough. We all commiserated. How many other villages are similarly attending their own wake today?

It wasn't until dinner, in the safety of our kitchen, that Dad talked openly.

"We'll be all right. We've saved a good amount from the markets," he said.

Lina and I recognized each other's pain at seeing Dad unsure about how we'd survive. That was even more painful than the prospect of losing the farm itself.

According to the letter, government representatives would be passing through Zana on Sunday at one p.m. to hold a meeting in the main square so anyone could ask questions.

"They're only interested in taking names so they can get a head start on troublemakers," said Mum. Dad didn't argue. But I had a feeling he was already decided on going anyway. From Mum's expression, she knew it as well.

On Sunday, just before one p.m., we arrived at the square. The whole village was there. A well-groomed man in his mid-fifties with a slight paunch, expensive suit, tie, and cap walked to the center of the square. He stepped onto an upturned wooden crate and was soon flanked by a weedy young man carrying a clipboard and an ominous, tall, and burly man, a cap pulled down low over deep-set eyes. Yet another man, equally the bully type, was leaning against a car parked to one side of the square. Some children played at taking a closer look at the car, but a mere glance from the man leaning against it was enough to keep them away. The man in charge kept checking his wristwatch. I'd never seen a metallic banded wristwatch before; it glittered and twinkled proudly in the light. They looked like nasty clowns overflowing with their own self-importance.

The atmosphere was quiet and somber. As people whispered among themselves, they glanced at the clowns, their eyes filled with anger and disgust. Had they been free to do so, I'm sure they would have ripped these officials to pieces.

The clown in the expensive suit put his hands in the air, gesturing everyone to be quiet.

"Thank you for coming," he said through a condescending smile. I wondered if he'd look as arrogant without the thugs by his side.

The buffoon gushed torrents of verbal diarrhea about how the country was making tremendous progress, how the Party was bringing farm production into the twentieth century, and how there'd never been a more exciting time to be Yugoslav. People groaned, rolled their eyes, and muttered obscene things under their breath. Catching the backchat, the clown with the clipboard began fidgeting excitedly, but appeared unsure of what to do with his excitement.

"The government is liberating land capital to increase productivity to benefit the many, instead of only the elite landowner class," he declared, inspiring gasps of incredulity laced with poisonous spite.

"I didn't realize we were the elite landowner class," whispered Mum, dryly.

"What would you know about productivity, you lazy Communist pig!" came a disembodied anonymous shout from someone hiding on the other side of the walls of the square, to approving laughter rippling through the crowd.

We all tried to place the voice but couldn't work out who it might be.

"Who was that? Show yourself!" demanded the official speaking.

"Go fuck yourself, you traitorous parasite!" came the emphatic response.

The thug leaning against the car burst into a sprint to the other side of the square. He leaped up and grabbed at the top of the wall in an attempt to pull himself over. He was very athletic, and it was a valiant attempt, but the wall was too high. Undeterred, he sprinted out of the square the long way, in search of the anonymous heckler.

Emboldened by the heckling, the crowd became increasingly vocal. Val was into it, but Dad was not. Mum was worried and holding on to Val, much to his consternation. Lina reached for my hand.

The thug near the official shuffled in eager anticipation of having heads to crack. Surely, he had a gun. Were we going to have to run? *I've already seen enough shooting; we don't need anymore.* The official put a hand on the thug's shoulder, signaling him to stand down. The other thug strode back into the square, shook his head at the official, and went back to his post by the car. If they ever caught the heckler, it wouldn't end well for him.

"Thanks to the nationalization, for the first time in the nation's history, all manner of consumer goods and services will become available, all at affordable prices. While it's expected all patriotic farmers will happily embrace nationalization, a means of opting out has been preserved," said the official. I'd never seen so many people become so quiet so quickly. This was what people had been waiting for. Dad had been right, again.

The good news quickly turned sour. Farmers opting out had a choice. On the one hand, they could submit to criminal prosecution for undermining state policy objectives with conviction assured. They'd have to pay a hefty fine, serve a six-month term of imprisonment, and receive a permanent criminal record. On the other hand, farmers could volunteer to provide three months' unpaid hard labor, while undergoing Communist re-education, living at a commune working nationalized land under the supervision of state-certified farming experts. In other words, the opt-out choices were imprisonment and slavery or imprisonment and slavery. More with a criminal record and less without one.

"The state, in its magnanimity toward recalcitrant farmers who are yet to culturally mature to the point where they can embrace the nationalization, has decided not to charge those farmers undergoing re-education for lodgings and tutelage," said the official.

Some shuffled provocatively at the naked insult, straining as their wives held them back. The clown bullies, ready for action, put themselves between the official and the agitated crowd. The meeting became rich with violent possibilities, which the goons looked eager to embrace.

"If they've got guns, I bet the crowd could take them before they got off a single shot," opined Val.

"Be quiet before someone hears you," responded Mum.

The official, for his part, was enjoying poking the bear.

"Those of you wishing to opt out and volunteer for labor camp, step forward and make yourself known," he said.

Dad looked knowingly at Mum, then at us kids. Tears rolled down my cheeks. Mum and Lina were crying as well. Val huffed and folded his arms in frustration.

Dad, along with several others, approached the official. Under the watchful eyes of the goons, Clipboard Man handed out paperwork, the rest of us looking on in dejected silence. *How inhuman to make people fill in forms asking the state to take them into slavery in exchange for not stealing their land.*

Dad and the farm were just about one and the same thing. We were all part of the land, and it was part of us. The thought of giving any part of it up was intolerable, as was the thought of Dad going into some kind of prison camp, again. Who knew what they'd do to him, or even if once there, he'd ever be allowed to leave.

As unbearable as it was, we all knew there was no stopping Dad. Clipboard Man dutifully made sure all the forms were completed. The sounds of sobbing and wailing from many farmers' families were loud enough to draw the officials' attention. The officials gazed out over the mournful crowd with approving smiles, drinking in the sorrowful sounds like a conductor sublimely pleased with their own ability to direct an orchestra toward the desired melodiousness.

CHAPTER 8

SECOND DISAPPEARANCE

A couple of weeks after the village square meeting, another letter arrived. This one, addressed to Dad. As soon as I collected it, I knew what it was but didn't want to face it. Official correspondence was never good.

Finding Mum and Dad in the kitchen, I handed the letter to Dad. Seeing how upset I was, he opened it. When he handed it to Mum, she went bright red.

"Bastards!" shouted Mum, throwing the letter on the kitchen table in disgust.

Lina and Val came to see what she was cursing about. Lina picked up the letter.

"You must report at the time, date, and location appointed herein to commence your re-education. If, at the appointed time, it is determined you are absent without lawful authorization, you shall be deemed subject to immediate arrest and criminal prosecution," said Lina.

We knew this was coming, but it didn't feel any better now it'd been made official. Hugging Dad, I sobbed. I buried myself in his arms as I felt his hand lovingly stroke my head.

"They can't be any worse than the Fascists and besides, I'll be back soon."

Dad put on a brave face, but I could feel his pain in the way he held onto me tightly.

"I can't believe they're taking you again," I protested, Dad hugging me tighter. An incredible heaviness descended onto all of us.

If it wasn't for all of us hardly leaving each other's sides the rest of the day and evening, I don't know how I would have coped. We went to bed early. Neither Lina nor I could sleep.

"Why can't governments just leave us alone?" I asked.

"Sooner or later, they always come for the men and the boys. They can't help themselves," responded Lina.

"It's governments that need re-educating, not Dad!" I said, incredulously.

"At least this time, it's not at the end of a gun," said Lina, straining for a bright side.

"I still see those guns. It's pretty low when it becomes possible to find comfort in any letter like that," I said.

"I still hear the men yelling in Italian, boots stomping around downstairs. From the window, we watched soldiers running all over in the dim light."

"I thought I was dreaming," I said.

"A nightmare—Dad in the courtyard, hands and ankles in chains. An Italian soldier holding a pistol. I screamed. Violent shivers radiated outward from my spine, surging throughout my entire body. I gulped air but felt like I was suffocating. Dad lifted his head."

"To reveal a swollen bruise on his cheek," I recalled.

"Another soldier marched Mum out of the barn. She was crying. Seeing the chains, she waved her arms in helpless agony. Dad lifted his head, but the soldier yelled at him. You ran to Dad, put your arms around his waist, and held on tightly. A claw grabbed you. You dropped to Dad's feet and hung on. I can still see Dad's teary eyes looking back at you with limitless love and a bottomless sadness. My heart was breaking, torn open. It was like all our lives were being spilled out right there onto the ground," recalled Lina.

"The soldier threw me away from Dad like I was a pillow. You, Mum, and I all cried, shaking, holding onto each other. The soldier marched Dad into the street, put him into line with the others. Old men and boys. I was shocked they'd take them so young. For so long,

I wished Dad had escaped with the others who'd run away to join the partisans," I said.

"They didn't even give them time to pack any clothes. Mum ran and got Dad's big warm jacket. They marched down the road, Mum running behind. She'd only just managed to tie the sleeves around Dad's neck before getting pulled away," said Lina.

"They were so rough. So many women by the roadside, crying and watching. Watching them marching away."

"Walking back toward us, Mum kept looking back, waving her arms in hopelessness, her face contorted with grief," said Lina.

"In that moment, it dawned on me we might never see Dad again. That was the first time I remember that suffocating feeling. It was so bad, the sadness, the weight of it was horrendous."

"We tried to catch you," said Lina.

"The sadness in me was too heavy. I felt myself going, I lifted my arms toward you, but there was no strength left in them. I fainted," I said.

"I remember you coming round."

"I couldn't stop wailing, lost track of how many days were just a blur of tears."

"I'm scared to think how it was for Dad. He's never told us much about it."

"I'm not sure he ever will."

"Val does his best to encourage him, although I'm not sure it's for the right reasons. At his age, I suppose it's understandable."

As we lay in bed, we wiped each other's tears and agreed the day they took Dad had been the worst day of our lives.

I knew from my memories of what had happened the first time that we'd be worrying about Dad every minute as long as he was away. It was like a fog one had to live through, making everything gray. The sadness of not seeing Dad around, not being able to touch him or feel him nearby, was already gnawing away at my mind. I could scarcely imagine how bad it was for Mum, yet I knew that same sadness was in all our hearts, and I knew it was just endless. Anyone who has ever really loved anyone apart from themselves has that depth of sadness in them. And the crying when Dad left. . .I just couldn't stop crying for days. I wasn't sure I could bear it, and yet we were about to go through it all over again. This time, Val would also get to experience it, which made it all the worse. If there was some way I could endure the sadness for everyone, I would have.

Just after Dad had been taken the first time, something strange happened. Lina and I saw how the older women of the village dealt with it. We'd always thought of them as tough, just like our own Mum, but with their men gone, they seemed to take on an even more steely resolve. They didn't so much become hard as nails, as reveal they'd always been tough as nails. The pathos in their eyes was still there, but they kept going. They were stoic. They never complained and got on with the business of making things run. Even when they took small pleasures in helping each other, the sadness and longing in their eyes was never far away.

There was something else underneath their stoicism, apart from sadness. They were seething. They would never forgive or forget, constantly sharpening their anger and resentment into weapons, sharp as any blades. Their very thoughts were an arsenal which they turned to supporting the partisans in any way they could.

A few days after the Italians took Dad, the men who'd escaped came back with some horses and donkey-drawn wagons. We were so glad to see them, and we cried again, out of happiness but also sadness. They bristled with weapons, retrieved still more from places I knew not where, and loaded them onto wagons. They loaded a lot of supplies and left in a big hurry. There was more crying as they left. We knew some, if not all, would never come back. The village felt empty without them just as my heart felt empty without Dad. Everything, absolutely everything, was uncertain, and we were not sure if we would survive. For some reason, that prospect didn't worry me anywhere near as much as losing Dad. I constantly thought about him, prayed for him, and wanted things to go back to the way they were before. I felt as long as he'd make it back, we'd be okay.

Weeks later, a modicum of relief came by way of a letter from Dad. He was in a prison camp in Trieste where he'd been put to work as a cook. Apart from the relief, silly me, I kept thinking about how I might be able to send him some of his favorite tobacco and Rakia. It no longer mattered he'd had a stomach ulcer since he was twenty-four years old; I just wanted him to be happy. When I got too tired to think, I occasionally cradled his bottle and tobacco in my lap and stared out the window for hours.

Months later, Dad wrote us he'd fallen ill. Dad was never sick, never took a day off. For him to write he was in bed scared us senseless. Reading us the letter, Mum cried.

"I can't forget the time those papers fell from the cupboard as we had dinner," I said.

"You mean flew. It was like an invisible hand threw them," replied Lina.

"It was bizarre. The first one I picked up was the letter from Dad about his being sick. Over several minutes, a deathly cold, dark, heavy feeling filled the entire room. I felt I was suffocating. It was like I couldn't speak."

"You didn't need to. We all felt the heaviness. Mum led us into the lounge, and all three of us piled into Dad's favorite chair. Mum whispered a prayer to the Blessed Virgin Mary and asked her to look after Dad, along with the rest of us."

"Suddenly, loud cracking came from the wooden shelves in the lounge. A shiver ran down my spine. We looked at each other as if the world was about to come crashing down. Mum went back to her whispering prayer."

"After a while, everything seemed back to normal. As normal as it could be."

"It was so surreal. To this day, I don't know what it was."

"I thought it might be Dad's spirit crying out for help."

"God, I hope this time is different."

"Amen."

About a month after that night of the flying paper and crackling cupboard, an Italian soldier on a motorbike had come to our house to hand-deliver a letter. It was from Dad. He'd been near death while bedridden but wrote for us not to worry. Mum had held onto the kitchen table with one hand and buried her forehead in the palm of her other hand. Lina and I had hugged her. At the time, we'd instantly connected Dad's latest brush with death with our strange experience, only to write it off.

Dad's wellbeing had been infinitely more interesting than any inexplicable experience. Countless men and boys were dying in Italian prison camps, and we'd keenly held onto any thin sliver of hope Dad would make it, so we'd kept praying. Praying had been one of the only things I remember making me feel a little stronger. Maybe praying could make a difference this time as well. But I wondered how we'd manage without Dad to help work the farm. The notion of God sending checks to us in the mail without us having to work for it didn't figure on my radar.

CHAPTER 9
ANIMAL FRIENDS

I was driving a car, knuckles white, roadside trees a blur. *Quick, grab another gear. Faster!* Suddenly, trees became buildings. I drove over several curbs, the concrete under my tires so new, it was still wet. *No time. Get ahead of the competition.* Dad was waiting at the finish. I didn't drive, let alone race. I slowed to a crawl. Was this real? Someone was spying on me. Was I dreaming?

Rubbing the sleep out of my eyes, I needed more rest but was too anxious.

Dad was leaving for prison today. Rushing downstairs, I found him sitting at the kitchen table, looking over a pile of paperwork.

"Dad, please don't go. Can't we sell some cows, pay a lawyer who can do something?"

Dad leaned back and shot me a quizzical look. Squeezing myself onto his lap, I put my arms around him, curled up, and cried.

"My dear girl, you were so strong the first time I had to go. You're older now, you'll be all right," he said softly.

"You don't know what it's like without you. It hurts too much. It's not fair!"

Raised eyebrows of studied surprise at my outburst gave way to a compassionate smile. He looked deeply into my eyes, into my soul.

"I know me being away in the war hurt you. It hurt me as well. I love you, all of you, more than anything in this world, more than I can ever say. But this is how we keep the farm."

"I can't take things casually like you. I'm not strong like you. I can't lose you again."

Dad stroked my hair, his tenderness opening my floodgates.

"When they took you away the first time, I thought I was going to lose you forever. When will it ever stop? I'm scared of what they might do to you," I blathered.

Cupping my wet cheeks in his hands, he kissed my forehead. "You are my beautiful daughter, and we love each other, and no one can take that away from us. You're much stronger than you realize. Only someone with the heart of a lion could face their feelings so directly. I know you're scared. I'm scared too. I don't think this is going to be like the war. But it's in God's hands. God gives me hope. You all give me hope. I feel so grateful to have all of you and the farm. I scarcely dare to dream of anything more."

"Why can't they just let us alone so we can be a family?" I protested.

"I understand. You're young. You dream, dream of freedom. I see it in your eyes. I'm so proud of all my family, especially the fine people my children are becoming. I'm so proud of how well you did while I was gone during the war. I love hearing what happened the first time you tended livestock, all by yourself! Come on, tell me again," he asked, smiling proudly.

Trying to distract me was a dirty trick. It made me love him all the more.

Mum, Lina, and Val came into the kitchen. "What time did Mum wake you up that morning?" asked Lina, rubbing my back.

"Two-thirty a.m."

"It was a pitch-black summer morning. How long had Dad been gone?"

"A few months."

"I was still sleeping. What did Mum say to you?"

"I told Anja to get up and take the cows and bulls out to pasture for a feed," said Mum.

"I thought I was dreaming. It took a few moments to register Mum was serious. Me! Alone! In the middle of the night! In charge of giants!"

I recalled.

"You weren't happy," said Mum.

"What seven-year-old would be? I was petrified," I said.

"Mum was nice but was having none of it," said Lina.

"It was going to be too hot during the day, and there'd be less chance of running into hungry and homeless partisans running around stealing whatever they could," said Mum.

"I wasn't sure how I was going to manage all those cows and the bulls. Reluctantly, I got up, shaking so much my little fingers had a hard time with buttons getting dressed. I was scared I'd lose the lot, including myself."

"I was trusting you with the only cows and bulls we had left. Apart from our land, most of our wealth was in your hands," said Mum.

"You gave me buttered toast and green apples for breakfast, made sure I ate it all, told me to be careful and to come home quickly once the animals were fed. You kissed me and sent me into the night. The tranquil air against my cheeks did nothing to cool my nerves. It was fixing to get really hot at the first lick of morning sun. In the barn, I took a long stick and timidly whacked the heavy breathers with my stick. Once Aristotle stirred, they all stirred. Mooing sleepily, they followed Aristotle into the yard. I gave Aristotle a decent whack and to my surprise and disappointment, the whole group started leaving the yard. I wondered if any of us would make it home."

"They would have still been half-asleep, but they knew exactly where to go," said Mum.

"Not that I could have done much if they didn't."

"Lumbering along that same path was their life. All they needed was you to tell them they had to do it," said Mum.

"I was so scared, a pine marten would have made me jump out of my skin. Eventually, we got to the feeding area. They fanned out. None were lost, but I counted anyway. I stood in the middle so I wouldn't be the first taken by a bear or wild boar and prayed trampling hooves had scared the snakes away. Aristotle came to graze near me. His breathy masticating helped relax me some. But if I stood still for long, my legs would start shaking. Scanning constantly for movement other than cows. . .I thought the moon looked oddly bright."

"You were so brave. Like luxurious black velvet splashed with sparkling diamonds, the night sky shows itself just as beautiful to a pauper as to a king. I'd look up at that same night sky and think of you," said Dad.

"I thought of you too, Dad. The serene stars seemed far off and uninterested in little girls like me. I prayed to God, Jesus, the Holy Ghost, and the Blessed Virgin Mary to keep us all safe and deliver me and our livestock safely home. I prayed for God to send an angel to watch over us. Moments later, several shooting stars crossed the sky. Suddenly, one changed direction."

"What do you mean, changed direction?" asked Val.

"I haven't heard this before," said Mum.

"It got bigger. . .as if coming toward me."

"You were dreaming. A frightened mind in the night plays many tricks," said Mum.

"It felt like a dream, one in which a forest fairy had come to say hello."

"There's no shortage of fairies around that clearing," said Lina.

"How did you feel at the time?" asked Dad.

"The light was very beautiful. I stopped shaking."

"How close was the light?" asked Val.

"Close. . .far. . .I couldn't tell."

"What happened?" asked Val.

"I felt warm and heard buzzing, like a mosquito. Next thing, a giant strip of sky had already gone from black to deep blue. I didn't want to hang around for bears, foxes, and boars, so I gave Aristotle and the others a few good whacks and kept scanning. Walking between them, I could just make out the forest where people said fairies lived."

"Is that it?" asked Val.

"I don't remember anything else, except the musky tang of cow dung."

"How were you feeling at that point?" asked Dad.

"Hmm, agitated. I tried distracting myself by thinking about how nice it was going to be when we were all home."

"How long was the light there?" asked Val.

"I don't know."

I didn't give it a second thought at the time. On the way home, I was too busy moving between the cows, doing my best to make sure everyone kept to the track. The forest was alive with birds chirping, dry twigs and leaves cracking beneath bovine hooves. They were so massive but so gentle, each one an individual and all of them like dear friends, especially Aristotle. Every so often, it felt like someone was nearby. But I was sure it was just my terror playing tricks. As long as we kept moving steadily, the terror was just bearable. I understood Val's curiosity but didn't dare mention any more of my experience lest it provoke more wide eyes.

"On seeing our front yard through the trees, I heaved a sigh. The herd glided arrow-straight toward our yard. Half in, one of the bulls stopped to eat some grass. As the rest piled into the yard behind Aristotle, this other bull went for a stroll up the road. Running alongside, I whacked him on the neck to turn him. He flinched but kept walking. Grabbing his tail, I pulled, but he was oblivious to the human insect buzzing frantically at his expansive rear. In desperation, I hung off his tail, feet fully off the ground, pleading. Finally, he stopped. I went from abject misery to absolute joy. With both hands on the furry hardness of his neck, I pushed with all my might to turn him. It didn't work, but after hitting him with the stick a few times, he turned and quickly headed down the road, rounding into our yard."

"That's my girl," said Mum.

"After closing the barn, I realized I was dripping with sweat and exhausted but so relieved."

"I came out to see for myself," said Mum.

"When I saw you, smiling, your arms open, my chest almost burst open."

"You couldn't hold it in anymore."

"I ran to you."

"We hugged so tightly, and you cried. I told you I was so proud of you."

"Those words unlocked something even bigger than my relief."

Mum's approval filled a huge underground cavern in my heart with light. A huge cavern where yearning for Dad, pride, bitterness, fear, and sadness were all mixed together. All those feelings rushed through my little body and out as a flood of tears and yelping. My little torso convulsed as I cried with my whole body. With feelings like those, unlike the bull, there was no tail to grab onto.

"Now I remember. You told me you'd seen fairy lights. But I didn't think to ask. By the time Dad came back from the war, you were a veteran at getting up at three a.m., stocking the kitchen with wood for the stove, fetching water from the well, baking bread, chopping vegetables, which you hated, cooking minestrone, sewing, and fixing anything broken," said Mum.

"To survive, we had to keep working. Watching you taught me that. Every day, I saw how hard you worked, and I wanted to do the same, and every minute, I thought about Dad. I don't want to go through that again."

Reliving that story reminded me not only how much I loved Dad, but of how hard it was to make the farm work without him. Him leaving again made everything feel unbalanced. Being older didn't make me need him any less. If anything, I needed Dad more than ever, in a different but even deeper way. As I perceived more of the world, I could see more how special he was. He was more than Dad. He was a compass inside me, showing me my way in life. At least this time, we could hope he would be treated better. Still, his absence would also put the farm out of whack for a season or more. With Dad away, anything could happen to Dad or our farm.

Sitting around the kitchen table, we strategized how to make the farm work as productively as possible while Dad was away.

Maybe I could get a job. I didn't know how, or who would give someone like me a job, but maybe I could try anyway. I had better keep that idea to myself for now and just focus on getting through the rest of this morning.

Turning to Dad, Mum asked, "Do you want to see what we have planned for you this morning before you go?"

CHAPTER 10
RADIOS ARE FASCINATING

Behind mournfulness, Dad's eyes sparkled with anticipation at the surprise we'd prepared. The whole morning of Dad's departure for prison was like that: painful and beautiful. Lina, Val, and I sprang into action. We ran a hot bath, and as he washed, we helped Mum make a special breakfast. The stairs creaked as he came down. Dad surveyed the spread laid on in his honor. The spread seemed a pitiful gesture. Given his every striving was to provide for us, there were no words for the pain at the departure of our wise and humble king. To willingly go to a prison camp to do hard labor so we had a chance at keeping the farm made him even more of a hero than he already was. Each of us in our turn hugged him deeply and repeatedly kissed him, wet cheek to wet cheek, as he chided us for making a fuss.

Sitting at the table, we held hands, prayed, and gave thanks, Val leading a prayer for Dad's speedy and safe return. We passed plates loaded to the brim with the very finest from our farm, the work of our loving hands. Cured meats, olives, roasted peppers, scrambled eggs with fried Kranjska klobasa, tomatoes, mushrooms, and spinach, covered with our own parmesan in the style of Parmigiano Reggiano, of which Dad was very proud. The smell of brown toast with lashings of butter, garlic, marjoram, rosemary, parsley, and thyme in the morning was blissful. In a special treat, it was all to be washed down with our own vino. Notwithstanding the fine food, the conversation was sparse and the tasting bittersweet. Watching Dad enjoy the meal was all the nourishment I yearned for. To finish, Mum poured Dad his special coffee sludge.

Dad patted his stomach. "Thank you. What a wonderful breakfast. I'm going for a smoke."

We were too sad to say much of anything as Mum cleaned up. From her fussing, I could tell she was angrier than anyone.

Through the kitchen window we watched a cart pull up with a couple of men on it.

"I'll be back down in a minute," said Dad, his usual calm self, at least outwardly.

Outside, the strangest thing happened. As Mum chatted with the men, a dark cloud dropping a fine misty rain rolled in and hovered over the forest, not far away. From my angle, it looked to be hovering right over the cart. Dad came bursting out the door carrying a small sack of clothes. As he approached the cart, a faint but distinct rainbow formed, the end of it landing right in the cart. Dad threw his sack onto the cart. I couldn't take my eyes off the rainbow as Dad gave each of us a hearty hug and a kiss.

"Keep your chins up and keep working the farm like we discussed."

Dad embraced Mum, and they shared a long kiss.

"Thank you for breakfast."

As Dad climbed aboard, the cloud appeared to approach, the colors of the rainbow brighter. I could hardly believe no one else seemed to notice. Mum was stoical, a crestfallen Val was putting on a brave face, and Lina and I were both a teary mess.

Through my tears, amazed, I kept looking at the rainbow and Dad seated right at the base of it. *I must be dreaming.*

Dad, up high on the cart, regarded us with unruffled serenity. His gaze pierced my chest, soothing and steadying me. What was I going to do now that my rock was leaving?

He blew us kisses as they headed out. We blew kisses back. Would I ever see my wonderful Dad again?

I looked on, stupefied, as the rainbow followed Dad. The cloud and rainbow melted into nothing as the cart ambled down the road. As

Dad and his colorful apparition disappeared, a gaping hole in my heart opened. The emptiness was like an old enemy once vanquished, now returned with spiteful vengeance. Dolefully walking back, I pondered the rainbow. It looked as real as real could be, and beyond the implied promise of a reunion, in this life or the next, I wondered whether it mattered whether I'd imagined it or not. I dared not ask anyone for confirmation of the sight, instead putting my arm around Mum, content with resting my head on her shoulder.

In the ensuing weeks, productivity on our farm declined, as expected. Somewhat less expected but unsurprising in retrospect was what the Communists did to our village and many others while the men were gone. Families not participating in the nationalization often had their crops and produce stolen or burned. Some families got letters claiming payment for so-called unpaid taxes. Some people were beaten when they complained. Bribes paid to officials who came warning of thieves were enough to make sure thieves knew which properties to leave untouched. For some families holding out, it was too much. They walked away from farms, leaving their village homes deserted. Generations of work lost forever.

After the government took its pick of land from willing nationalization participants, it took its pick of land left by those it had pushed off. Leftover farms forgotten about by the state were abandoned, often invaded by itinerant squatters. Our kind couldn't expect much help from the law, and many of the old friendships and networks were destroyed. Once the bottom-feeders moved in, villages weren't the same. Perhaps that was the plan.

The Nazis ethnically cleansed by trucking men and boys off to be worked to death and killing many who remained. Making room for the Lebensborn meant liquefying the deplorable masses. The Communists did their best to flatter their former enemies by imitating them.

With Dad gone, we focused on growing enough to feed ourselves, fearful either the state or a prospective squatter might erroneously claim fallow farmland was deserted. Trips into Italy chancing bandits and corrupt border guards was too dangerous. Val was loyal, strong, and eager, but he was too young to risk putting in harm's way. We kept to working small plots close to home, and almost every day did small amounts of work on the more remote plots. We'd leave one of Dad's unwashed shirts, an old smoking pipe, and a few personal items on each plot. We'd often return to see a shirt or pipe had been moved or gone missing.

When I couldn't sleep, which was often, I'd lay in bed, look out the window at the stars, and wonder how Dad was. I'd fantasize about how nice life could be and how grateful I'd be if a way through presented itself, no matter how strange. Suddenly, I realized I already had the answer or at least an answer. I'd been so stressed I'd forgotten about my idea of getting a job, a well-paying job. With that kind of money, we didn't need risky trips to Italy. I could buy food, clothes, and tools, maybe even a good rifle. I didn't particularly like guns, but with a rifle, we could protect ourselves and our land and hunt game. Val certainly wouldn't need any encouragement in applying himself to learn how to use it, but he'd need a good teacher. Mum wouldn't be happy, but I'd rather see her unhappy than homeless and starving. There was just one problem. Who, in a Communist country where only the well-connected got well-paying jobs, would give a Catholic Triestini a chance? The more I thought about it, the more ridiculous it seemed.

*

October, 1954, I turned seventeen. There was no time or money for a party. Who would I have invited anyway? Most families we'd known in the village who'd resisted the nationalization had been decimated and scattered. As one of the last holdouts, we were already considered subversives by the Marxists, making us even more untouchable. Who among those few still precariously hanging on would willingly risk guilt by association by attending a birthday party? So much suspicion hung in the air, people hardly spoke to anyone who wasn't family.

I was no stranger to social distancing. My own grandmother on my

Dad's side had refused to see me for years after I'd been born, continually claiming I was illegitimate. Her passionately open recalcitrance got so bad no one could stand it. Once, when Lina and I were still quite young, Grandma came and made a big show of giving Lina candy but none to me. When Lina asked Grandma why she wouldn't give me any candy, Grandma told her I wasn't really her sister. Lina, the darling, spat the candy out onto the dirt.

"Why'd you do that?" I asked Lina. I'll never forget her response.

"Because you're my sister," answered Lina, hugging me tightly.

Grandma sure went off in a huff that day. She spread so much gossip about me, in the end no one wanted to be her friend. No one talked about Grandma around Mum if they knew what was good for them. I didn't know if Dad ever forgave her.

I felt the hurt. How could I not? But I still loved Grandma. I couldn't help it. I was always polite to her and always wanted the best for her. More than anything, the whole drama just made me sad.

Ironically, I was the only one willing to spend the last few days of her life with her. She lay in bed, not able to do much else except talk barely above a whisper when she had the energy. Staying with her in her little house, I cooked for her, fed her, cleaned her, and forgave her as I hoped she could forgive me. For the first time, I felt like I got to know her, and the lovely side of her I always knew was there. I couldn't have cared less about an apology. By that stage, all that stuff seemed unimportant. Perhaps it always was unimportant. In the end, it was so nice to chat and share kindness with her, and it was my privilege to look after her. Holding her hand as she passed, I felt bitterness at all the years wasted as a fundamentally good person lay trapped behind senseless innuendo and malice. That waste cut me a lot deeper than anything silly Grandma had said about me.

Having a birthday party was the last thing I needed. Besides, I had much more exciting ideas in mind.

Getting up extra early, quiet as a mouse I washed, combed my hair, and put on my nicest clothes, the ones I normally only wore to church.

After a quick breakfast, I left a note on the kitchen table. All it said was I'd be back in the afternoon. I was determined to do everything I could to find a job, knowing full well I had no idea what I was doing and that I'd have next to no chance. The only thing in my mind was a picture of how grateful I'd feel to get a job, any job.

To me, Sezana was a metropolis. The notion a couple thousand people could, or would even want to, live in one city was laughable. Riding my bicycle along the deserted road in the dim morning light, I prayed to God, Jesus, and the Blessed Virgin Mary over and over again that my dream of getting a job to help my family would come true.

After a forty-minute ride, I coasted into Sezana figuring the thing to do was head for the biggest buildings, see what kind of places were about, pick one, go in, and ask about work. If I got a no, I'd hit the next one, and keep coming back until someone relented. If there was a tailor or dress shop, I would definitely ask there.

As I floated past what looked like a factory, a massive sign perched on the top caught my eye. The big red stylized letters read *Astro Radio*. Dismissing it, I rode on, but the sign somehow called to me. Radios were made of lots of little bits. I could be good at putting all those little bits together.

Stopping the bike, I thought about how radios picked up signals, ideas from far away. The concept was intriguing, exciting, futuristic, and radios were popular with rich Communists. The more I thought about it, the more I heard it calling.

The front gate was open, and the lights inside were on. Wheeling my bike past the gate, I immediately felt anxious. I might as well have been asking for a job where they build space-rockets.

Scared of embarrassing myself, I hesitated and turned around. Leaving, I asked myself why I'd bother to come at all. I thought about Dad, Mum, Lina, Val, and the farm. A big, busy factory might have all kinds of work—cleaning, cooking, packing boxes—and need lots of people to make it run and offer lots of different opportunities.

Riding back through the gate, the building suddenly became huge, almost overwhelming. The red bricks and tall, white, wooden-framed windows loomed. A feeling of being watched gripped me. Even in the dim light, the building looked dirty, the brickwork chipped and rough, like the place had seen better days. Perhaps they didn't build rocket ships here after all.

The sign on top of the building towered, each of the big letters as tall as a tall man. At the end of the sign was a red star with a hammer and sickle. Okay, I was not keen on the hammer and sickle insignia.

Remember what you came here for.

Heart in mouth, determined to follow through, I kept putting one foot in front of the other.

As I looked in through one of the large front windows, an older man with graying hair suddenly appeared in the dim interior light. The sight of him staring back at me startled me. Recoiling, I fell off my bike.

Luckily, a hedgerow broke my fall, and nothing was broken. I felt certain I'd ruined my clothes, perhaps torn my dress, but I was more worried about getting arrested. I got to my feet, and to my relief, my clothes were still in one piece. Brushing myself off, I lined up the gate for a quick escape. Picking up the bike, I got on, and instantly got an even bigger fright at finding the man in the window now standing next to me. Again, I recoiled. If he hadn't taken hold of my arm, I was sure I would have taken another tumble. His arrival was so silent, it was like he'd flown like a bird rather than walked. As soon as I was steady, he released his grip, calmly observing me from behind black-rimmed glasses, blinking like an owl.

He moved in front of me, blocking my escape. But seeing his eyes, I no longer felt scared, just embarrassed.

"I'm sorry, I didn't mean to disturb you."

"You're not disturbing anyone," he said, his tone striking me weirdly. "You're obviously looking for something. Why don't you tell me what it is?" He spoke like no one I'd ever met before: perfect diction but with a subtle accent I couldn't place.

"I'm looking for a job," I offered timidly.

"Well, you won't find one flailing about in the shrubbery," he said, looking me up and down like a scientist attempting to classify a wayward specimen. "Who referred you here?"

"Nobody," I answered, as he furrowed his brows in disappointment. "So why this particular place?"

There was something strange in his manner, like a pleasant but discordant note in a new song. Perhaps he thought me a thief. Instead of becoming defensive, his oddness aroused a directness in me I wouldn't normally be game to pursue with a stranger.

"I was riding past. This may sound strange, but something stopped me. When I looked at the place, I had an urge to drop in. Maybe there's cooking or cleaning work here I could do?"

Something clicked. Looking me up and down again, his mood lightened to bemused skepticism. "Cooking or cleaning, you say," he repeated, as the look of skepticism on his face softened further but didn't dissipate completely.

Sensing I'd made a mistake, I moved my bike to go around him.

"If you really want to ask about work, I'd be happy to unlock the front office. You can wait in the foyer. When the office girls arrive, you can talk to them."

I'd made such a scene, I felt obligated to at least go through the motions of being rejected by the office girls. Initial optimism became trepidation as I carried the bike up the concrete stairs to the large steel-and-glass front doors. Waiting for him to unlock the door, I had the urge to leave. Just as I drew breath to tell him I'd changed my mind, he swung the door open and gestured for me to enter. He walked off before I'd gotten a good grip on the heavy steel-and-glass door, quite a fancy if well-worn thing. Electric lights flickered to life as I fumbled with the door, which banged loudly against my bike several times as I dragged it inside. He winced painfully at the banging and appeared relieved when the door closed without any broken glass. Quick as a flash, the owl-like man disappeared behind a counter and down a dark hall.

The foyer gave off an unnatural, spooky vibe. After pacing around for a while, I felt tired and sat on a nearby chair. As soon as I sat, my eyes became drowsy. Shadows milled about around me. I wanted to move so I could see what was making the shadows, but I couldn't.

When I woke, the morning light shone bright and warm through the windows. Workers trickled in through the front gate. I was still alone, thank goodness. Where was my bike? It was neatly on its stand. I thought I'd left it lying on the floor at my feet. On my lower right shin, there was a spot of crusty blood. I must have nicked myself falling over. Dabbing at the tiny wound with a hanky, I watched the workers arriving. None came through reception; instead, they all disappeared around the side of the building. Most dragged themselves along in a slow and tired gait. Some chatted, a few even shared a laugh.

Suddenly, two young ladies emerged from the hallway and took their seats behind the reception counter, one shooting me a brief look. They glanced at one another in recognition that an outsider was on their turf. They were very well-dressed, attractive even, in spite of all the paint heaped onto their faces like it had come off a spatula. They pretended to ignore me and went about their work. How plain I must have looked to them, a poor country girl, which I was.

Eventually, I plucked up enough courage to approach. They typed and shuffled papers busily and continued ignoring me. I was scared they'd shout at me to get out. A couple of times, I drew breath as if to speak but couldn't. *Have I come this far and waited this long, only to be ignored?*

In exasperation that I might as well get my rejection out of the way, I blurted out, "Hello," which they pretended not to hear. While working up the courage to say something that might get their attention, Owl Man came out from the hallway just enough so he could get a good look at me. He was assessing me. In the full morning light, his age showed. He looked handsome in a fatherly kind of way in his cardigan, thin necktie, and gray slacks. He gave me a thumbs-up, smiled, put an index finger to his puckered lips, and left. It seemed the thing to do was to stay put and wait quietly.

One of the receptionists finally stopped working and smiled at me with disdain. "Can I help you?"

"I'm looking for work; can you please tell me if you have anything available?"

"Who told you to come here?"

"Nobody," I replied innocently. She looked at me with disgust, like I was trash.

"Do you have any experience or qualifications?" The tone in her voice hardened, as if she had no intention of helping and every intention of torturing me so I'd never come back.

"No qualifications, but I grew up on a farm, I'm very good with my hands. . ."

"Good with your hands. . ." the other receptionist repeated mockingly, giggling. I didn't appreciate her insinuation but didn't want to pay her the compliment of becoming agitated.

"I mean I can clean, cook, and sew very well with a needle and machine," I said, firmly.

The interrogating receptionist rolled her eyes and huffed dismissively. "We have no need for your, err, handiwork here, but here is a form. Fill it out and if a suitable position comes up, someone will let you know."

It was clear enough the form, once filled out, would only end up in the rubbish. She only wanted to put me through the humiliation of filling it out anyway. The other receptionist contracted a case of the giggles, so much so that she stopped typing.

"Don't worry, I'm sure you'll find work in town, if you're good with your hands," she said, laughing loudly.

I felt like melting into my shoes and was about to hand back the blank form when another man came out from the darkness of the hallway and handed the interrogating receptionists some papers. The giggle-pot receptionist suddenly went quiet and straightened herself up.

I recognized him immediately as Dad's Communist acquaintance from White Sunday. He looked up at me with a blank face and turned to walk off. Suddenly, he stopped, turned, and came back over to the counter.

"Anja?"

The two receptionists stopped working. Slack-jawed, they looked at him and then at me, waiting to see what I'd say.

"Yes," I said quietly.

"Anja, Joe's daughter from Zana?" he enquired tentatively, with the hint of a hopeful smile.

"Yes," I said, unsure whether to return his smile.

"I almost didn't recognize you," he said, apologetically. "You probably don't remember me, but we met a while ago at the harvest festival. I spent quite a bit of time with your father that day. He told me about you. He's very proud of you."

"Yes, I remember."

"I very much enjoyed the performance you and your sister gave. You were both wonderful. You have an amazing voice."

"It's very kind of you to remember."

"So what brings you to our factory?" he asked, eyeing the job application form in my hand, making me feel even more self-conscious. As he eyed the ogling receptionists, they instantly resumed working.

"I came into town to look for a job, any cleaning job. This was the first place I came to," I said sheepishly. "I'm sorry, I didn't realize I'd run across anyone who knew my Dad. I'm not looking for any favors. I'll be on my way," I said, abandoning the application on the counter. Impatient to leave, I briskly made for my bike.

"Anja, wait!"

I froze to the sound of footsteps rushing closer.

"Don't be silly. You've come all this way; you might as well at least stay long enough so we can have a decent chat. I can't promise anything, but you can come to my office, and we can talk about it over a cup of tea. If there's nothing for you here, at least you can leave knowing you tried. If you tell me a little more about what you can do, I might even be able to point you in the right direction. Sound fair enough?"

Recalling the way Dad had talked about this fellow, I felt myself relenting at his civility.

"Don't worry, it will be all right. Come on, get your bike, and follow me."

His eyes brimmed with simpatico, the kind one might feel for an animal entangled in a trap. He waited attentively as I collected my bike, gesturing for me to follow him down the hall.

As I passed behind the counter, the receptionists both gave me the same look of disgust. Taken aback at their easy hostility, I averted my gaze.

Wheeling my bike down the hall, I was surprised to see Owl Man standing in a doorway, watching, and smiling as we passed. He came and went almost like an apparition. He felt kindly on some level, but I was struck by how opaque he also felt to me. There was something eerie in his smile, tinged with knowingness. Between Owl Man, Dad's acquaintance, and the receptionists, Owl Man scared me the most.

A couple of executive types coming the other way stopped chatting as they drew near. I felt their eyes on me and couldn't bear the thought of looking at them. I felt a knot in my stomach; they were sizing me up like I was lunch. Finally, Dad's Communist acquaintance stopped at a doorway.

"In you go," he said, his outstretched arm gesturing for me to step into the blackness that was his office.

CHAPTER 11
THE INTERVIEW

The office was modest. My bike seemed uncomfortably large in the space, but I didn't dare leave it in the hall. I quietly leaned it up against a row of filing cabinets dominating one side of the room. My interviewer slowly navigated his way around the other side, taking care not to knock any of the neat piles of papers stacked high on various cupboards and precariously perched around the edge of his desk. Behind the office desk and paper stacks begging to be knocked over, a large, colorized portrait of Tito took pride of place on the wall. The portrait was in a religious style, featuring dreamy hues which made the father of the nation look decidedly saintly. The rest of the wall was blank, with nothing to distract from the weight of investment in that portrait.

"Please, Anja, make yourself comfortable. Can I offer you a cup of tea?" he asked, as I perched myself on the edge of one of the wooden visitors' chairs.

"Oh, no thank you."

Ignoring my refusal, he picked up the phone and ordered kopriva and kamilica tea and potica cookies.

"I hope you don't mind if I smoke. Would you like one?"

"No thank you, I don't smoke."

"I have a bottle of Rakia in my desk. I can offer you a little if you like?" he asked, armed with a playful smile and a cocked eyebrow.

I laughed nervously.

"No, thank you. I don't drink."

"As you wish," he said, smiling, leaving me wondering whether I'd passed or failed this part of his test.

"How is your father?" he asked, lighting a cigarette.

Unsure how much he knew, I was unnerved by his question.

"I hope he's okay. He's in a camp for a few months because he didn't give land for the nationalization," I said.

"Nasty bit of business that nationalization. I'm not surprised he opted out," he said with surprising candor, his tone suggesting he already knew where Dad was.

"I've been thinking the best thing I could do would be to get a job."

"I understand. I hope you and the rest of your family are not too worried about him. I've heard the camps are a bit rough, but your Dad's resilient. I'm sure he'll be okay."

"Thank you for your kind words."

"Please, excuse me for asking, but if your Dad's not on the farm, wouldn't you be needed there rather than out here looking for a job? Is something stopping you from working the farm, your health perhaps?"

"My health is good."

"You're not running away from home, are you?" he asked, through half-squinting eyes.

"Everything with me and the farm is as good as it can be without Dad. Apart from missing him terribly, production is down, but until Dad gets back, it's more about protecting what's ours than maximizing output. I'm looking for a job on top of my work on the farm."

"Pardon me again. You seem like a petite girl; what exactly is it you do on the farm?"

I did my best to avoid embellishment. "I tend animals, help with planting, weeding, harvesting, transport to market, and making cheese and wine. I help maintain things like fences and forest tracks. Around the house, I help clean, cook, fetch water. I make clothes, do knitting, darning, and quite enjoy embroidery when I get the time, which isn't often. We all do whatever needs doing, but I like it best when we're doing things together."

"What about school?"

"I almost finished primary school," I said, sheepishly.

"You didn't finish? Why?"

"After the war, when the teacher said I could read and write better than kids a couple of years ahead who were finishing, my parents took me out of school. There wasn't time and no money to pay for books, travel, and fees for high school."

"What did you do if you weren't in school?"

"I worked on our farm and other people's farms," I replied, slightly defensive.

"What kind of work did you say you were looking for?"

"Anything really. Cleaning, sewing, cooking—whatever you have that might be suitable. I'd look forward to learning as much as I can," I said, with gusto.

He'd listened intently and smiled at my enthusiasm. "I have to say, the resilience and drive of youth never ceases to amaze—at least, some youth," he said, puffing on his cigarette.

Having humored me, I expected he would politely tell me I was wasting his time.

"Do you know how I know your father?"

"No," I answered, trying to hide a growing expectation of failure.

As he was about to let me down gently with a story, the phone rang. After a brief conversation, he slammed down the heavy black receiver.

"I'll be back in a moment," he said, exasperated, as he shuffled his way out the door, careful not to disturb the neat piles of papers. The lingering smell of cigarette smoke reminded me of Dad. I couldn't imagine Dad smoking a cigarette from a packet. He always insisted on rolling his own. It was his little ritual. I wondered what Dad might be doing, whether he was all right, and hoped he had some way of getting tobacco.

I felt awful about having stopped at the factory, wasting this man's time, and awkward about staying any longer. Before leaving, I'd write a note apologizing for interrupting his busy schedule and thanking him for his generosity.

The notepad and pencil on the desk were out of easy reach without risking knocking over papers. There was no one else there, but I still felt like someone was watching me. Midway through shuffling around the other side of the desk, the high-pitched sound of stilettos reverberated down the hall, a fancy woman's footsteps. *The tea and cookies!* Not wanting to appear nosy hovering over a desk in a place I wasn't supposed to be, I quickly doubled back. Somehow, papers went flying. *Shit!* Quickly replacing them as best I could, I sat in the guest's chair in the nick of time.

There was a knock at the door but no pause for a response before it opened. In came one of the dragons from the front desk, armed with a tray of teapots, cups, a small bowl of biscuits, and a look on her face like she wanted to kill me. She deposited the contents of the tray onto the desk with a swift deftness suggesting she was no stranger to avoiding the piles of paper. Her eyes lingered on the pile of the papers I'd disturbed and flashed me a look of sharp disgust.

"Treacherous Triestini bitch," she hissed under her breath as she left the room. Of venom, I was sure she had plenty. The smell of fresh tea and the sight of biscuits made me salivate profusely, but I didn't dare touch either.

Returning, my host apologized for his absence, and I apologized for having knocked over some papers while waiting in his office. Pouring me a cup of tea, he suggested I forget about the papers. Insisting I take a biscuit, he didn't relent until I'd taken two.

"Ah, yes, your father and I," he said, reclining back into his chair as I munched and quietly sipped my tea, imagining I'd concealed how thirsty or hungry I was.

"Has he told you how he and I met?"

"Ah, no."

"Well then, let this story be our little secret," he said, shuffling in his seat as if he was settling in.

I didn't have time for war stories. I needed to find a job!

"I met your father in the war, in the prison camp. Countless died there. . .starvation, torture, disease, being worked to death. They did as they pleased with us. Your father said the only thing that saved him was being put to work in the kitchen, on account of his fluent Italian. After, they trained him to be a nurse's assistant. He even deployed with their troops, but it wasn't a promotion. He described the carnage he saw as a kind of mass suicide. . .stealing, prostitution, violence, rape. . .anything you could imagine. Children and old people picking over piles of rubble, rubbish, and bodies. They'd eat anything. . .broth from leather belts and shoes stripped from the dead. He said he saw and smelled people cooking meat in places where the only source of protein would have been the dead."

"He's never mentioned much about the war."

"For your Dad, there were no rest breaks; sleep was often denied him. He said he lost count of how many mangled and diseased people and soldiers he'd nursed or watched die. Eventually, a chest infection got him."

"Oh."

"They told him medicine was too valuable to use on his kind and told him he'd be shot if he stopped working. When he was coughing up blood and too weak to stand, they eventually told him they had no food to waste on a dying captive and suggested he find somewhere to rest. He knew what they meant. He found an empty bed, but they refused it to him, saying beds were only for Italians. The only resting place he found was a disused cleaner's storeroom."

"My God."

"He slouched on one chair and put his legs up on another. Your Dad lay there, barely conscious, coughing up blood onto his soiled shirt and pants and the floor, waiting for death. On the second day, he heard a big commotion, lots of shouting and running. He was too weak to care. He said things went suddenly quiet. Slipping in and out of consciousness, he saw his departed parents standing in front of him, come to collect him. He told me in that moment, thinking he was about to die, he felt an unbelievable gratitude to God for giving him such a wonderful life.

As he felt life was soon to leave him, he was filled with joy at being your Dad, and sadness he'd never see you again."

"Oh, my dear papa."

"He heard faint sounds, voices. . .American voices, and saw soldiers with guns in the doorway. To him, they were angels sent by God. He was too weak to speak. Your Dad told me he often prayed to God to bless those GIs. They nursed your Dad, gave him an English/Italian phrasebook, which he devoured."

"He's very smart, my wonderful papa."

"They were impressed enough that an American officer offered your Dad work, making it clear no one would force him and that he'd be looked after. Your Dad didn't hesitate."

"He came back so much later than everybody else."

"He never told you why?"

"Not really."

"He isn't the kind to say much, but he did important work, traveling with them, looking after the wounded but especially as an interpreter. Your Dad has a knack for languages. True to their word, the Americans treated him well, even with dental work."

"His teeth still look great. Dear God, I hope he's all right." *Stop crying!*

"Your Dad liked practicing his English with the GIs and enjoyed their jazz music. He'd tell me they could accomplish anything. Of that, I have no doubt he was right. I'm sorry. I didn't mean to make you cry."

"*I'm* sorry. I wasn't expecting to hear those things about my Dad this morning."

"I know, it's all right. Take a moment if you need."

"Aren't the Americans supposed to be our mortal enemies now?"

"It's complicated."

"Shouldn't peacetime make it simpler?"

"Peace? I'm not sure anyone knows what that is. You'd be surprised how far down into the roots that soaks. That's why you have to make sure you know who you're talking to, and you never know who might be listening," he said, smiling cryptically.

"Honest people shouldn't have to watch what they say."

"A fine sentiment but not always practical, as I'm sure you already appreciate. Anyway, soon after I arrived at a camp where your Dad was at, I became ill, some kind of gastrointestinal thing. Things were a bit touch and go for me."

"Which camp?"

"I can't say."

"Oh, I'm sorry. I didn't mean to pry."

"It's all right. Your father looked after me. He always downplayed it, but I know I wouldn't have made it if it wasn't for him. After I got better, I got to know your father. I began to appreciate how truly good, decent, and wise a man he is. It's important to me that you're aware of my opinion in that regard."

"Thank you."

"Apples often tend not to fall far from the tree. Seeing you this morning with an employment application, I wanted to get an idea for myself what kind of person you are."

"I'm an ordinary person."

"You're the kind of person who's listened patiently while I've prattled on about old war stories of so little interest to the young these days."

"I'm so glad you've told me more about what my Dad went through. My brother is always trying to get him to talk about the war."

"You've been honest yet discreet, including about your emotions. You don't drink or smoke. You're loyal to those you care about. You're hardworking, and I can tell you're focused on your mission, even if you've yet to really see a lot of it. All you need is a chance. Is that something you think might interest you?" he asked as I withdrew slightly, embarrassed by his personal assessment.

"Well?" he asked.

"Ah, yes, of course! I'd be happy to clean or cook, just tell me where and when I need to report," I said, excitedly, but still a little teary from hearing about Dad.

"No," he said, "cooks and cleaners are essential, but I think you'd be more useful making radio parts and assembling radios. How does that sound?"

"Ahh, I wouldn't know the first thing to do."

"No matter. We'll teach you."

"Thank you, thank you, thank you!" I screeched. "When can I start?"

"When your father gets back. By all means, take a few days after he gets back, but don't leave it too long."

"Oh, but if you have any cleaning or cooking work available right now, I'd be more than happy to start with that."

"No, look, I admire your spirit, and I know you're keen. But I've got people coming out of my ears wanting to do that stuff. What I need is initiative that hears a calling and can follow where it leads, smart people who can learn and work. In fact, I seriously doubt there's any cooking or cleaning work going in town either, especially for a Triestini, no disrespect. My advice is to sit tight for a few months; it'll go quicker than you realize. Trust me, it's better this way. Do we have a deal?"

"Yes. Thank you very much," I said, happily, but deflated at not having work right away.

"Well, you've got a long ride ahead of you, so I'd better let you go. But, before you go, let me tell you something," he said, ominously, "because of what we do, the Party is strong here. Almost everyone in this place came specially recommended, and even then, I'm picky. It would be wise for you to keep a low profile. Crucifixes don't go well here."

"I'm a Triestini. I know what it means to be low in others' eyes." My initial doubts returned with a vengeance. I wanted to give him an out. "Look, if you're giving me a job just because you know my Dad or it's going to cause you trouble, maybe I should look elsewhere."

"No!" he said, squaring up. "It's true I took an interest because of my connection to your father, however, I interviewed you, and I saw something worth pursuing. If I hadn't, believe me, I wouldn't even offer you a cleaning job. On my say-so, you have just as much right to be here as anyone else. If you want the job, it's yours. Offers like that don't come along every day. Think on it carefully. If you decide not to take it, no hard feelings. But if you decide to answer the calling, bring your best because no one will give you an easy ride here," he said, softening his firmness with an understanding smile.

Since when has anyone ever given me an easy anything?

To my delight, he put out his hand. I grabbed it and pumped it hard, several times, which broadened his smile. Reaching into his coat, he took out a business card. Handing it to me, he told me to see myself out, went back to his seat, and buried himself in his papers like I was already gone.

As I walked toward the foyer, the sound of typing from the receptionists got louder. The sound stopped as I wheeled my bike through the foyer. I didn't dare look as I left. Outside, I realized he hadn't even told me his name. When I turned over his business card, it was blank except for the name, Vultre, and a telephone number. Very strange.

What was Mum going to say when I got home?

CHAPTER 12
CONGRATULATIONS

My mission accomplished, I rode out of the factory slowly, surprised but thanking God for my quick success. It wasn't often I came into Sezana. As much as I tried to take in the sights, the stories about Dad's wartime experiences and the pain of it kept erupting in my mind. It made me think about my own experience. The bullets ricocheting off walls, the smell of gunpowder, screaming, people dropping, the rotting flesh, the burning, and finding horrible things in the clean-up. At least we'd come through, by the grace of God. For all the things I'd seen, I couldn't bear to think what it must have been like for Dad to volunteer to go back into all that when he had the chance to come home. Knowing made me feel closer to Dad, and that was always going to be a good thing.

As a young girl at war's end, missing Dad terribly, it was hard seeing the other dads come home. Even if I could have explained to my younger self why Dad did what he did, I'm not sure it would have made any difference. I wanted him back; no explanation would have sufficed for any delay. Learning how to deal with the anger, hurt, and pain at him not being with us was not an easy lesson for a young girl. Neither was living with paranoid doubts and shame that a part of me wondered whether maybe he wasn't coming home because he didn't love us anymore. It was only years later I could put the labels to the feelings that raged through me at the time. Now that I knew more about what Dad had gone through, it made me love him all the more and feel even prouder and more grateful to have him as my papa.

If I could speak to my younger self, I wouldn't tell her not to be upset. I'd tell her the opposite: it's all right to be upset, to doubt, and be uncertain. It wasn't weakness; it meant I loved Dad and always would. I'd tell her as she got older and found out why he had to come home late from the war, it would only make her love him all the more. Maybe that way, my younger self, scared and wondering if she'd live from one day to the next, would have been able to feel unpleasant things without feeling trapped by them. Who knew?

As I coasted into the courtyard of our home, Mum turned away from hanging out washing to give me a good long look. "Where have you been all day?"

"I went to Sezana looking for a job and was offered a position with the radio factory. I start when Dad gets back," I said, dismounting the bike.

Mum froze, wet dripping shirt in hand. "You did what?" she asked, incredulously.

I started to repeat, but she interjected, obviously displeased. "I heard you. Are you kidding?"

"Dad's Communist friend from White Sunday was there. He interviewed me and offered me a job."

"What Communist friend? What's his name?"

"Vultre," I responded, handing her the business card he'd given me.

She recognized the name but became even more agitated. "No, this is not the right way. First you should discuss with me," she said adamantly.

I became defensive. "Well, I can do more than what I'm doing on the farm. I'm so proud of how hard you and Dad work. I just want to help. Please let me help. Besides, we need the money," I responded, trying to put the best spin on it.

"You don't realize what, or with whom, you're dealing. That's why you should discuss things first," said Mum, getting huffy.

I pressed my case. "This job will change things. We'll have more money, and if I can do more than work on the farm, why shouldn't I?"

"You should be more patient. This situation with the farm will not last. The farm will still be here. We need to make sure we are here as well. Your plan will not work out the way you think."

Dejected, I started walking my bike to the barn, but Mum wasn't finished. "Family and land, all together, are worth more than a few dinars from the city. We don't make radios because we don't need them. Most of what comes out is just empty propaganda."

Pointing toward the roof of our house, Mum recalled, "When you were young, the ceiling beams needed replacing. We dismantled the roof, put in new beams, and replaced the tiles. Do you remember how determined you were to help?"

"Yes."

"When the roof came off, Dad insisted on building the stone walls higher, and you insisted on lugging rocks and slate tiles. I watched, equal parts amazed and horrified, as my eleven-year-old daughter collected and lugged rocks from the countryside in a wheelbarrow. People were shocked at this thin, little girl heaving rocks around. You were too eager, even then. You tied and slung bundles of slate over your back and climbed the tall ladder up to where the men were working. Again, people would look on in amazement. You got angry when the wife of one neighbor complained."

"I told her I could do it."

"We told you to stop, but you didn't listen. Do you remember what happened next?" asked Mum, quietly and gently accusing me at the same time.

"Yes," I said, squeezing the handlebars of the bike in frustration.

"A few days later, you started bleeding. At your age, how could you know why? You were too ashamed to tell us and too good at hiding it. A week went by, then two. You got weaker and weaker. You told us you'd caught a cold, but you got paler and paler. Finally, you couldn't hide it anymore, could you?"

"No."

"One day, spraying grapes, you collapsed."

"I refused to stop."

"Exactly. The next day, Dad had to physically restrain you from working. Finally, you told us you'd been bleeding for over two months. Dad quickly sold some cows so we could call a doctor. You began fainting, over and over. I was screaming, but you didn't wake. We were petrified we'd lose you. What on earth was going through your mind at the time?"

"I was floating near the ceiling. You were crying."

"What are you talking about?"

"Looking down, I felt sorry for you. I looked so peaceful on the bed."

"So you mean you passed over?"

"I don't know. A beautiful swirling light opened above me, and a warm feeling washed through me. Floating toward the light, I felt happier. As I got closer, so much joy surged through me, I wasn't sure I could take it. Suddenly, I felt I was falling, so fast I was scared of hitting something. I remember the smell of stale blood and urine. Opening my eyes, a strange man stood over me. 'Welcome back,' he said."

"The doctor."

"When I saw the stethoscope, I wanted him to leave. We couldn't afford it."

"Over several days, he gave you injection after injection."

"I couldn't work for eight weeks. I couldn't stop thinking about the light. I wanted to see that light again."

"You shouldn't wish for something like that. I wish you'd talk before running off and getting yourself into trouble."

I still felt guilty about the loss of production I'd caused and how much money my parents had to spend on repeat doctors' visits, vitamins, and minerals. It cost a fortune. For weeks, I watched in frustration as the rest of the family trekked off to work, and I'd be stuck in the house. When I was well enough to be left unsupervised, I'd stroll in the forest or chop wood for exercise, at least until I'd get dizzy. I was happy to keep those bouts of impatience to myself.

At the time, the thing that hurt most was Mum ordering me to spend more time playing and less time working. Playing seemed useless to me.

I wanted to be out in the field working. I was scared to admit it even to myself, but if it wasn't for the expense and fright I'd given everyone, it was almost worth it just to see that incredible light. Stupidly, as far back as I could remember, I always felt lazy if I wasn't pushing myself.

"We shouldn't have let you start so young. It was my fault. I asked too much of you, and I'm sorry for that. Now you're so damn impatient to get things done. I don't want to see you get hurt. The Communists will not last forever. The job at the factory will not be as you expect. It might be tough here on the farm now, but that will change."

"I like working, and besides, I'm not a little girl anymore. You say things will change, but when? In a hundred years? Fifty? Even if it's only twenty, it might as well be a lifetime. Maybe it's stupid, but I see how hard we work, especially you and Dad, and it hurts to see us always ripped off."

"Good decisions will not come when fear and impatience are motivating you."

"If the job doesn't work out, I'll get another. Mum, I don't want us to fight. I'm sorry, I love and respect you more than I can possibly ever say, but I'm going to work in Sezana," I said, softly, resolute in my chosen course.

"You're afraid of losing Dad again. You're afraid of not having enough money, but you're too young to really know what's what. I understand the war and then the Communists ruined a lot of things for people like us. I still feel like it's Dad and I's fault you've grown up too fast, but to us, you're still a child. This is just another corner in life we have to navigate. Sooner or later, our differing opinions will come up against reality. Some have to learn the hard way, especially the fearful and the impatient. You'll see."

"Dad is going to make it, he has to, and I want something to still be here when he gets back. Without more money coming in, how can we stop them from pushing us off? How will we keep going?"

"They can never steal the best of what this family has: our love for each other. I bore you for nine months, I gave birth to you in this house,

I nursed you, and I hold you as close to me as I can, always for as long as I can. One day, if you're ever a mother, you'll see what that means. No matter how we disagree, no matter what you say to me, no matter how wrong you might be, my love for you will go beyond everything and anything."

"I've never doubted your love for me. I couldn't wish for a better mum."

"Come here, my dear daughter."

I couldn't hug Mum quick enough. The warmth of her body pressed up against mine, her deep breathing, and her quickly beating heart nourished me, and I could feel her love for me. When her arms released their tight grip, I put the bike away. Walking into the house, we caught each other's eye. She looked like she was feeling sorry for me. From her point of view, I was about to do something that would almost surely hurt me, and she was powerless to stop it. It wasn't exactly the congratulations I might have hoped for, but I felt the love in it just the same, just as I felt an irresistible urge to prove I was right.

CHAPTER 13

SLEEPOVER

Getting through Dad's absence was excruciating but somehow, we made it work. He came back the same way he'd gone—on the back of an oxcart. On the appointed day, Mum was busy around the house, while Lina, Val, and I pretended to be busy. We were really taking turns looking out for the cart. Eventually, Val called out, and we raced outside. Pulling into the courtyard in the late morning sun, the cart did a neat little U-turn to reveal Dad perched high on the back. He looked emaciated, dirty, and exhausted, but he was smiling. My heart lifted because I knew he was unbowed and triumphant. The sunshine had come back into my life, and it again brought me back to life.

Running to the cart, we helped our triumphant king disembark from his Balkan limousine. The bright sun shone painfully down from behind him, like a burning halo. I could just make out the outline of his smile, and the faintest impression of it warmed me from the inside out. Gingerly placing his feet on the ground, we looked him over.

We were speechless at his gauntness. It made his normal taut and thin muscularity look Herculean and luxuriously plump. He'd aged noticeably beyond anything justified by the normal passage of time, like they'd sucked years out of him.

Dad's bony hands reached out eagerly across the silence to caress and squeeze each of us, as if wanting to make sure his eyes were not lying. The pungent aroma of his long-stale sweat filled the air between us, but I couldn't care less. We all gently dove into a single teary and passionate embrace. Dad drew away, suddenly self-consciousness at his own aroma, a smell to which he himself had obviously become oblivious.

"Let's go inside and get you cleaned up," said Mum.

Mum thanked the men for bringing Dad home. Dad suggested they stay overnight since they had another day's ride ahead of them. There was something about them I didn't like but couldn't put into words. Mum didn't look happy at Dad's suggestion but said nothing.

Lina, Val, and I scurried about, fetching feed and water for their beast and water and firewood to make warm baths for the men. We peeled and chopped vegetables and put them into the cooking pot. Dad insisted the guests wash first, and he tried to help the three of us fetch water, but Mum screeched at him to sit down.

Throwing out the putrid wash-water from the visitors, we wiped the bath down with vinegar and put fresh warm water in for Dad. Mum put some of Dad's old, clean clothes out for the visitors. The kitchen filled with the smell of frying onions, garlic, and bacon to add to the minestrone. Mum put in rosemary, thyme, and a few other things, but she was making the minestrone overly watery. When I had the temerity to question her, she chided me and shooed me away from the stove.

Our next job was to wash their dirty clothes. Showing us what to do, Mum scrubbed at their undergarments with warm soapy water. After rinsing, she soaked them in vinegar and then simmered them in a big pot for about five minutes. Using sticks, Mum transferred the steaming clothes to a large washboard and scrubbed them again in cold soapy water before rinsing and finally hanging them to dry in the afternoon sun. All the clothes were liberally sprinkled with holes and rips which Mum said she'd fix once they'd dried. Lina, Val, and I copied her example with pants, shirts, and jackets. Dad emerged into the yard to watch us work. This time, we shared a proper hug. I felt the side of his bony ribs heave in and out, his warmth rubbing against mine. In my arms, he felt little more than skin and bone. I was so happy to hold him again and so angry at what they'd done to him.

In the early evening freshness, we gathered the still-slightly-damp clothes from the outside line and hung them next to the fire in our loungeroom. Dad insisted our visitors sit in the most comfortable chairs by the fire. As Lina, Val, and I stood near the doorway looking on, the three men sat quietly, staring into the fire, silently processing their emergence from what must have been a harrowing ordeal.

Calling the three of us into the kitchen, Mum kept us busy by checking on the animals. By the time we finished bedding them all down for the night and got back inside, dinner was on the table. Hardly anyone said a word over dinner, which suited me just fine. I understood the need to be hospitable, but I still didn't feel good about our visitors. After dinner, we washed up. Even the visitors helped out.

As we congregated in the loungeroom over cups of tea, Mum took to darning the clothes, the fire crackling in the background.

"It's good to see color coming back to your faces after a bit of proper food and some rest," said Mum optimistically.

"It couldn't have been good in the camp?" asked Val, tentatively searching for a ghoulish story.

Even though I wanted to kick Val, I nevertheless found myself on the edge of my seat for any news about what they'd gone through. To our surprise, the man who'd been driving the cart started laughing.

"What's so funny, Ivarn?" asked Mum, bemused.

"I'm so sorry. Both Victor and I are very grateful for your hospitality. Had we continued on, we'd be sleeping rough and begging for food. I can't thank you enough, but the notion I could put into words how bad it was, well, if one didn't laugh, only tears would come out," he said.

"It's me who should be sorry. It was rude of me to ask," said Val.

"Not at all, young man. It's a perfectly reasonable question, especially for a young, intelligent person like yourself. The camp was horrific. I don't know how we survived. Your Dad somehow knew what to do and yet be funny at the same time," he announced as the other chap, Victor, nodded in gleeful agreement. Dad shrugged dismissively, which only made me more curious.

"What do you mean, funny?" asked Val.

Ivarn searched his memory. "Well, just last week, your Dad defused what I thought was going to be the best fight I'd seen in a long, long time."

"How'd he manage that?" asked Val, sniffing out an exciting story.

"The three of us had been sent to help a couple of other guys cut up a huge tree that had fallen across a road about thirty minutes' walk from camp. We could hear the shouting well before we could see them. They were arguing about how to cut up the tree. Everyone was always starving, yet those guys still had the energy to argue. It was nuts."

"Even after we arrived, they kept arguing. They liked having an audience," interjected Victor, who'd barely said a word since arriving. His manner began to make me wonder if he was all there.

"They were swearing, calling each other names, insulting each other's wives. But when they started insulting each other's mothers, I thought, okay, it's going to be on here any minute," said Ivarn.

"Is that when the three of you stepped in?" asked Val, eagerly.

"Not quite. Your Dad walks between them, stops a few meters away, undoes his pants, and relieves himself. They stopped arguing, in shock. Doing up his pants, your father turned to us and said, 'Hey! Do you remember that cow we saw last week? That cow laughed at you after you stepped in cow shit. I could use a cow like that. I'm gonna make an offer on that cow.' Catching on to his joke, I replied, 'That sure was one smart cow.' By then, the argument was history. Your Dad asks the guys, 'So how are things here? You need any help?' They weren't sure what to think. It's only then your Dad tells them we'd been sent to help and how it would be great if we could finish so we could get back before dark. Before long we were all cutting away at the tree."

"Don't listen to these guys, especially Ivarn. He tells tall tales for a living," said Dad.

"I love tall tales, what kind?" asked Val, turning to Ivarn.

"I used to be a journalist, in politics. I had money, an office, nice clothes, a fancy car, a holiday house near Split. . .mistresses," he said, bowing his head in shame as Mum looked away. She wasn't overly fazed, except for hissing at Val to stop giggling.

"I thought I had it all worked out until I forgot, or discovered, my place. Either way, I started asking unwelcome questions. It wasn't long before the speaking and party invitations dried up. Colleagues and friends deserted me. My bosses stopped publishing my stuff. They started telling me where I could go, even who I could see. There were threats on my life, my family. I was interrogated by officials who accused me of subversion, false reporting, not paying taxes. It was a grab bag of lies corroborated by former friends and allies, happy to slander me and prey upon my carcass. The state makes up its own stories to suit the reality it manufactures."

"What do you mean, manufacture reality?" I asked.

"I mean our Communist state manufactures lies like a butcher makes sausages. People think they believe something and then speak it, but it's the other way around. Control what people are allowed to say, and their beliefs will follow. Control the sausages, and the stomachs will follow. Injustice becomes rationalized and normalized, and like magic, reality itself changes.

"They changed my reality. My writings were withdrawn from circulation, book by book, pamphlet by pamphlet. Libraries were scrubbed clean. If they could have gone back in time and erased my birth, no doubt they would have done that too. They wanted to eviscerate any mark I'd made. My life fell apart. My wife left, took the kids, said she couldn't raise them in that kind of environment. I couldn't blame her. They would have killed me if it wasn't for a mistress pulling some strings. Eventually, even she could no longer risk associating with me.

"I resigned myself to living as a hermit, a prisoner on my farm with only books that didn't officially exist for company. Then the nationalization came. Kids playing at revolution wanted to take my farm. I refused, opting for the prison camp instead. Without something to leave my kids, I wasn't sure what my purpose in life was anymore," he said, forlorn.

It wasn't quite the story Val was hoping for.

"How do you know your farm will be there when you get

back?" I asked.

"I don't," he readily admitted. "A mistress, wife of a Party official, wonderful woman, said she'd see to it. I'll find out soon enough," he said with a touch of resignation.

I wanted to ask about his wife and children but couldn't bring myself to do it.

"Was it worth it? Speaking out, I mean," asked Mum.

Ivarn smiled knowingly. "I don't get to see my kids enough; that really hurts. For all my failings, I can still look at myself in the mirror as someone who spoke at least some truth, some of the time. Whether that counts for anything, others can judge."

"Where do your writing ideas come from?" I asked, trying to hide my disgust at noticing Victor seemed to be having his own silent conversation with my legs. The fact my legs were hidden under a dress seemed to matter not.

"The same place all ideas come from," continued Ivarn.

I wanted to listen, but my attention was distracted by something in my mind clicking into place. My uneasy feeling from the time I met them suddenly made sense, and it had something to do with Victor's odd behavior. Mum and Dad had also picked up on Victor's wanton gazing and from their raised eyebrows, it was apparent that they were clearly unimpressed and concerned. Ivarn, by apologizing on Victor's behalf and blatantly telling him several times to look away, was clearly embarrassed at Victor's leering. Ivarn did his best to persevere with sharing his views on philosophy and human psychology.

"Philosophy is interesting, but not much use to us here on the farm," observed Mum. Victor let out a loud belly laugh. He laughed so hard he almost keeled over.

"Poor Ivarn, all that education, only to end up in prison," said Victor, laughing rudely. His emotionality, as well as his creepy perving at my chest, hips, and legs, was increasingly disturbing. It was hard to tell if he was simply arrogant or had some kind of disorder. I didn't want to find out.

"Well, you two have a long ride ahead of you tomorrow, and I'm sure we could all use a good night's sleep," said Dad, calling an end to the evening's entertainment.

"Excellent idea. I'm sure we've all had more than enough," replied Ivarn.

After retiring, I lay in bed thinking about Ivarn's life and his ideas, but most of all how good it was to have Dad back. There was a quiet knock at the door. Lina, who was still up putting her nightgown on, answered. It was Val.

"Dad told me to sleep next to Anja for the night, just in case."

I chuckled nervously, trying to make light of it while secretly happy Val was sleeping in my bed. I dared not tell him, otherwise I'd never hear the end of it.

With Val and Lina to protect me, I nodded off.

*

In the woods, something was chasing me. *Dare I look? Oh, my God.* It was a strange animal, a hideous cross between a bear and a fox, baring glistening teeth. *Run!* Suddenly, I was in a clearing. What was this place? I didn't recognize the trees or bushes. I didn't want to be in here. This was no good; there was nowhere to hide. I was scared. I couldn't see anyone else around, but where were those voices coming from? It was my family; they were calling me. "Run!" they yelled. Squinting, I could just make them out at the far end of the clearing. They were waving frantically. If I ran really fast, I might just make it. Oh, my God, the monstrous animal was gaining. I was almost there, but the monster was so close. *No! No!* Its paws were running up my legs. My skin was crawling. I was losing it. Panic. I was falling, sheer terror. I was screaming—why wasn't any sound coming out? Its ugly hands were on me. I was paralyzed. Help! I was moving now, struggling and flailing about. *Fight back! More! Harder!*

I woke up and turned over. A dark figure loomed over me at the side of the bed. I felt hands touching my legs, clutching at the blanket.

"Be quiet, be quiet," whispered the figure. I recognized the voice as Victor's.

A shudder convulsed throughout my body. I screamed so loudly I thought it would fill up the entire night. A dim light from a kerosene lamp suddenly filled the room. Lina stood behind Victor, also screaming. Victor tried to slip his hands under the blanket. Suddenly, I was yanked hard from the other side of the bed. It was Val pulling me out of bed, well away from Victor's reach. Val moved me behind him and stood in front of me, ready for a fight.

The bedroom door flung open, and Dad came rushing in, Mum close behind holding another lamp. Dad rushed toward Victor, who was still sitting on the edge of the bed, motionless, his hands still stretched out to where my legs had been. Dad pushed Lina—who was now screaming more than me—out of the way. He splayed his feet, crouched, and twisted his torso, swinging his fist out wide as if he was about to swing an almighty ax into the side of a tree. Victor buried his head in his hands and rolled his body up into a submissive ball. Dad, his face still filled with a wild rage, paused.

Instead of punching Victor, Dad grabbed him by his pajamas and shook him so hard, the crackling sound of material ripping could be heard over the shouting. Dad savagely dragged him across the floor and out of the room, Val and Ivarn close behind. Dad thundered at Victor to get on his feet. Dad continued yelling at Victor, telling him off. There was such a commotion as they proceeded down the stairs, I thought maybe Dad had thrown him down.

My skin crawled as the thought of what had just happened began sinking in. Shock and disgust welled up inside of me. I couldn't stop shaking and started crying. Mum and Lina put their arms around me. Eventually, I got back into bed, just barely, but couldn't lie down, so sat up.

Dad came back into the room. Ever so softly and gently he took me into his arms, stroked my hair, and told me everything was going to be all right. Victor had been tied up and locked in the barn, Ivarn staying with him to make sure he didn't escape. The rest of us went back to bed and tried to get some sleep, although I'm pretty sure none of us slept. I know I didn't.

Late morning, Mum woke me gently, but I still got a fright. I'd slept in, surprised I'd slept at all. Mum explained Ivarn was waiting downstairs in the hope he could briefly speak with me before he and Victor left. She told me I didn't have to speak with him if I didn't want to.

I found Ivarn standing by the kitchen sink, staring out the window. He looked awful, like he hadn't slept a wink. Through the window, I could see Dad and Val standing next to the oxcart, upon which was perched Victor, hunched over, and looking into the bottom of the cart.

"I wanted to apologize to you, Anja. Last night was unforgivable, a terrible and shocking thing. Had I known Victor was going to behave in such an extreme way, I never would have agreed to us staying overnight. I hope you're not too shaken?"

"It wasn't your fault. I'll be okay."

"There's no excuse for Victor's behavior. Since he lost his family in the war, he's never really been all there," said Ivarn.

"The war took so much from so many," I responded, cutting Ivarn off. It was difficult to listen to any more about Victor. Mum stood next to me and put her arm around me.

"Well, we'll be on our way," said Ivarn, picking up on my discomfort. "Thank you very much, Anja, for giving me a chance to speak with you. Again, I'm truly sorry for the disturbance we caused you."

"I wish you a safe journey."

"You know, you have quite an intellect, Anja. Before I go, I wanted to give you this," said Ivarn, reaching into his jacket pocket and handing me a thick booklet. "When they began expunging my work, I wrote a summary of writing on my favorite authors, Jung, Rousseau, Steiner, many others. I'd like for you to have it, Anja."

"I couldn't possibly take this," I protested, surprised by his gesture.

"I can write another when I get home. But this one belongs to you now."

With that, he said goodbye and walked out. I watched as he shook hands with Dad and Val, then got on the cart. After the cart disappeared, Dad and Val came into the kitchen. Dad gave me a hug.

"Do you think that maniac, Victor, will come back?" asked Mum.

"I don't think so. I made it clear I'd shoot him on sight if I ever saw him again. I think he got the point," replied Dad.

Dad told me not to worry, that he wouldn't actually kill him, just that he'd scare him if needed. I wasn't sure whether Dad was serious, but in any case, I gave him a big hug.

A debate ensued about the booklet Ivarn had given me. Mum said it was full of crap and a danger just having it in the house. She wanted to burn it, but after having a look at it, Dad said I could keep it as long as I didn't talk about it to anyone or show anyone.

We spent the rest of the day talking about Dad's time at the camp. They'd been fed one meal a day and had been worked from sunup to sundown. Often the food was stale or rotten. They slept on the ground. Many people got sick and died. The people running the place didn't do much that was productive. Mostly they'd drink and sell off as much of the camp tools and equipment—and anything else they could get their hands on—on the black market and then blame it on the inmates. Inmates that complained got taken to prison. They'd come back to the camp with stories of torture and of others who'd been beaten to death.

While in the camp, Dad had thought about ways to improve the farm. That was my Dad! He wanted to increase Rakia production. I didn't like the idea at all. His plan was to construct a special camouflaged shed to house a larger distillery, hidden deep in the forest. He told us we were not to ever go near it on pain of a beating.

There was no need to threaten violence to keep us away. When Dad was young, his eighteen-year-old cousin had come to grief when the distillery he was tending set fire to the stable housing it. Dad's uncle had reinforced the stable to keep thieves out. But the solid iron bars on the windows also blocked any quick escape. Dad's uncle helplessly listened as his only son was burned alive. The whole building went up. Afterwards, he went into a deep depression, passing away only six months later. They say he died of a broken heart.

It was common for people to get hurt by their own distilleries. They'd often explode, get stolen, or their owners would get into trouble with the law, especially when they attempted to expand. I was keen to do what I could to prevent Dad from going down that path.

Even though Mum and I joined forces to oppose Dad's plans, he remained adamant. It was only after I told him I'd been offered a job that he relented. Much to Mum's consternation, Dad was thrilled about my job opportunity. However, he also agreed with Mum's assessment that I didn't know what I was getting into.

"They say it's a very strange place, that factory. Vultre won't tell me what they really do there. But if she feels called to work in the factory, the only way for her to learn how to manage the risk is to try it. If it doesn't work out, she can always leave the job," said Dad.

Not surprisingly, while Mum remained unconvinced, I could hardly wait to get started.

CHAPTER 14

INITIATION

Just before bed, the Sunday night before my first day at the job, Dad handed me a metal can with a miniature wall clock inside it and two metal mushrooms sprouting out the top. He told me it was an alarm clock. I'd not seen an alarm clock before. It was very futuristic. Dad proudly showed me how to use his new gadget. We laughed at the ugly sound it made when the alarm went off.

"I know you get up early already, but anyone who works at the pleasure of others lives by one of these. You should set this to wake you up, just in case."

"You shouldn't have spent the money."

"It's all right. Consider it a vital tool of your new trade. I'm going out for a smoke; have a good sleep. I'll see you in the morning before you go," said Dad with a sanguine smile as he disappeared into the night for a puff. Lying in bed, I looked across at the clock and wondered how I'd sleep with the faint ticking and what the following day would bring.

Just before four in the morning, I fumbled off the alarm before it had a chance to make its terrible noise. Getting up, I was as quiet as possible. The floorboards creaked under my feet as Lina softly wished me a good first day. I thanked her and told her to go back to sleep.

In the crisp air, I drew water from the well and quickly washed by the moonlight coming in through the bathroom window. After getting dressed, I went to the kitchen, the smell of breakfast making me salivate. In the faint glow of the kerosene lamp, Mum was making me breakfast. Seeing her doing her best to help me, even if she didn't agree with me working, touched me deeply. She smiled knowingly and motioned for me to sit at the table. Dad also appeared to see me off, which gave me as much—if not more—nourishment than the food.

The adrenaline and self-doubt flowing through my body had me so wired, I hardly noticed my lack of sleep. I slurped hurriedly at my hot, milky bowl of coffee, the sweetness surprising me. Mum's crusty, fluffy bread, dipped in milky, sweet coffee was divine, as was the hot semolina swimming in fresh, boiled milk topped with honey. Mum was certainly spoiling me. She wrapped a green apple, some bread, cheese, olives, and several slices of prosciutto in a hemp tea towel and packed that into a well-used, thick, brown paper bag for my lunch. She cried as I kissed her on the cheek.

"Please be careful."

"Thank you, Mum. Don't worry."

Outside, Dad was savoring his tobacco. As we shared a hug, I kissed him on his stubbly cheeks, and we gave each other a big squeeze. He smiled at me proudly.

"Be careful."

"Thank you, Dad. I'll do my best."

"I know you will. Be careful more so of smiles than frowns. If it's no good, just come home. You heard a calling that took you there; listen to it if it tells you to leave."

I loved having his reassurance and needed it more than any-thing. It was still night as I took off on the bike toward Sezana, my way illuminated by moonlight and the rhythmic dim light from the friction-powered headlight. The air was still fresh, and I'd given myself plenty of time, so I pedaled slowly, carefully looking out for bears, wild boars, and potholes. Earliest sunlight appeared as I reached the deserted outskirts of Sezana, whose streets were all mine. At the locked factory gates, I waited. Soon came the jangling of keys from a man walking toward the gate. It was the same owl-like old man I'd met before. *Does he live here?* I didn't dare ask.

Unlocking the gate, he said, "I remember you. Welcome." Together we walked toward the ominous-looking factory. I remembered how he'd been nice to me, and he seemed friendly enough, but he wasn't saying much, so I kept quiet.

"I'll unlock the foyer, so you can wait."

It hadn't changed since the first time, except I'd forgotten how eerie it felt. Sounds of doors being unlocked echoed from down the dark hall. I walked over to have a closer look at a portrait on the far wall, the sound of my footsteps filling the space. The portrait was yet another of Tito, in full military dress uniform, smiling broadly, holding his pipe. He looked mature but youngish, relaxed, a leader in his prime, a whiff of mystery behind the smile. I liked the picture; it flattered and dignified him.

Light from car headlights momentarily filled the foyer. In minutes, Vultre emerged from the hall, another early bird. He glanced in my direction, and a smile of recognition flickered across his face as he busied himself behind the reception counter.

"Good morning," he said, brightly, waving his hand for me to come to him.

"Good morning," I replied, enthusiastically, wheeling my bike toward him.

Passing the reception counter, I noticed two black typewriters, two black telephones, and four black trays of papers on the recessed workbench. The typewriters looked spindly and ominous in their quiet morning slumber, like giant metal spiders, their great arrays of legs sitting above countless round eyes. Thankfully, their mean operators were absent.

"Follow me," said Vultre, drawing me down the long hall, small offices hanging off either side. On my first visit, I hadn't noticed how run-down and unkempt this part looked compared to the foyer. The few light fittings were just bare globes dangling at intervals from the ceiling. Our farm had no electricity, so it still seemed futuristic compared to what I was used to.

The starkness of the artificial light bleached everything a drab gray.

The floor featured the same off-white linoleum squares as the foyer, but here the lino was dirty. In places, it was flaking and had worn right through to the floorboards. Most of the doors to the offices were open. Walking past, I caught glimpses of mismatched desks, chairs, cabinets, and boxes, and more trays of papers. The walls were painted a pale green that struggled to be seen over the bleaching light. The once-white ceiling presented an assortment of aged yellowy stains, cracks, and an uneven patchwork of repairs. A busy but unloved place. Apart from the documents, if it went up in smoke or was bombed, I don't think anyone would care. Maybe that was the idea?

After suggesting I leave my bike in his office, Vultre led me to the end of the hall to a metal door with a large round window in it, like an oversized porthole on a ship. People—some dressed neatly and others in dirty overalls—took turns swinging the big door open both ways as they heaved their way through. It was like no other I'd seen, with rivets running up and down, multiple large horizontal locking bolts, and a large spring bolted to the top from the metal door frame. Parts of the spring were so dirty and greasy that the coil resembled a thick tube of dirty blackness, like a big snake with a partially exposed skeleton. The black snake hissed and groaned every time someone swung the door.

Two portraits hung on the wall near the big metal door. The bigger portrait was another of Tito, again holding a pipe and in full military regalia, but with a deathly serious expression, as if warning of doom behind the door. The smaller portrait was of another man. *Nikola Tesla*, read the inscription. I thought it strange the Communists would have his portrait on the wall, given he'd gone to America. Vultre held open the big door and motioned for me to go through.

A bleaker, grimier, but more impressive world opened up. It was a large, cavernous warehouse with a ceiling so high, birds could have freely flown about. Exposed brick walls supported high, metal-framed windows up to the sheet-metal roof, supported by a metal beam skeleton. In the foreground were metal lockers, a kitchen with running water, and beyond that, rows of long benches with lots of people working away. Bright boxes of light blazed away above the benches even though it was daytime.

Vultre led me to the far end, passing bench after bench. There were lots of wires and cables running from strange gizmos, radios in various stages of assembly, rolls of wire, and bits and pieces of small metallic-looking things. It was noisy and chaotic but exciting. I turned to look back at the big, metal, swinging door. It was small in the distance and hardly visible behind people milling about.

What caught my eye was the massive red picture painted on the wall above the metal door. An angularly stylized man and woman leaned forward, their outstretched arms reaching up toward a red antenna towering above. At the top was a hammer and sickle, and radiating outward, a circular array of red lightning bolts. Art or propaganda? Surely both. It was immediately unsettling, nothing like the homemade, rustic, life-affirming folk art I was used to.

Our art celebrated cycles of life, beauty, nature's mysteries, and people. To Communists, it was kitsch. To us, it aroused contemplation and gratitude, intertwining the viewer and the world.

To my eyes, the art above the metal door was cold, abstractly jarring, shockingly impersonal: a grandeur of emptiness depicting manufactured people enthralled and consumed by technology, a technology constantly obliterating any humanity with red bolts of poisonous mental radiation. I was taken aback at how blatant, grotesque, and overwhelming it was, attack presented as celebration. I was not sure if I'd ever seen a more pompous, death-affirming, and hideous eye sore. *Better keep my mouth shut about it.*

"How do you like our mural?"

"Oh, it effortlessly dominates the space. Amazing how a few angles can convey so much." *Keep your face straight, Anja, not a muscle out of place!*

As Vultre walked me back toward the big metal door, we passed through fast-flowing rivers of people rushing this way and that, each one an individual blood vessel in the veins of a giant mechanistic organism. Was that what I was to become?

The blur of activity in this dilapidated, oversized shed was muscular and stimulating. The air itself was frenetic, tight, and purposeful. Its dirty messiness was well-hidden behind the relatively clean, serenity of the foyer. The ugliness reminded me of the alarm clock Dad had given me. But this alarm was beyond my power to switch off. The relentlessness of it pounded my brain. I might as well have been on another planet. So many ideas exploded in my mind, and it was even stranger because they didn't feel like mine. But where were they coming from? I was not sure I could keep up.

People there rushed to save time, but the rush only distorted and stole all time. On our farm, we strove to harmonize the rhythm of our lives with nature, the seasons, the moon, the weather, the crops, and the animals. All was inseparable, all flowing into and out of one another. Our farm was itself a kind of clock, and we worked according to its time, and in exchange, the time we experienced was our own. The land took from us, mostly in sweat, sometimes in blood, but it also gave so much more in return. It held many dangers but also joy. That life was rich, and we celebrated that richness in our culture.

The factory felt alarming and bizarre. People looked constantly hounded by a rhythm with no natural stability, no natural inclination to settle at a particular harmonic; there was only acceleration. Whereas farm work could rejuvenate as well as be exhausting, the people here looked exhausted, beaten with no prospect of rest. Was this hell? I thought I heard a faint call to leave now, but I chose to revisit it later, at least that was what I imagined I'd do. For now, I needed to see more.

The factory produced radios, but more significantly, it produced culture and identity. What else was the mural about? If the mural couple and the scurrying about were any indication, this new Communist culture was no improvement on the old. But for the steady income the factory promised, everything else so far seemed retrograde.

I'd only just arrived and already, the place made me angry. The state squeezed people off their farms, away from nature and independence, and into these shacks to bounce around like bocce balls. Seeing a worker sycophantically stooping and bowing while being verbally abused didn't inspire confidence. This was progress, prosperity for all? Perhaps Mum was right, especially if all the radios emanated was propaganda about marching to the beat of ridiculous drums.

Sensing the tour was coming to an end, I did my best to look happy about the vibe. I didn't come here for happiness; I was here for work, for my family.

"Come meet your supervisor, an old hand who'll oversee your training."

I nodded eagerly.

Learning something new and complicated from people who looked tired and scared made me apprehensive. Remembering Dad's advice, I was on the lookout for nasty people who smiled a lot. I already guessed navigating predators in this place was going to be an even more amazing achievement than learning how to make the radios.

As we approached one of the workbenches, several people looked up at us and then smiled at each other. The smiling bench-sitters exchanged a few words, which I couldn't hear over the background noise. I figured I'd already found my nasty types.

Suggesting I hang back, Vultre tapped a man on the shoulder, and they started talking. He looked to be in his mid-forties, graying hair, solid build, like a wrestler who'd wrangled a monkey or two in his day. They seemed easy company, like they held each other in good regard. The other man turned, looked me up and down, and smiled. *Another smiling nasty type?*

Vulture called me over and introduced me to Giuseppe, the boss of about a dozen people, now including me. Giuseppe made small talk, at speed, most of which I missed. I tried making up for it by smiling politely as I shook his clammy limp hand. I wasn't expecting a dead fish.

Vultre promptly excused himself. Giuseppe, or Talking Smiley as I wanted to call him, led me away from the bench to another area he described as his office. His office was just two large, tall sheets of plywood joined at right angles with a high horizontal sheet of wood set into one "wall" that served as a table, under which sat a high stool. There was a tall, thin cabinet, a shorter, fatter, heavy, lockable filing cabinet, like some of the ones I'd seen in Vultre's office, and a couple more stools. His desk was strewn with papers. More sheets of paper were haphazardly pinned to his office "walls." There was a row of similar such "offices" lined up near the end of each workbench. Most people sitting in them were men, but some were women. *Wow, could women be bosses too?* All the people at those desks had to do was turn and they could see down the entire workbench that was their team.

Talking Smiley motioned for me to take a seat as he sat at his desk.

"So Anja, tell me a bit about yourself."

The question immediately aroused my disgust and fear. I figured he had to know at least a little about me, which was more than enough to know I didn't really fit.

"I live with my parents, sister, and brother on our farm in Zana. I like looking after our animals. I'm looking forward to start working."

It was the longest introduction I thought I could give without mentioning anything about myself that constituted political heresy. He smirked smugly and nodded, as if he already knew, wasn't interested, and enjoyed seeing me squirm as I tried to avoid talking about my background.

He seemed comfortable in himself and in his surroundings. But as he began jabbering on about himself and his career, I found it difficult to get a sense of who he really was. He seemed friendly and unfriendly at the same time, a slippery smoothness smeared over everything about him. If a snake could smile, he'd be it. He then got to it.

"I'm always available, talk to me anytime, but only if needed. My people are all adults. I expect everyone to sort things out and keep everything flowing. I don't have time to get involved with the day-to-day of the bench unless it's necessary. Olga and Meduser, they're my experienced seniors who'll teach you. I want you to feel welcome. But understand, I've got a good team. They work well, and I don't want you changing the dynamic."

I now knew Talking Smiley was more unfriendly than he was friendly. If nothing else, I was eager to start earning, so the prospect of being shown how to "keep things flowing," and being left to get on with it appealed.

Talking Smiley led me to the farthest end of the workbench he commanded to my spot. Everyone looked busy as we went past, but again I felt the stares. He motioned to some people at the far end, and two women immediately approached.

Olga, the older, looked to be in her early sixties, short and pudgy, hair almost completely gray. A brutal and somewhat imperfect crew-cut accentuated her width. I couldn't see any attempt to embellish or hide aspects of her appearance, which gave me the impression Olga wasn't terribly interested in her presentation, beyond looking clean and tidy. Her handshake was firm, her hands were rough worker's hands. Despite her austere looks, Olga had a thoughtful, calm, and pleasant disposition, which lent her a degree of dignity. She smiled faintly and welcomed me to the team. She seemed genuine, even if she didn't radiate much warmth. Her expression was economical, as if the years had taught her to only give out enough to achieve the desired end but no more.

Meduser looked to be in her late forties, a bit too well-groomed for a factory worker, like she was trying to hold back the tide. She smiled at me with faint disgust. Her gray roots betrayed long wavy hair, colored dark. She had a barrel-like torso and not much shape. Like Talking Smiley, she featured a wet fish in the handshake. I couldn't ever remember getting two of those in one day. Unlike Talking Smiley, she made sure to scrape my palm with her sharp nails on the release, like a barb on a fishhook. In containing any visible reaction to Meduser scratching my hand I did my best to make it clear I was not interested in biting down on her barb, which to me felt like a provocation. Unlike Olga, Meduser seemed to be fighting the future. Her beauty routine and the expense must have been quite something to behold. Her steadily crumbling but still somewhat intact infrastructure suggested charms well on their way out. No matter, I was not here for beauty tips. I was here to catch fish, not be one. I'd have to watch her.

As they chatted, Meduser was overly lavish in voicing her agreement with whatever Olga and Talking Smiley said. I'd only just met Meduser, but her grasping demeanor, preened appearance, and insecurity was already annoying. I imagined she saw herself on the rise. Olga, on the other hand, seemed like someone who didn't particularly feel the need to impress. Like Olga, Meduser seemed superficially friendly, but her friendliness had to fight its way through aggression masking inferiority. It was like Dad said: let her smile tell you what she's about. Her words may lie, but her body won't.

It was clear Meduser was Olga's right hand, Olga was Talking Smiley's right hand, while he was one of Vultre's many right hands, and I was on the bottom. There was so much deferential hierarchy in the place, I felt like I'd just joined an army, a radio-making army. In front of Talking Smiley, both Olga and Meduser emphasized how keen they were to help me, which only made me more skeptical. I didn't much expect bonding. My expectations beyond money were limited, and I itched to get started earning it.

"Anja's all yours now, ladies," said Talking Smiley to Olga and Meduser. "I want her up and running pronto," he decreed, backing away and holding up his palms while blowing heavily, like he'd off-loaded an unwanted weight.

With Talking Smiley barely gone, Meduser, slightly taller than me, leaned in. "I for one am not happy you're here, remember that. You don't belong here, you little Triestini bitch."

I froze against the hum and buzz of the factory, making sure I'd actually heard what I thought I'd heard. Meduser's frustration and anger had been clear from the moment I saw her. But it was the pleasure she took in discreetly but firmly emphasizing her displeasure that was unnerving. In my gut, I wasn't really surprised, but I doubted someone like her would be so eager to show this opinion off to me if it wasn't shared more widely. It added to my uneasy feelings about the place, about the people. She was obviously comfortable in front of Olga, but not Talking Smiley. Perhaps Meduser didn't want a higher-up to see her as she really was?

Olga, who'd heard what Meduser had said, shrugged and looked at the floor, only slightly embarrassed, not at Meduser's rudeness, but that I'd witnessed her endorse it. I didn't sense Olga had any interest in actively joining in the attack. But she certainly didn't want to spend any social capital on maintaining civility, certainly not for my benefit. Seeing the two of them felt more like I was watching one friend not wanting to get in the way of another friend, rather than superior and a subordinate.

Not taking Meduser's bait, I looked coolly at her and politely asked, "Nobody wants me here, and yet here I stand. Why is that then?"

Meduser's face crunched itself into a look of disgust, and she fidgeted tensely, like she was a bomb about to reach the end of its fuse. I imagined my calmness had offended her, even more than my ethnicity. A smile tried escaping the corners of my mouth at the thought my serenity in the face of her naked aggression would frustrate her. Meduser shook her head, snorted dismissively, and stormed off. Suggesting I wait by the bench until Meduser returned with tools to show me what to do, Olga headed back to her end of the bench as if nothing had happened. I'd been blatantly attacked by one supervisor, but more significantly, I couldn't rely on the other to maintain minimal decency. As for Talking Smiley, I didn't think he was sincere or remotely interested in anything other than radio production. He didn't want me changing the flowing dynamic.

Waiting for Meduser's return, I surveyed bustling workers, contemplating how alone I was. If I was going to stay, I'd have to find a way of not chafing at abuse, even though I wanted to scream at the unfairness. I could resign, but then what? I'd have no money to help my family. Dad had said I could leave, but just the thought of giving in upset me. Vultre was probably right; without Party connections, I'd find it difficult to get any job in Sezana. I could go to work for next to nothing on someone else's farm. But getting harassed or worse by some under- or oversexed farmer didn't appeal. I hadn't allowed Meduser to get a rise out of me, and as long as I kept cool, she wouldn't have an excuse to not teach me. Once taught, I could earn.

Meduser lazily dragged a trolley with a big suitcase of tools and old broken-up radio parts. I sat at the bench, and she stood over me, hands on her thin hips, barking instructions. Her curtness, willful impatience, tendency to throw tools and snatch them out of my hands, along with throwing my work onto the floor, made her resentment at having to show me anything clear enough.

I kept calm. But when she was interacting with me, Meduser often looked like she was on the brink of having an outburst. She'd get a frustrated look in her eye, especially whenever my work showed improvement. I could have sworn Meduser hated teaching me anything not because I couldn't pick up what she was showing me, but because I *was* picking it up. It was like she wanted to punish me for learning and probe for my breaking point. Her aggression felt cunning, evil even. But I still saw some restraint in it, like she needed a justification others could approve of before fully unloading. I urgently needed to find out more about how that dynamic worked. Otherwise, my family and I would be hexed and vexed into poverty by a misguided woman determined to act like a hag at every turn.

Dad's advice came to mind: the importance of behaving out of self-respect even where it wasn't possible to respect others' behavior. Dad's words still ringing in my ears, I resolved to have the audacity to be hated and keep cool. Acknowledging Meduser's rudeness, I continually refocused on the real task, picking up what was useful and discarding the rest. As I continued in my determination, Meduser became ruder and pushed me harder. The better I became at assembling the dusty, old broken parts, the more she tried to break me, to disassemble me. As unfair as she was, I had to respect her energy and her determination. I couldn't openly defy her, but I could redirect my own reaction to her abuse. The ruder she was, the more I leaned on and into the task, leaving her with a choice. Either she could calm down and reclaim the anger she was projecting at me, or she could let it erupt and be consumed by it.

Emotions were Meduser's tools, but they could be mine as well. There was no doubt in my mind that she wanted to learn how she could use her tools to destroy me. All I wanted was to learn how to translate my motivation into building marketable skills. It felt like we were both in unfamiliar territory. The task she'd been given was to teach me how to assemble radios, but as far as I was concerned, her combativeness and hostility toward me made it clear she had no intention of helping me, even if that was part of her job. Maybe what she really wanted was to teach me that I was helpless and hopeless, to undermine my self-confidence, and destroy my ability to learn. After all, not that long ago, she'd called me a bitch and told me I didn't belong. The enthusiasm she put into being rude toward me made me think she was the kind who took pleasure in my pain. Perhaps she was hoping I'd quickly lose my temper and ask to be put out of my misery. Could that be where the enthusiasm in her aggression came from?

For all I knew, Olga and Talking Smiley were in on it, letting Meduser push me into giving them an excuse to say I wasn't up to the job. If I gave up, they'd be free to savor having gotten the better of an unwanted Triestini bitch. Perhaps I could deny them that pleasure.

As we continued working on the radios and each other, it occurred to me that in giving myself permission not to be totally distracted by Meduser's hatred, I'd freed up just enough attention to learn a surprising amount. Meduser abruptly announced she had to get back to her own work and left. The suddenness with which Meduser broke off teaching me anything more for the day left me wondering whether she'd temporarily had her fill of taunting me.

With Meduser gone, I was able to fully focus on practicing the assembly procedures, determined to need her further instruction as little as possible. A loud buzzer echoed through the factory and people began drifting away from the benches. I looked up at the clock and saw it was already midday, lunchtime. Some people socialized, but nobody looked at me or said a word. I was invisible, or they were robots, or both. At least I had the lunch Mum had lovingly prepared to look forward to. Enjoying a stretch, I was desperate for the toilet and to get a drink. But when I came back, my lunch bag was gone, stolen. Shit! I should have realized. My stomach grumbled loudly, and I had no money to go out and buy anything. Worried about my bike, I rushed to check it was still locked up. To my relief, it was still there. I spent the rest of my lunch break practicing radio assembly and trying to forget my hunger and anger.

After lunch, Meduser grunted an order at me to go to a meeting room on the other side of the factory. In the room, half a dozen workers milled about. No one returned my greeting as I walked in. Deflated, I sat silently at one of the tables.

An old man came in, introduced himself, and said he was going to tell us about factory rules on behavior, socialist worker management committees, and safety. It was nice propaganda. Employees were expected to behave respectfully at all times, had a say in how the factory was run, and were supposed to put safety first. He told us to turn our chairs toward each other and introduce ourselves. They sounded normal, and my spirits lifted at the prospect these might be a nicer bunch than the others. Last to speak, I was embarrassed everyone could hear my hunger pangs. I needn't have been. I hardly got beyond my name.

"Ah, you're Anja, the Triestini," said a young man.

A woman piped up, "I've heard about you. You're on Olga and Meduser's team. I'm told theirs is one of the best assembly teams here. Being a Triestini, how are you going to stop yourself from dragging them down?"

Yet another woman piled on, "It won't matter. Soon enough, we'll be putting her out with all the other trash."

I knew the old man's talk was little more than talk, but I had to admit I was horrified at how brazen the abuse was. My tormentors smiled smugly as they got up and left. Everyone else remained quiet except one person, sniggering. The show over, they all got up and left. The last person to leave, a middle-aged woman, paused before walking out. By the kindly look on her face, I hoped she might say something nice.

"Triestinis have been around a long time. But nobody cares. We took over because our science is better than your superstition. None of your kind has ever given the world anything of value. When you realize you're truly nothing, only then will you be ready for Communism, if there are any of you left. Progress has passed you by, and don't for a minute think you'll be able to rely on your looks to get by. If you're smart, you'll leave this factory and stop wasting our time and yours," she said, dripping with paternalism. It was just me and the old man who'd given the talk on factory rules. He said nothing and left.

Sitting alone, I felt empty. A part of me wanted to cry, but I knew that's exactly what they wanted. I had the strangest feeling at least one person was waiting just beyond the doorway, waiting to hear the sound of someone caving in. I thought about the promise I'd made to myself earlier in the day about staying focused, and I tried to understand. For them, the truth was I was beneath them, someone vainly resisting the inevitability of giving in to them. I'd never thought of my looks as anything, let alone something to rely on. In a way, it was a compliment even if not a very nice one.

I hadn't realized how impossible it was for them to see me as I was. They'd put me in an invisible prison of unchangeable projections, per-haps inescapable. If so, they were prisoners too. In their eyes, I didn't know my place, a public nuisance to good folk. Apparently, they were doing me a favor by telling me how it really was. My urge to cry evapo-rated. Looking down at my chest, I saw the cross around my neck was plainly visible. It must have worked its way out from behind my shirt while I was working. Kissing it, I tucked it behind my shirt and headed back to my spot on the bench.

"How was your meeting?" asked Meduser, gloating.

"Good to know, but I've heard it all before," I answered, not wanting to give her any satisfaction.

"Get back to work then," she said coldly, disappointed at my resilience.

I resolved to continue matching Meduser's hostility with a relentless desire to learn my way to independence from her. Notwithstanding my resolve, a part of me wondered how long it would be possible to last in a place where everyone either ignored me or seemed against me.

Suddenly, a loud siren blew. It was three-thirty p.m. My first day was over. Work and shenanigans had so engrossed me I'd lost track of time. Everyone made for the exits like it was a sprint. None of my supervisors, nor my co-workers said anything to me on their way out. Emotionally exhausted, hungry, and spent, I packed up slowly.

The day had been filled with firsts, most on a spectrum between mildly unpleasant to downright abusive. But the work itself seemed good. It was going to take a good deal of practice to get really proficient at assembling. The place had only moments ago been a hive of activity and now it was so silent so quickly. I contemplated which might be worse: working on other people's farms, dodging farmers' unwanted advances and the pitchforks of their jealous wives, or this place. *What we do for money. . .*

"Good first day?" asked the Owl Man, appearing out of nowhere, smiling faintly.

"Just wonderful. I'm grateful to have made it here. I'm learning to make radios, and I've got a paying job, so I'm very lucky."

"Mmm, must you leave right away?"

"No," I said uneasily, suppressing hunger pangs.

"If you have time, I could show you a few tricks, if you like?" he asked, smiling brightly.

The offer made me forget how tired and starving I was. "Why are you helping me?"

"Let's just say I think you deserve a fighting chance. Fair enough?"

"Fair enough," I responded, still unsure about his intentions.

"Now, we don't have all night. I want to get to bed at a reasonable time. Drag that box of rubbish and tools over here. They really did give you the worst of everything, didn't they?" he asked, rummaging through the detritus.

Owl Man looked over the work I'd done, then looked me up and down skeptically.

"Not bad, all things considered."

I could feel myself warming to Owl Man's backhandedness, but I couldn't tell whether he actually expected much of me. Pulling up a stool, he gestured for me to sit. He proceeded to show me how to properly use a soldiering iron to connect electronic components on a board. Slow and smooth at first, he began speeding up. For a mature gent, he could work surprisingly fast. Suddenly, his movements became even faster. He twitched like a hungry bird stabbing at seeds in the grass. Each movement deft, deliberate, and economical. So quick, yet each movement flowed imperceptibly into the next.

Noticing I was suitably amazed, he set up new components on another board, cleaned the hot tip of the iron by gently scraping it on a wet sponge, and slowed right down so I could see as he talked me through each step. I noted how careful he was to only melt a tiny bit of wire at a time onto the tip of the iron. It was like an upside-down way of dipping a quill pen; he kind of drew the radio into being.

"You see, just like needlework, no?"

"Oh, I don't know about that. You make it look so easy." How did he know about my needlework? He and Vultre must have been talking.

"I can see you're thinking ahead about the marks you're trying to make. Yours is a strategic head."

"I don't know about strategic, but I've got a head."

"A good head. Come on, your turn."

The muscle memory was different than needlework, and I knew it would take time to digest, but it was by no means impossible. I was very careful not to melt too much wire, and my attempts were very slow.

"Yes, good. Slow is good at first. Always quality first; keep going."

Examining my work, Owl Man seemed quietly surprised, which unnerved me.

"Is something wrong? How bad is it?"

"Hmm, a few mistakes. But better than a lot of other work I've seen. You know, you could become quite good at this if you keep at it."

Relief swept over me, followed by a chaser of giddy delight. Owl Man explained my mistakes, places I'd put down too much molten metal or not enough. I eagerly drank in his advice.

"Your body still needs oxygen when you work. Remember to keep breathing. Relax and concentrate on your objective. Keep practicing and give your body time to learn the rhythms and techniques."

Owl Man handed me more parts to assemble. As I implemented his suggestions, my determination soared. A small speck of white light opened up in the tunnel that was my future. Hope began mingling with my dream of making money for my family. Owl Man fed me pointers on how to sit to minimize strain, adjust the light box, arrange tools and components so they were easy to hand in the right order. He explained how keeping parts clean and minimizing heat running through components kept them reliable. He got me to mimic him, showing me where I could pick up speed.

"You have to think like molten metal, understand how hot it is, where it's coming from, and where it's running to. All these parts come together to make a living thing. Your job is to help them be friends. For now, focus on technique. The perfect assembly is out there; when you're ready, it will find you. Think of each mistake between now and then as a gift along the way propelling you toward perfection. Your thinking righted, your breathing steady, and your body flowing, thinking vanishes, your action occurs all its own, then real speed comes. In time, you'll create your own techniques, perhaps even advance the art."

I smiled in humble gratitude for his wisdom. He'd treated me like a human being, and I felt like the place might just work for me, if I could survive.

"You know, you can tell just by looking at the finished result who did the work, how they felt at the time. You can even guess how long the radio will last, just by looking at it, just by thinking about it."

"You maybe, not me."

"Perhaps we shall see. Now, it's time for you to go home, eat, rest. There is no obligation, but tomorrow after work, I will show you more if you like?"

"Yes, I like!" I said, appreciatively, "but I don't even know your name."

"In here, names are not always names. A bit of advice. Don't let pointless chirping from some get to you," he said, his kindly look soothing earlier hurts.

I wasn't entirely sure he understood the depth of hatred directed at me and still had an uneasy feeling about the strength of my hold on my new job.

"Quickly, let me show you a trick," he said, handing me a piece of paper and a pencil. "After I look away, quickly write down one color and one animal that come to mind, fold the paper, and don't let me see it."

I did as he asked. He didn't even wait for me to finish writing before announcing, "White and owl, right?"

"How did you. . .?"

"A good magician never reveals his tricks. In return for being such a good student, from now on, you can call me White Owl."

"But that would be silly. Why not just tell me your name, or give me a more reasonable name?"

"It's silly like most names are silly. Around here, people on the floor don't need to know. So let's stick with White Owl."

I almost fell off my chair.

"I'll meet you here same time tomorrow. Off you go."

I left in a daze.

CHAPTER 15

DINNER FOR ONE

Riding home in near pitch-black darkness, I was exhausted and hungry. But also wired with fear of what might be lurking in the wilderness at the side of the road and the wilderness at the factory. Turning into our courtyard, I glided past Dad out smoking, his customary final before bed. I heard him go inside as I put the bike away in the stable. In the kitchen, I found him sitting alone at the table with the clock he'd given me, a bowl of what smelled like minestrone, some bread, and a green apple.

"Everyone's asleep. Mum left some minestrone for you; it's still nice and warm."

I rushed into his arms, his embrace making the tension pour out of me. As did the familiar smell of his tobacco and Rakia nightcap that often went with his smoke.

"Eat. You look tired."

I ravenously shoveled the minestrone and bread into my mouth while trying to look dignified. I had to remind myself to breathe and chew, not just gulp and swallow. Warm and tasty food in my belly made me feel alive again. I was so hungry. Dad patiently watched as I demolished the meal.

"Well?"

"You were right; the ones that smiled were the worst. But almost all were nasty. They don't know me, yet they hate me. It makes no sense. Instead of teaching me, most did their best not to. Someone even stole my lunch, but there was one older guy who was nice, and after work, he stayed and taught me a few things. He's going to teach me more after work tomorrow."

"I can't say I'm surprised. Are you?"

"No, but the hatred is incredibly intense and so blatant."

"Like I said before, only you can judge what you should do. Things are a bit tight around here at the moment, but at least we've still got the farm. Things will improve over time, and there's certainly no pressure from anyone, especially me. I know Mum would be happy if you didn't go back."

I didn't feel any pressure from anybody to work except from myself. Dad was optimistic about the farm. I wasn't so sure. He was still recovering from prison, and I didn't much like his idea about significantly scaling up Rakia production. Apart from the production risks, there was the danger that came from dealing with corrupt officials and avoiding others prosecuting sizable homebased producers, not to mention thieves and jealous competitors. Besides, if I didn't pursue the factory opportunity, who knew when another like it would come along?

"Apart from being hungry all day, I'm all right. I'm so lucky I came across that older guy."

"What's his name?"

"Well, it was the strangest thing, he said it was some kind of secret. It was weird, he made me play a game where I had to make up a name for him, but somehow, he guessed it, first. . .or, ah. . .it felt like, I mean, I think he read my mind. . .I don't know," I said, laughing skeptically. "Either way, I'm supposed to call him, owl. . .err, White Owl. . ." I shook my head at how silly I must have sounded. "He was kind but a bit strange. Now that I think about it, there was something unusual about his eyes. I'm sorry, I'm tired, I'm not making much sense," I said, chuckling at my own confusion.

"Hmm, interesting. Maybe things will be clearer once you get some sleep," replied Dad, giving me a quizzical, deeply contemplative look. "How much are they paying you?"

"A base rate of four thousand dinars per month, the trainee rate. If

I pass probation, the base jumps to five thousand per month. A few years in, most assemblers get proficient enough to earn a base between six thousand and seven thousand per month. If an assembler doesn't produce post probation, they don't get paid."

"Not bad numbers."

"Right now, I just want to focus on learning as much as I can about the job."

"Sounds like a plan," said Dad approvingly. "It hurts to see you suffering. If you decide that you won't stand for what they're dishing out, there's always the farm and there's no shame in that. I'm proud of you either way."

Hearing him say that made my heart pump with happiness, but in my mind, there was no question that I was going back.

"I better get some sleep. I have an early start tomorrow, and I'll probably be back late again," I said, making my determination clear.

"Keep your lunch in your pockets; keep them buttoned up if you have to. You won't last long on an empty stomach. Sounds like you'll be keeping different hours now. If we don't get a chance over the week, we'll talk more over the weekend. But if you want to talk before, don't be afraid to wake me up. I don't care what time it is."

"Thanks, Dad."

He kissed me on the top of my head and went off to bed. I lingered in the kitchen, finishing my apple, eating the core, seeds and all, leaving only the stem. Taking my clock, I dragged myself upstairs as quietly as I could and crept into bed. As soon as my head hit the pillow, I was out.

By the end of day two, I was assembling actual radios. I took care to work just as Mr. White Owl had taught me, ignoring what I suspected was purposefully bad advice from Meduser about assembling technique. On the odd occasion Talking Smiley examined my work, he'd tell me I was doing pretty good for a probationary employee. Meduser quickly appeared whenever he stopped by and never missed an opportunity to remind him I was slow compared to the experienced assemblers, as if that were a sin. She seemed annoyed by everything I did as if worried I might make the job work, at the same time wanting to appear to be helping me. Keeping my lunch with me always, even in the bathroom, meant I had something to eat, and I took great solace in having at least one ally. Without food and a friend, I don't know how I would have survived the first week. Why was Mr. White Owl helping me so much?

The rest of the six-day work week flew by in much the same way as the first couple days. On Sunday, following the end of my first week, I slept in to find the curtains still drawn, strong daylight seeping at the sides. The clock confirmed my fears. What kind of farmer's daughter slept in until after ten? I felt so guilty.

I'd barely seen any of my family the whole week, and I could hardly wait to get out into the field with them. I bounded into the kitchen and saw that, to my delight, a bowl of porridge had been left for me. Smiling at how much honey had been put in the porridge, I really craved the sweet company of my family. The house was painfully quiet otherwise.

While I was washing up after breakfast, Mum, Dad, Lina, and Val appeared with a couple of visitors I hadn't seen in ages. "Oh, gosh, what a sight for sore eyes!" I said gleefully.

CHAPTER 16
BREATHE DEEPLY

Teresa and Pepe laughed when they saw me.

"When we heard you got a job at the radio factory, I told Pepe we had to come see you. It's so lovely to see you; it's been too long! How's it all going?"

Ashamed, I wondered if they were informers. Teresa and Pepe were only from the other side of the village. Their family was one of the few other landholders to successfully hold out against the nationalization. We were so close by and yet so busy simply surviving, it was rare to find the time for a social call, especially when the weather was good for working land. Teresa was originally from Zana, but Pepe was from the opposite side of Slovenia, near Croatia. Not having any children, they stood out in the village like nobodies' business.

"I'm good. It's lovely to see you too. Mum, Dad, I'm sorry I slept in."

Waving away my apology, Dad told me not to worry. Mum and Lina began putting together a morning tea as the rest of us sat around the kitchen table, which only made me feel all the more guilty.

Teresa and Pepe were closer to Dad's vintage than mine, very hardy people who'd been partisans during the war. It was nice to see them, but why today?

Reading my mind, Dad fessed up.

"I invited Teresa and Pepe over so they could tell you about how Teresa, as a Triestini woman, dealt with prejudice at her work many years ago."

Mum burst out laughing as I did my best to suppress my alarm, wondering what Dad had told them. I appreciated the effort but was embarrassed at the prospect of being lecture-worthy.

"Teresa, please excuse my husband, he means well. . ." said Mum, to Dad's displeasure.

"What's wrong?" said Dad, defensively.

"Oh, I'm happy to talk about it. There're no informers in this house and besides, your parents are so sweet together," said Teresa, winking reassuringly at my discomfort.

Teresa and Pepe fell in love while working in a partisan hospital hidden in the mountains. Teresa was a nurse and Pepe was part of the security detachment that transported patients.

"It took me some time to come around to the idea we'd make a life together," said Teresa. "There was a war on, so I lived from one minute to the next. Like a puppy, Pepe instantly fell in love with me as soon as he saw me. It was quite pitiful really. I wasn't expecting it, but I guess it was fate," she said, teasing Pepe.

Pepe teased Teresa in return, "She's such a superstitious partisan. It was pure chance I got assigned to the hospital. But once there, how could I miss her? She did so much of the talking at staff meetings. She drowned everyone else out."

Teresa punched Pepe in the shoulder. "Well, someone had to speak up. Improvements weren't going to happen on their own!"

Turning to me, Pepe confessed, "As I listened to Teresa speak at that very first meeting, I knew then and there I would marry her."

"He was so obvious, it was almost embarrassing, making all sorts of lame excuses to ask me questions or talk to me."

"No, I didn't. The truth is, I bought her attention. I straight-out bribed her into paying attention to me with chocolate. You see, she's making things up to make herself look better."

"If you want the truth, the truth is I liked Pepe from the start. He was relaxed and fun and had a cute smile. But you know, it was a long time before I let him into my heart."

"I had to use all my sniper training in being patient."

"It was more like you wore down my resistance."

"It wasn't me that was trying to wear you down, it was those other folks who didn't like having a Triestini around. They thought the Italian part of you might betray people."

"Oh, my goodness, at first people questioned my trustworthiness, decision-making, and constantly viewed everything I did with suspicion. Anything I did right was really because of someone else, whereas anything I did that could remotely be twisted into a negative would immediately be cast in the worst possible light. It didn't matter if it was about what kind of bandages I used on patients' wounds, how I changed dressings, how I helped patients move about, anything and everything—all things large and small were grist for the gossip mill."

"At first Teresa ignored the hostility. After a time, it did wear her down. Eventually, she stopped caring. There was a war on, and they needed good people. So she only devoted energy to whatever task she was focused on."

"Rarely, people who were initially hostile came around. Mostly, people saw things confirming their prejudice. I came to accept I couldn't change anybody."

"So how did you cope?" I asked.

"Of course, I was hurt and upset. But I kept seeing how the patients had much bigger problems than I did, and there was so much to do. I hardly had time to think. I just persevered and made the best contribution I could."

I admired how philosophical and committed Teresa was while acknowledging her own feelings.

Teresa offered me advice. "There are people at the factory who are not nice and there's no point expecting them to be otherwise. Don't let them tempt you into behaving badly. Regardless of what work you're doing, your job is to remember who you are, maintain your self-respect, and stay close to your family. You're so lucky you have a family that supports you. Each of you knows real love that only a family can share. That's possibly a lot more than many of the nasty folks at work will ever have. Do your best and keep on the right path, and you'll prevail regardless of how things turn out."

I loved listening to Teresa. She was living proof overcoming barriers was possible, even if curing prejudice was impossible. In the war, she constantly lived on the edge of life and death and understood stress sometimes made people forget their prejudices and other times, made people cling to it more dearly than life itself. She kept reminding herself what she valued and why she was there. The prospect of changing hearts and minds came a distant second.

"The funny thing was, by the time the war was over and the hospital closed, a few who hated me at the start came to love me like I was family. I even left the place with a husband!"

It was fascinating to learn more about Teresa and Pepe, even if I couldn't imagine anyone at the factory becoming like family.

"Do whatever you need to protect yourself from nasty people. But if you can, keep an open mind just in case. People can surprise, both to the downside and the upside. It's not possible to predict but think about how you might handle whichever way they go."

I wanted to ask how they were going to make farming work after the nationalization, but I couldn't bring myself to ask. I felt sorry for them. They'd given so much for their country only to be repaid by the government attempting to steal their land.

Val was unusually quiet, so I asked him what he made of Teresa's stories. Val lit up.

"Breathing is very important," he said.

"What do you mean?"

"Earlier today, Pepe and Dad took me into the forest with some of Pepe's hunting rifles. Pepe taught me about sniping for game. Breathing is important to getting a good shot."

Guns weren't my thing, but I made a mental note of Val's eyes sparkling when he talked about rifles and hunting. I wondered how much a good gun cost. *We could use the extra protein.*

Pepe encouraged Val to view hunting as something primarily

happening in the mind. It was key to calm the mind, so the right focus emerged, breathing not only air, but also appreciation for the animal and the forest, the soul, and God. Val beamed as Pepe spoke. He'd obviously acquired a taste for hunting and had found a suitable teacher.

"Killing for food is all right, but all the mystical overlay is superfluous," teased Teresa, as Pepe laughed loudly. Their passion and humor were uplifting and forced me to contemplate the possibility of being able to stick it out at the factory.

As Teresa and Pepe got up to leave, we hugged and said our farewells. They were quick to suggest if I ever felt like talking about things, I was always welcome to visit. I appreciated the offer, but a part of me still couldn't help wondering if they were informers. In any case, the chat help put my own troubles in perspective, which was a welcome relief. Their values, persistence, forbearance, and love for each other made me feel honored to have spent time with them. Thanks to my parents, I felt like I'd already seen those qualities in people I truly trusted and loved.

"Did you get anything from Teresa and Pepe?" asked Dad, after they'd left.

"I think so. If a person hasn't got much control over their environment, there's not much to be gained from ruminating over unjustness. Do the needful without expecting things to change but stay open-minded. There are almost always others who have it better or worse. Be grateful for what you have and stay close to family."

"Very good. That's how we run the farm. Always remember, you can leave if you want."

I gave Dad a hug. How would we make enough money if I left?

Over the following few weeks, factory life settled into a familiar routine. Long bike rides to and from work. Me, working hard, keeping my lunch in my pockets, Mr. White Owl helping me on the downlow, while Meduser did her best to make me leave. Most ignored me, except for the odd pervert more interested in talking to my chest than my face.

However, just when I thought my routine had completely settled, someone sorely tested my newfound appreciation for proper breathing and emotional poise: a man, my first ever romantic foray. It all started as I was embracing the luxury of buying bread at a new bakery close to the factory.

CHAPTER 17

QUICK STEP

'd stopped off at a new bakery close to the factory after work to buy bread. It was the first time in my life I'd paid for bread. I ended up getting more than I'd bargained for that day. The dancer from White Sunday was standing in line to buy bread, almost close enough to touch. Visions of how he'd intertwined grace, poise, and strength on stage at White Sunday flooded back. Enthralled, I momentarily forgot what I'd come there for. I giggled with excitement, and the same lightning bolts of hot interest I'd felt at White Sunday surged. Those lightning bolts must have shot clean out of my eyes and knocked him on the back of his head because he turned and looked right at me. Performing a casual double take, he seemingly confirmed some recollection. Without hesitation, he left his place near the front of the line.

Taking my breath away, his loveliness effortlessly crossed what only moments before had seemed an impenetrable void: the distance between strangers. One stranger, a thoroughbred dancer for Communism, the other, a Catholic farmer's daughter. Socially, he may as well have been crossing the iron curtain in one balletic leap. Gently parking himself at the edge of my personal space, he smiled, making my toes curl with anticipation. He hadn't even made an utterance, and already I was his, and I was ashamed.

"Hello, you're the wonderful singer from White Sunday, aren't you?"

It took a moment to register he was referring to me, so besotted I was at hearing the melody in his voice. His authoritative tone hooked me deep and aroused yet more excruciating excitement. Not only had he remembered me, but he was talking to me. He was so natural in his speech, gestures, and approach, making it seem we were old friends, so wonderfully low-key. His manner and presence were at once settling and unsettling in their novelty, and there was a delicious ambiguity about his motivations I longed to surmount. I yearned to flirt but wanted even more for him to go first.

"I don't know about wonderful, but I sang with my sister. Still, it's nice of you to say, thank you." I had to stop smiling so much.

"You probably don't remember me. I was one of the dancers."

Of course I did, but I liked that he was not assuming. "There were so many people there that day. But I do remember the dancers being very good." *Play it cool, but not too cool.*

I couldn't help but smile, and he returned my smile, his eyes entrapping my gaze. I felt a rush of blood as his interest and the meaning in his smile remained unspoken. He was so confident, relaxed, and calm. He wasn't looking me up and down; rather, he savored my eyes with his own, probing my thoughts deeply while sharing his. Him seeing me as I saw him was captivating.

Advancing in the line, we made small talk, allowing the initial frisson to pleasantly simmer. Occasionally, my arm brushed against his as we jostled along in the crowded line.

When he wasn't dancing, he worked part time in his uncle's accountancy practice. He lived in a village not overly far from Zana and had finished work early for the day. I told him I'd recently started work at the radio factory. He teased me a little about how, looking at my garb, he imagined I might be a French painter or sculptor in the country incognito, coming to the bakery to get my baguette. I found the comparison laughably absurd but pleasantly exotic. He was charming and achingly beautiful, his deep blue eyes and masculine yet youthful voice spellbinding. I would have laughed at any joke he cared to make, baguette or no baguette.

Loaves in hand, we lingered outside the shop. Chatting, we couldn't take our eyes off each other, carefully appreciating every glance and inflection like different facets of a jewel. Laughing at something he'd said, I instinctively put my hand on his forearm and blushed at having directly touched his body. He pretended it was nothing, but I saw the way he smiled when I touched him.

He asked if we could meet at the bakery the following Friday at the same time. Naturally, I said yes. When we shook hands in parting, he introduced himself as Janez. I savored wrapping my lips around his name as I repeated it back to him. Hearing him say my name made me swoon. I could hardly wait to see him again.

*

In those first few weeks at the factory, I'd hardly seen or heard from Talking Smiley, not that I was complaining. One day, that changed. As the lunch buzzer blared, Talking Smiley came barreling in my direction, scattering subordinates like an overly proud rooster. *I must be in the poop now.*

"I've been looking at your numbers. For a beginner, very impressive. Keep it up."

I just about fell off my perch.

"Thank you very much." *Thank you, Mr. White Owl.*

"Quality control says your connections are good. You're economical with solder, parts wastage is below expectations while speed of unit output is above expectations. With continued application, before long, you could become a reasonable operator, assuming you stay focused," he said, smiling in a way that made me doubt his sincerity.

"Thank you very much," I said, coolly.

"It's lunchtime; get some fresh air. I assure you, work will still be here when you get back. Do you have your food?"

Was he telling me he knew why I kept my lunch in my pockets?

"I have my lunch right here," I said, patting my bulging pockets.

Talking Smiley looked at my pockets and walked off, his eyes bulging, as if I was strange. Despite feeling like an idiot, I appreciated the small mercy of a civil conversation. Pushing my stool under the bench and turning to head out for lunch, I came face to face with Meduser. She'd surely overheard everything. Looking angry, Meduser faced me squarely, feet splayed, hands on hips, her beady eyes fixed on mine, trying to throw her evil eye straight through my heart. She wanted me to feel her displeasure and definitely didn't want me getting any attention, not from anybody, let alone from a boss-rooster.

My heart beating faster, I made a point of calmly walking to the kitchen, taking my time to wash my hands. Hoping she'd be gone, I looked to find her still there, still glaring at me. She really wanted to destroy me.

Not wanting to show I was intimidated, I strolled toward the rear entrance, keeping my gaze down so as not to provoke her. Squeezing my right hand into my already bulging pocket, I secretly made bull's horns to ward off her evil eye. Walking past, I felt her still crackling with hostility, desperate to goad me into giving her an excuse to attack. She reminded me of a vicious dog, oscillating between utter submissiveness toward the master holding the leash and hateful bloodlust toward anyone else. If Meduser wasn't flashing me her sharp canines, she was cowering submissively at Talking Smiley's feet.

Like any trained attack dog, Meduser knew she needed her master's permission or a justification before she could let slip her leash. I didn't want to do anything to give her that justification, but I couldn't help wondering how far she'd go to manufacture it herself. Was Talking Smiley using her as a stick? Just how much of her hostility was her own?

Emerging outside for lunch was like emerging from a cave. As I squinted in the natural light, the clean air and pleasant breeze were refreshing. The day was only half done, yet the workers propping themselves up against the side of the factory looked lifeless and oblivious to the joys of natural light. How long was it going to take before I looked like they did?

At my after-work lesson with Mr. White Owl, I made sure to let him know Talking Smiley had been impressed with my work, and I thanked him profusely for his help. He wanted me to celebrate by going home early, but I insisted on staying back so he could teach me more. I rode home at the customary late hour, exhausted as usual but a little happier.

"You know, for someone who had a very successful day, you still seem a little down. Why is that?" asked Dad, seated across from me at the kitchen table.

"Almost everybody is nasty. Is it like that in other places?" I asked, playing with the little bit of food left in my bowl.

"Can't say for sure," said Dad ruefully. "Factory workers are under pressure; more is always demanded for less. On the farm, we control what we do, how we do it, and we can express ourselves freely. Factory workers have none of that, and it makes them depressed."

"If we were allowed to profit from our own farm like we should be, I don't think I'd want to work in the factory."

"Nobody would. As workers are drained, so Communist bosses are nourished. They pretend to care, but make no mistake, they squeeze workers like a dairy farmer squeezes udders. Here on the farm, our work and nourishment are as one because we work as a family. Despite what they'd have you believe, there's no family in the factory," said Dad.

Coming into the kitchen, Mum chimed in, "Many bosses abuse workers, especially the decent and good ones like you, whereas they support the crooked ones."

"But why?"

"Because they know the crooked ones will always owe them, and in the end, that matters more to them than someone who does a good job. You may not realize it yet, but your body can already feel it, which is why you're sad even though you've been praised, because there's a part of you that knows the praise comes from a screwed-up place. It'd be best if you quit now and stayed here. Seeing you suffer is killing me!" said Mum, almost screaming.

Mum had a point.

"I agree, Mum," I admitted, trying to calm her. "I can already see how a lot of people are false. They say I'm welcome, but it's obvious I'm not. They say they'll teach me, but the ones that are supposed to don't. Many act as though their job is to kiss the boss's ass while making radios is something they do on the side. It's disgusting."

"So why work there any longer?" demanded Mum.

"I sometimes wonder how many lies the government delivers using the radios we make. But if it helps put food on our table, I'm going to keep doing it."

Mum listened, a horrifically tortured look on her face. However, Dad looked at me with a mixture of surprise and pride. Huffing skepticism, Mum left the room, while Dad looked on compassionately. Mum was implacable but grounded in all the wincing beauty only the ugly truth could offer. Dad was alive to the contradictions but seemed to only demand I make up my own mind, eyes as open as possible. We were all right in our own way, but a little life still ebbed out of my heart. My rationalizations couldn't change the facts. I could either exist on a farm the government was doing its best to destroy and watch my, and our, future wither away, or I could watch it wither away in a factory. At least the latter offered relatively more money, after tax.

I tried imagining tens of thousands of people around the country like me, being displaced off farms into factories. My mind couldn't comprehend the enormity. Trying to comprehend suffering in big numbers was like trying to keep track of grains of sand lost in the tide. It was impossible. In the grand scheme, we were all specks thrown here and there. Only love was strong enough to keep us connected across fortune's crosscurrents and only God could comprehend the enormity of his own creation. What I could comprehend was the sabotage aimed at me and those like me, the prospect of my family not having enough to eat. I could well comprehend the personal suffering of family and friends I loved and how much that hurt me as well.

My suffering in the job wouldn't just be felt by me, it would be felt by Dad, Mum, and anyone who loved me. Not being alone was comforting, but it also made me feel guilty about the hurt sticking it out at work might cause, was already causing. Yet, I had no intention of leaving the factory.

Dad said something that shook me out of my melancholic thoughts. "Your insight and resilience impress me and remind me of your mother," he said, a cheeky smile filling the cold void in my heart.

"Mum speaks out of love," he continued. "Your job is risky. In the end, she may be right. However, it's good you experience more of life than just this village. You're a talented girl, and you have a good heart. You must decide, make your own path. We are here for you. We love you and are proud of you."

Dad's words filled my heart to bursting. He stretched out his arms to me. I went and sat in his lap and gave him a big hug.

"Listen my child, factories are full of informers, bum-licking back-stabbers who will be friendly to you. Be polite in return, but remember, in factories, there are no friends, only temporary alliances of convenience. Keep your wits about you. You cannot trust those you find there."

Having poured yet another dose of antiseptic into my brain, he gently cupped my cheeks in his rough farmer's hands and kissed my forehead. Dad's advice was always good advice. His presence was always nourishing, and his love pure and undiluted. In that moment, I honestly wondered how many people on earth I could trust as much as my Dad. I imagined we were at least two specks of God's sand, forever connected by our love for each other.

Safe in Dad's embrace, I entertained a fancy and imagined what it would be like to see myself happy in my job and doing well. My thoughts quickly flew to buying things for us, extra clothes, meat, vegetables, even though I hated vegetables, and bread, multiple times a week. How wonderful it would be to be able to afford to buy meat!

Contemplating delicious delights, my thoughts raced to the bakery and how I'd been regularly meeting Janez there. There was no one I trusted more than Mum and Dad, but I couldn't face telling them about Janez, not yet. He was still my little secret. At the same time, the need to tell someone about him was bursting my insides so bad I was expecting organ failure any moment.

When I retired to the bedroom, Lina was still up, pretending to read a book.

"You're up late."

"I could hear something going on downstairs. . .How's Mum coping with your job?"

"I know she's worried out of love. It's not her opposition to the job I'm worried about most right now."

"Let me guess, you've found a boy."

"What! How did you know?"

"Don't ask silly questions."

"Do you think Mum and Dad know?"

"They haven't asked me anything yet. Don't worry, my lips are zipped tight."

"Gosh, I really have to work on my secret-keeping."

"Were you not planning on letting me in on your little secret?"

"No, I mean, yes. I'm sorry, I've been wanting to tell you, it's just we keep different hours these days. I've missed you, everybody," I said as we shared a hug and held hands.

"Yes, I've missed you too. Now, who is he and what's he like?"

"The dancer from White Sunday. He's dreamy."

"Get out! Have you had sex with him?"

"Not yet, but I'm not sure how long I will hold out."

It felt so good to unload. I showed Lina some dance moves Janez had taught me. We sometimes practiced in his uncle's office when no one was there and when I wasn't getting tutelage from Mr. White Owl. Dancing was so much fun it took my breath away and my mind off everything. We'd move furniture to make room, Janez would play folk music records, and he'd teach me how to really move. What blew my mind was when he'd bring a bag of proper dancers' outfits like those I'd seen at White Sunday. My favorite was a flowing purple dress with green borders, puffy white shirt, and tight black vest. It was so beautiful, so professional. He looked handsome in his brown leather knickerbockers, white shirt, signal red vest, and black round hat. Dressed up, we'd wildly cavort our way around the room for half an hour, doing our best not to break anything.

Janez showed me his uncle's secret stash of American records in a filing cabinet. Next to bottles of whiskey, rum, and gin were Frank Sinatra, Dean Martin, Ella Fitzgerald, Chet Baker, Harry Belafonte, Peggy Lee, Django, Elvis Presley, and too many others to remember. Apart from a sip to taste, I never touched the booze. For me, dancing to that music was intoxicating enough.

Janez taught me swing, rock and roll, cha-cha-cha, rumba, and the tango. Of all the dances, the tango was the most delicious. Rubbing against his firmness while in his commanding embrace and the way we looked at each other was intense. He'd get me wound up so tight, we'd be so hot and heavy, my head would feel like it was exploding as well as the rest of me. Janez knew about my Catholicism and was always a perfect gentleman. He understood that if anything was going to happen, he'd have to let me initiate it. I don't think I really appreciated how dangerous it was. Our liberty as well as our reputations would have been at stake had we gotten caught. But I was willing to take the risk. Having dancing to look forward to helped get me through those early weeks at the factory.

"He's been telling me I pick up dance moves quicker than anyone he's seen. According to him, I'm a natural dancer."

"That sounds wonderful. . . .So how do you feel about where it's all going?"

"I don't really know, and I feel so guilty about that. But on the other hand, I'm just enjoying myself. It's obvious to both of us there's a magnetism between us. The longer I hold out, the more unbearable it gets. Sometimes I can almost see sparks flying between us when we dance. I feel so much desire for him when we're dancing, like I never knew I could feel. I'm not sure how much longer I can hold myself back."

"Oh, my goodness, that's so intense, but there's something else. What is it?"

"Well, it's silly, but I keep having this recurring fantasy."

"What do you mean?"

"There's so much I want to get for us, things we need, but I also dream about something I'm scared to admit."

"This is me you're talking to, Anja."

"I think about stretching the money from the factory to get some gorgeous heels and a nice little dress and going out dancing with Janez, maybe even buying some petrol for his Vespa."

"Well of course you can. As long as Mum doesn't find out. You deserve some fun but let him buy the petrol."

"He's so much fun, I can barely stop thinking about him."

"When are you seeing him next?"

CHAPTER 18

PROBATIONARY ROMANCE

Meduser's constant stream of belittling, abuse, and undermining continued making factory life hell. It was a constant battle to keep my spirits up. Thanks to Mr. White Owl, my wonderful Dad, and my dance dates with Janez, I made it through the probationary period. Meduser's disappointment was palpable. Even Talking Smiley and Olga seemed grudgingly amused by my survival, itself a victory in the face of overwhelming opposition. I'll admit to discreetly nibbling a little schadenfreude in Meduser's honor. I kept taking the high road. It was one of the few defenses against her continuous pecking. She wanted me to get down in the mud with her, where her seniority and sadistic nature gave her the advantage.

My work team, wanting to at least give the appearance of good manners, held a morning tea to mark my transition out of probation into permanency. I was presented with a letter confirming my appointment along with my identification credentials and was amazed at how quickly the novelty wore off. As I smiled politely through half-hearted applause, a nearby rubbish bin caught my eye as the most appropriate filing cabinet.

The modest spread of homemade prekmurska pie and medenjaki biscuits was popular. Sweetness disappeared quickly in sour times. The sight of Talking Smiley eagerly filling his cakehole in between bouts of laughter ruined my appetite. I declined to eat until I was badgered into taking something before it all disappeared. I took the smallest broken leftover I could find and took the same approach to the chit-chat that went with it. Small talk, affectations, and forced laughter weren't things I grew up with, but they were on tap in this place. At home, instead of small talk, if we weren't discussing the farm, trade, and markets, or the endless duplicity of officialdom, we were discussing the soul, the world, and the afterlife.

Chomping on a piece of biscuit at work made me appreciate Mum's biscuits all the more, and the love that went into them. It was amazing what she could do with a bit of flour, butter, some dried grapes, and honey on those rare occasions we had any.

The work morning tea was like a little party except I couldn't imagine anyone, including me, wanting to be there. People made the most of having a sanctioned opportunity to put down tools and talk garbage. The clock was calling, and I couldn't wait to get back to work and keep earning at a higher rate. Most in the team were superficially congratulatory, but the politeness was uncomfortable and not terribly warm. Beneath the surface, they were commiserating with each other about the fact that a Triestini had made it, and they worried I might stick it out. I had every intention of doing just that.

Talking Smiley seemed largely above their hatred of me. As long as unit output was where it needed to be or above, I don't think he cared about much else. He went through the motions, cracking jokes at which people laughed too much.

"I wanted to acknowledge, Anja, how much you've learned about making radios and also about our systems and culture in such a short space of time. No doubt due to Meduser being such a good teacher," he said, downplaying my role in my own learning.

"Thank you so much, comrade Giuseppe. It is only in emulating your superior leadership as much as I can that I've been able to get through to impart anything at all," said Meduser, desperate to make me appear as stupid as possible.

Meduser continued heaping lavish praise on Talking Smiley, every word dripping with supplication. Everyone listened quietly to her drivel. Averting my gaze to hide my rolling eyes, I noticed a few glanced at each other in recognition at how thick she was laying it on. At least some people hadn't lost complete sight of reality. Even so, all followed enthusiastically when Meduser led applause in honor of Talking Smiley's leadership prowess. I grudgingly joined in.

It wasn't that I hated Talking Smiley, or anyone else for that matter. It was the way they behaved that drove me nuts. Watching anyone wallowing so gleefully in the groveling directed at them wasn't pleasant. For my part, I couldn't see what he'd done to deserve it, apart from be the object of people's desire for approval. His need to identify with the power of his position undermined everyone's integrity. My real teacher was Mr. White Owl. I discreetly looked around for him, but he was nowhere to be seen. If I wanted to celebrate with anyone, it would have been him. He was wise like Dad but strange, unlike Dad.

Talking Smiley was right about the importance of processes and culture. Even if it was toxic, the better I knew all that stuff, the better chance I stood of surviving. These people had written systems and processes for everything. Systems applied to pre-arranged schedules and expected flows of consumables to be fashioned into radio components and pre-made radio components for use in assembly. Systems for finished products, quality assurance, fixing faults, even repairs under warranty. All of it accompanied by paperwork and endless forms to be filled out. Paper systems constantly swirled around everything, running in parallel with the real world.

The paper world they created was supposed to be a world of perfection without surprises, while still being an accurate reflection of the real world. I couldn't understand how. As long as the words, grammar, and sentences of their paper world looked good to them, that was what they cared about most. For my colleagues, the paper world was in fact their real world. They behaved as though it was more real than they themselves were. The factory was primarily a place for producing words on paper; the radios seemed incidental. It was totally upside down, collective insanity, a kind of madhouse.

If the paperwork said a finished radio had been checked and was working fine, that was more important to people than if the actual radio itself was working. Sometimes this was by accident, at other times by design. Phantom radios were a case in point. A phantom radio was a radio that existed on paper but not as an actual radio. Whether this was because someone had stolen it or because it had never existed in the first place or because someone wanted to up their numbers was impossible for me to know for sure. Other times, there were real radios but with no paperwork. These were radios that didn't exist, made for who knows whom, for who knows what price. They still played nice music.

Countless forms of one kind or another got piled up on desks, bench tops, and many other flat surfaces. Once a pile got big enough, it would be placed in a box and then stacked into piles of boxes. Once the pile of boxes got big enough, the pile of boxes got taken out the back of the madhouse and put in a big shed with lots of other boxes. Once the shed got full, they'd burn the boxes in a big furnace. People treated paperwork like fish. When it was new and fresh, they seemed interested, but it quickly got stale and rotten so as no one wanted to be anywhere near it.

Weeks flew by. Occasionally, if no one was around, Mr. White Owl would appear out of nowhere and show me another trick or critique my work. One day, he caught me as I was leaving and had a quiet word in my ear: management was impressed with my productivity.

"Management keeps tabs on how much materiel each assembler uses, how many parts each breaks, how many radios have to be fixed because they didn't pass quality control, how much time each assembler takes on average to assemble a radio, fix a radio, do paperwork for a radio, or waste time at meetings. They know who is friends with whom, who is having an affair with whom, even how much workers gossip and what they gossip about," he whispered.

I froze at the reference to having an affair—not because I was having an affair; I wasn't. I didn't want my clandestine tango interludes with Janez being exposed to some local tin-pot Polit bureau. It wasn't immediately clear which management or whom in management he was referring to. In any case, I thanked him, telling myself that, bar he and Vultre, there wasn't any kind of management that knew or cared I existed. As long as I could keep working, I preferred management not knowing I existed. I wasn't doing anything wrong. Why should I worry? Something didn't feel right. Of course I should worry.

At my next dance date with Janez, I became paranoid about us being found out. I told him I was scared and, as much as I hated the idea, thought it might be best if we met less frequently or took a break. Janez was furious. Grabbing me, he kissed me passionately.

Even though we'd been dancing together for a while, sometimes with such passion I thought our clothes would catch fire, his sudden anger and the vigorous thrust of his kiss came as a shock. Oh, God, was this happening?

The energy of his kiss sent pulsating fire deep into my body. My heart raced. My body ignited. Whatever fear I'd felt a moment ago was submerged in a torrent of wanting.

Pulling Janez to me, I returned his kiss with the full force of my imploring body. Things quickly spiraled out of control. His hands were all over me. I wanted his hands all over me and let him know it. That unleashed something that had been pent up for too long, and a different kind of fury consumed us. The thrusting of hands, our kisses and breathing—it all got so intense I thought we might both combust on the spot.

As we tore off each other's clothes, suddenly something didn't feel right. I tried ignoring it, but doubt kept thumping me until I had to acknowledge it. This was not the right time, at least not for me.

Tidying myself up, I did what I could to hide my embarrassment as well as guilt. In my head, I tried working out what just happened. In spending almost all our time dancing, there was so much about each other yet to be shared and savored. We'd danced around the experience of really getting to know each other. I knew little about his family, apart from them being committed Communists. I began laughing.

"What's so funny?" he asked, tucking in his shirt.

"I feel like such an idiot."

"No, you're not."

"We're obviously attracted to one another, but we know so little about each other. Maybe we should stick to just dancing less frequently for now if that's possible?"

"I'm not sure if it's possible. You said it yourself—we're obviously attracted."

"I just need for us to know each other more."

"What would you like to know?"

"I don't know, little things, big things. I'm sorry. It was silly of me, forget it."

"No, it's all right. Go on, say it."

"I don't know where to start."

"Maybe try a little thing."

"Okay. I know what some of your family does for a living and that you're committed Communists, which is amusing considering you and your predilection for Western music and liquor. Isn't that against whatever the Communist teachings are?"

"You're right, maybe we should just stick to dancing?"

"Oh, shit. Now I'm really sorry."

"I was just kidding. Okay, if we're playing that game, how do you square your Catholic faith with the actual behavior of your Church?"

"What do you mean?"

"Here's an example: didn't the Pope support Hitler in the war?"

"That's not fair. I'm not a spokesperson for the Pope, and it's got nothing to do with us, and besides, it's complicated."

"It's got everything to do with us. You asked me about adherence to Communist doctrine, why can't I ask you about adherence to Catholic doctrine? Life's not fair, but it's also not complicated. We like each other, and we should do what comes naturally." *It's not complicated for you because you're on top of society.*

We were an odd and unlikely couple. The way our bodies fit together when we danced was proof positive. I didn't want to lose that. Rather than fight, we found ourselves hugging and returning to the safety of a quiet slow dance.

If dancing had become our small talk, it was the only small talk I'd ever enjoyed because it involved so few words. Even if today wasn't the day, the anticipation of what might lay beyond still killed me sweetly. But if Janez and I couldn't progress beyond dancing, I wasn't sure I could give myself to him. Our differences, or perhaps our mutual fear of tackling them head on, prevented a deeper intimacy. In our moment of passion, the weight of my faith had descended upon me and spoiled it. Janez had tried to hide his disappointment, but it was written all over his face. I felt guilty about letting him down.

Before long, it was time to go, and our movements toward each other became awkward. I hugged Janez, willing the awkwardness to pass. In his arms, I felt confused and held back the urge to tear up. I hoped other moments, both for deeper knowing and passion, would present themselves. We parted politely but without saying much.

To my disappointment, following that experience, while buying bread at the bakery, I often looked around for Janez, but he was nowhere to be seen. I often thought about the times we'd had and wondered if I should try to find him at his uncle's office but couldn't bring my desperate self to go there. If what Mr. White Owl had said about all of us being under surveillance from management was true, I didn't want my private life and its failures coming under the purview of my employer. Surely, I was being paranoid even thinking such a thing.

The level of detail Mr. White Owl had gone into about surveillance was disturbing. On the surface, the madhouse seemed so chaotic and shabbily run. Tribal nepotism, favoritism, sycophantism, all kinds of *isms* seemed to have the run of the place. If they were collecting as much information as Mr. White Owl claimed, surely, they could have made the place run better.

Back at the factory, after work, when everyone had gone home, Mr. White Owl was still catching up with me sometimes. I was sure it was a coincidence, but after Janez and I petered out, Mr. White Owl seemed warmer. His eyes were still mysterious in a way I couldn't quite comprehend, but I was glad to still be getting his coaching and happily obliged his desire to share some banter. I began to imagine he genuinely liked my company. Sometimes, he'd sit next to me at the workbench, and we'd have a little race to see how quickly we could each make a radio. We'd inspect and critique each other's work. I was a little surprised at how much I enjoyed it. Sometimes Mr. White Owl let me think I'd beaten him. He'd laugh when I told him as much.

With Janez out of the picture, I buried myself in my work. Once I got into a rhythm with it, just like the farm, I tended to forget about everything else, and time seemed to fly. It was even a little addictive. It was then I knew I was getting inside the task and the task was getting inside of me. It was like Mr. White Owl had said all along: it was becoming natural. I was thinking less about each movement required to complete each part of the process and more about how to link parts of the process together, steps and steps ahead of time. It reminded me more and more not only of the scythe, but also how I'd come to enjoy needlework or sewing. Reaching that point was a revelation. It was strange but also exciting to feel that outside the farm. I thought I saw Mr. White Owl recognize that transition in me, because when looking over my work, more and more, his eyes twinkled at me in a way I hadn't seen before, like shooting stars filling a night sky.

Just as I thought I'd gotten over Janez leaving me, it all went horribly wrong.

CHAPTER 19

DON'T ARGUE WITH THE BOSS

Days after my permanent appointment, things at work went sideways. I'd put in internal orders for parts and my paperwork would get lost or incorrect parts would get delivered. Sometimes, the wrong parts were easy to spot; other times, they were very similar to what I'd ordered but were still incorrect. When the correct parts came, they'd often look all right but still be faulty. Indeed, the first time this occurred, I hadn't noticed until I'd assembled several radios using suspect components. Luckily, the quick checks I did myself caught the bad units before they left my workstation. It got so bad, I stopped using the internal ordering system and personally delivered my paperwork to the stores clerk and got what I needed myself from the stores out back. The extra checks and getting my own parts added time to my production. It was annoying, but even with the additional time checking parts, replacing faulty batches, and doing my own quality control, I was still producing at a reasonably good rate, and I was only getting faster.

I was petrified getting my own parts the first few times. But the stores clerk and their runners seemed glad not to have to serve me and didn't try to stop me. They seemed happy that I always made sure my paperwork was in order, in contrast to their buddies. I couldn't be bothered complaining. Any complaint from me would be turned into criticism of the uppity Triestini who was either imagining things or looking for special treatment.

One night after work, catching up with Mr. White Owl, I let slip what had been going on with the parts. He interrogated me in a nice way, criticizing me quite harshly for not telling him about it sooner. Mr. White Owl never said anything to me about what he did, and I had no idea how he got the problems to stop, but I was very grateful just the same. I asked him about it, but he brushed my question aside and told me not to worry about it. After a week of not having problems with parts deliveries, I went back to getting them myself anyway. Having gotten a taste of getting things myself, I preferred it, much to the surprise of the store men.

The giant stylized portrait of the Communist couple in red that towered over the work area no longer held my hostile fascination. I wondered if its symbolic meanings had burrowed into my subconscious. Perhaps I was becoming institutionalized?

Questions and torture mingled with special moments in the madhouse during those first few months. My first payday was special, but the one that really meant something was my first payday that included a bonus for producing above the expected output band for my level. Every second Thursday afternoon just after knock-off time, the buzzer would sound loudly at three-thirty p.m. We'd line up in our work teams, and the paymaster would open a small internal window underneath the big red couple from which he would dole out the brown envelopes.

The whole factory was there, but it was very quiet. Nobody wanted to miss hearing their name being called. When I approached the paymaster's window, he made a notation in his ledger and handed me the extra-fat envelope. That very first payday bonus was incredible for the way the money felt in my hands. I squeezed the envelope so tightly and gave the cash inside a good sniff. The feeling of money in hand filled me with power and much determination to get another bonus. I felt strong enough to bend steel with my bare hands. I double- and triple-checked the name written in neat, flowing handwriting on the envelope. It really was my name, and it really was my pay and bonus. Maybe they hated me, but they still had to value what I'd produced and pay me for it. I tried as best I could to hide my smile, but I could scarcely conceal how happy I was. I got on my bike and peddled hard for the bakery. Instead of only one loaf of the cheapest bread, I bought two in the largest size, one crusty continental and one dark rye. I carefully counted the change, making sure I hadn't been short-changed, and couldn't wait to get home and hand Mum that bread.

"Today I got my first bonus pay," I said, handing her the brown paper bag loaded with two giant loaves. Mum was speechless as she took out a loaf. Putting her nose to the bread, she sniffed at it, and then took in a big whiff.

"It's not as good as the bread you make. Nothing could be that good, but with this, maybe you don't have to bake all the time."

Breaking open the loaf, she put a little in her mouth. Joy and skepticism swirled in her eyes. "Are you trying to make me lazy, child?" asked Mum with backhanded pride.

My eyes welled up at seeing her smile. Mum wasn't given to easy tears, but I could see she was teetering. Quickly regaining her composure, she gave me a hug. I hugged her back intensely. I think I would have gone through almost anything to get that bread for Mum. Tapping on the loaf she was holding, I said, "And when this is finished, I will buy more."

"So you really do want to make my baking redundant," joked Mum.

"I want to give you everything I can," I replied, happily.

"With this bread, I will make you lunch to take with you tomorrow," she said, her eyes twinkling.

From that first payday bonus onward, I was already planning bigger purchases. I could seriously contemplate more than occasional coffee, tea, sugar, and chocolate. Within reach could be pants, belts, dresses, shoes, socks, jumpers, jackets, even gunpowder. No one in my family ever asked for money or for me to buy them anything, but the prospect of being able to help filled me with such joy, they didn't need to. I was determined to provide as much as I could.

The only thing Dad bought to spoil himself was tobacco. Mum never spoiled herself, period. She was too skeptical for something as frivolous as bought conveniences. Dad almost cried when I bought him a pair of the finest-quality leather work boots. At first, he refused to wear them. He said they were too valuable, not just because of how much they cost and how long I'd worked to buy them but also because they were from me. After a while, I begged him to start wearing them. Once he finally started wearing them, he couldn't take them off.

Whatever I could see anyone in my family needed, I bought. It often took a little arguing to get them to accept things, but giving fulfilled me in ways I knew would stay with me forever. It made suffering the opposition at work easier. With pay coming in, there was less pressure on the farm. Best of all, Dad didn't have to contend with producing illicit hooch in volume.

Giving my all for my family felt good but giving my all at the madhouse still felt like something of a lie. Looking into the faces of other madhouse workers, it was obvious they were also lying. The bosses, all good Communists, were the biggest liars of all. What good could come of lies stacked endlessly on top of other lies? The madhouse was starting to give me a feel for where the country was headed. I wasn't about to ask any of my colleagues what they thought. To them, lofty questions were above my station. I didn't want to get caught up in interpersonal politics nor factory politics, so I avoided doing or saying anything, no matter how innocent or reasonable, at the risk it could be twisted into something provocative.

While I appreciated how supportive my family was, Mum was still demanding I quit. As long as I wanted the money, I had to keep working, keep tolerating, avoid the traps, and find small joys where I could.

After lunch one day, I found about a dozen radios on my bench and a note from Meduser. If she wasn't in my space and face, she was leaving notes, her way of trying to belittle me. Each radio had a red tag tied to it with a bit of string. Red tags were bad news. The units hadn't passed quality control and needed repairs. A red tag normally had some brief description of the problem, the batch number, and the unit number, along with the name of the person in quality control who'd checked the radio, and the assembler's name. Normally, radios with red tags would be sent back to the original assembler for rectification before they could go back to quality control for re-testing and hopefully, final clearance. My skin got clammy at the sight of so many red tags. Quivering with fear, my heart sank at the prospect of so many radios I'd assembled being sent back for disassembly, repair, and reassembly.

Apart from the drop in my numbers and the consequent drop in pay, the thought so much of my recent work wasn't up to snuff was gutting. I had become so careful and wondered how I could have missed making so many mistakes. Thinking perhaps some new way had been found to sabotage my work, I read Meduser's note: "You'll need to fix these before you can get back to your own work. Keep track of the names on each. Let me know when you're done." I breathlessly checked each red tag. None of the names listed were mine. These were not my radios! It took me a moment to realize she was expecting me to fix radios I hadn't assembled.

Meduser's demand I fix others' faulty work was so obviously against standard operating procedures, I was astounded at the audacity of it. She was effectively directing me to work extra for free, so others could be paid for work I did. I couldn't even really be sure how long it would take to pull them all down, confirm the faults, rectify, reassemble, and then resubmit for quality control. It could take ages, and there was every chance I'd find other problems, perhaps even placed intentionally. Contemplating the enormity of the task, I did my best to breathe and remain calm as a wave of anger swept its way through my entire body. *That bitch; how dare she!* Not only was her instruction unreasonable, but it was downright rude.

Until now, I'd not directly challenged anything, but this was a step too far. If I complied, not only would I be taking a massive pay cut, but I'd also be opening myself to further, more onerous requests. On the other hand, there'd be no guarantee things would go my way if

I challenged the instruction, notwithstanding standard procedures. *Breathe and think.*

Approaching Talking Smiley would put him in the position of having to defend the likes of me against someone he actually seemed to *like*—if that was the right word. And besides, he'd made it clear he didn't want me changing the dynamic. Olga was unfazed about Meduser's ongoing abuse, so appealing to her didn't seem like a promising option either. Making a formal complaint to one of the many worker relations representatives seemed laughable.

Taking a deep breath and having exhausted all the sensible options, my mind wandered to the silly solutions. Nothing else came to mind except going straight to Meduser and telling her I was not going to comply. That would be tantamount to an open declaration of war, going out with a bang. I wasn't sure what else to do. If I stayed polite, I could frame it, at least initially, as a request for clarification. It was flimsy, but that angle was the best I could think of. If I was going to lose my job, part of me wanted to give her a piece of my mind. *God, please help me to say what is right and best.*

Meduser's note in hand, I walked along the bench. From a distance, I could see Meduser working busily; Olga was sitting next to her, also working. My mouth dry, I swallowed a few times. Meduser ignored me. Olga glanced at me, looked at Meduser for a moment, and went back to her own work. Sensing Meduser was not going to acknowledge me unless I said something, I raised her note.

"Excuse me, Meduser, do you have a moment?"

She looked up, exasperated. Seeing the note, she looked across at Olga briefly and continued ignoring me. Olga shrugged her shoulders, the tiredness in her eyes almost enough to make me feel tired. Olga knew what was about to happen but was too old and worn-out to care. If she wasn't actively going to help me, at least she acknowledged my presence, which was more than a lot of others did.

"Meduser, I'm sorry to interrupt. I understand you wish me to fix the radios left at my workstation. However, our terms of employment stipulate each of us is responsible for repairing our own work when that work is not deemed satisfactory, as indicated by red tags. While it is not appropriate for me to fix others' work, I am happy to return the radios to each assembler. Once I've finished that, I'll certainly get straight back to work assembling my own units."

Walking away, I tried convincing myself I'd done it. I didn't get very far.

"Get back here," barked Meduser.

Meduser's tone stopped me in my tracks. She'd spoken to me harshly countless times, but this was different. It was like she was gargling gravel, her true spirit rising from the blackest pit of her bitter, bile-filled gut. She'd transformed, and I sensed the beast within her had been released. I knew the interaction I was about to have with her might get very fiery.

When I turned to face her, Meduser's eyes bristled with a mixture of rage and delight. Her nostrils flared in pulses like the veins in her neck. Her head tilted forward slightly like a bull making ready to charge. Her gaze locked onto me as she rose up off her stool, splayed her feet apart, and rested her clenched fists on her hips.

She'd obviously felt the day she'd been working toward so diligently had finally arrived, and she planned to enjoy her rage. I'd stirred her inner dragon, but for the first time, I could smell sulfur as hatred stirred in her guts like molten magma. I had no idea what I'd done to inspire such hatred, except exist and have the temerity to work. I couldn't understand her depth of feeling and had to admit it unnerved me. She would have killed me if she could have, but in that moment, I didn't want to let her see anything except a polite and respectful co-worker.

Doing my best to conceal my fear, I met her gaze and calmly walked toward her, stopping just out of arms' reach. The eager redness in her cheeks glowed all the more brightly with my approach. It seemed my willingness to look her in the eye only further aroused the beast, so I looked away frequently.

Breathing through the fear, I sensed something in her had given way, like she'd decided to finally give in to her desire to spew forth flames, even against her better judgment. As long as she didn't take a swipe at me with a stool or a tool of some kind, I had an uncanny feeling I still had a chance, in spite of expecting dragon flames were about to engulf me.

Meduser didn't disappoint, putting on quite a display. Her voice bellowed, shrieked, whizzed, and crackled like fireworks. "How *dare* you? Who do you think you are? You don't get to question anything here. You're not some kind of fucking Triestini princess, you little cow. You're just a shit-kicking worker. You don't tell me what to do! I tell you what to do!" And so on it went for what felt like an eternity.

Should I wipe her spittle off my face now or wait? I think I'll wait until she comes up for some air.

Letting her have at it, I took it all and held my ground. When she finished, I think she fully expected me to smolder away like some little cinder of charcoal and crumble into dusty nothingness. I think that's what everyone expected. She'd been going at it as hard as she could and mercifully stopped for a moment to catch her breath. From the look on her face as she huffed her way back to a semblance of composure, it wasn't certain whether she'd really had enough or was just refilling her boiler for another round of flame-throwing.

With the break in screechy transmission, I wiped Meduser's still-molten spittle off my face. Looking past Meduser to Olga, slack-jawed and mouth fully agape, I almost felt happy for Olga. For the first time in my experience, she looked very much alive and no longer so old or tired. I was glad she could still get excited about something.

Suddenly, I realized how quiet things were. It was quite a scene to behold people frozen, gawking at the carnage of a Triestini princess getting strips torn off her and then burned to a crisp. If this was what it was like being a Triestini princess, I was quite happy to leave it and just get back to work. So that's what I did.

Putting the note in my pocket, I turned and walked back to my workspace and proceeded to take each of the radios back to the assemblers listed on the red tickets. Each of the red ticket assemblers was surprised to see me delivering their radio back to them. Not one of them protested. What could they say? It was their workmanship, their red tag, and their responsibility to find and fix what was wrong. They knew it, I knew it, everybody knew it, and no dragon's huffing and puffing was going to change that. They could change the rules, but that would take time, and they'd have to say something to justify it, which Meduser had just made all the more difficult for them. Polite defiance it was then.

Half-expecting to get jumped from behind by an insane Meduser, I delivered the last of the suspect radios to the rightful repairer. I was barely back at my workstation when Talking Smiley, who'd no doubt witnessed the fracas, somberly directed me to follow him. As I marched behind, I could see Meduser sitting in his office, quietly steaming. He motioned for me to sit on the empty stool next to the dragon.

Watching intently as Talking Smiley took his seat, I mentally prepared for being fired and marched out. He rubbed his scrunched-up face with both hands, like a silverback gorilla unsure of what to do with two warring females in his troupe. The confused ape let out a long, heavy breath, and slouched in his seat uncomfortably, collecting his thoughts.

Talking Smiley looked across his desk at Meduser, exasperated. Turning my eyes as much as possible and my head as little as possible, I snuck a peek. She was less dragon, more scalded cat, desperate but still determined. She ignored me, firmly keeping her gaze on Talking Smiley, looking for a handle to swing him her way.

Raising his bushy eyebrows, Talking Smiley asked Meduser to explain.

"This girl is willfully disobedient, insubordinate, is impossible to teach, arrogant, and today created a disturbance causing a costly delay in the flow of work. You saw it yourself."

Meduser kept slinging insults and accusations, like a boxer swinging punches. Going for broke, she was putting her back into it, doing her best to knock me out for good.

I didn't interrupt. Talking Smiley seemed to be taking it all in without reacting.

Something weird happened. Instead of Meduser's complaining invigorating and energizing her, like it might if she were truthful, her emotions bled out, and she began to look spent. Talking Smiley gave her his full—if slightly impassive—attention. On any other day, he probably would have had no hesitation backing her, but even he didn't want to endorse her outburst. It was like he was reserving the right to cast her adrift if it suited his purposes, in spite of how hard she'd always worked to cultivate him. It must have disappointed her. Meduser's body withered as it registered his reservation as a kind of rejection.

I was expecting Talking Smiley to look angry, be angry, at me. Instead, he seemed surprisingly neutral. He didn't like that she'd let go control of her feelings.

As Meduser's blathering finally ground to a halt, she looked bleached and wrung out. She'd given it her all, but it was like her body knew it was all for naught. It dawned on me that staying true was more important than keeping my job. Meduser looked at me, expecting me to cave. She still didn't get it. Her mind hadn't realized what her body had been trying to tell her.

Talking Smiley gave me his full attention. My eyes met his gaze without shame and without expectation, not of support, nor approval. I hadn't attempted any cultivation. I'd made no investment other than work as hard as I could. If this was to be the end of my job, I could accept and face it with a clear conscience. All I was going to do was say my piece and let whatever was about to happen, happen.

"So Anja, I asked around while you were handing back the red-tagged radios. I just want to know from you, your side of it."

"You know factory policy regarding red tags better than I do. I respect that Meduser is my supervisor, and you are my boss. I know you're under pressure to keep production moving, and my job is to help you in that. I come here because I want to work as hard as I can, and because I want to learn. I look to people like you and Meduser to be my leaders and teachers. I want to have good working relationships with everyone. I especially look to Meduser, as my supervisor, to set the example of how to behave like a professional. Right now, I'm sad and confused because it's difficult for me to understand how Meduser's behavior today is professional or sets a good example. If others saw, perhaps they were also confused, but you already asked them, so you'd know more about that than me," I said, calmly.

Talking Smiley raised his eyebrows, seemingly surprised and impressed by my remarks. The mood shifted. I felt my position strengthening and turned in my chair to face Meduser, as if inviting her to respond.

Meduser looked annoyed. Perhaps it was dawning on her this was not going to go the way she'd envisioned when she'd written the note or when she'd first started flaring her nostrils. Her demeanor turned incandescent, like someone still confident they couldn't be hurt, even if being unreasonable.

"So what do you say to that, Meduser?" asked a curious Talking Smiley.

Meduser was white-hot. "I'm not listening to this shit," she har-rumphed and stormed off.

Talking Smiley allowed himself a brief but distinct smile, amused by the surprising turn of events. Sensing this wasn't going any further, at least not officially, I was relieved in part. For Meduser, the confrontation had been a loss of sorts, but for me, it was a draw at best. On the one hand, I'd successfully defended myself, but on the other, the thought that Meduser was able to get away with so much was concerning.

Sure enough, Talking Smiley dismissed me. "Okay, if that's it, you can go back to work," he said, as if nothing of any import had occurred. No double standard there!

Walking back to my workstation, I was happy at having come out of it with my job, but also angry that in order to survive, I'd had to put every foot right, while Meduser could afford to cross all sorts of lines with apparent impunity. I sensed my success at this juncture would never be forgiven by Meduser. She was certainly in the box seat in terms of thinking up new ways to torment me. As I'd expected, in the days following, Meduser, along with most of the team, stopped acknowledging me altogether. The atmosphere went from cold to deep freeze. At least ostracism and the occasional evil eye were nothing I hadn't already come across in my time at the madhouse. All instructions from Meduser were either delivered with extra terseness via a colleague or via further notes left on my part of the bench; no more notes about fixing others' red tags, though.

As far as hostilities went, in my gut I knew Meduser was far from done. I was right about it being a prelude to more conflict, but I could never have expected what happened next.

CHAPTER 20
PERFORMANCE BONUS

About a week after Meduser's outburst, early in the workday, Talking Smiley called a snap team meeting. Staying at the back, I kept as out of sight as possible. Talking Smiley announced that a secret productivity audit of the factory's entire production processes had just been completed. Apparently, the audit had been carried out by specialist consulting Party economic planners from Belgrade. They'd measured productivity down to the individual worker level, including radio assemblers. We were all to be given individualized written assessments of our performance as a means of motivating us to do better. Similar letters were being handed out to everyone in the factory. There were a lot of sullen faces. You could've heard a pin drop. Nobody spoke, except for a few people who swore ominously under their breath.

Talking Smiley grabbed a pile of letters from his desk and handed them out to each team member, including me. I looked at the envelope, my name neatly written on it. Everyone opened their envelopes and after a brief silence, people quickly started talking about their ratings. Not wanting to open mine, I instead watched others share their ratings, which varied from descriptions like "satisfactory" and "could do with improvement" to Olga, who received a rating of "good." Meduser's rating was "satisfactory."

People began dispersing until someone asked, "What'd the Triestini get?" Everyone in the team stopped and stared. The invisible deplorable had suddenly become the center of attention. I looked at Talking Smiley, partly in the vain hope he'd excuse me from participating. To my horror, he suggested I open my envelope. Reluctantly, I took out the letter and started to read to myself. An impatient Meduser lunged forward, her feet wide apart and her torso fully extended. She brought down her hand in a big swooping arc, snatching the letter out of my hands. The sound of her greedy hand slapping the paper, like a loud firecracker, startled me.

Meduser read quickly and loudly at first, then trailed off, ". . .for exemplary performance, and for achieving the top individual production figure over the audit period, you are awarded a financial bonus of. . ." She silently read what was presumably the amount but couldn't bring herself to say it out loud.

Clenching her hands into tight fists, Meduser tore my appraisal letter and violently threw the pieces to the floor. Turning to Talking Smiley, in a voice quivering through angry tears, she proclaimed, "You've got to be kidding me! How can she possibly deserve that? The rest of us have been here a lot longer."

Despite exploding, it looked like Meduser was holding so much more inside that desperately wanted out. There was complete silence, which in the madhouse was quite an odd sensation. Her eyes a mixture of anger and humiliation, she looked imploringly at Talking Smiley, as if accusing him of somehow causing this outrage and desperately begging him for an explanation. It was clear he had none to offer, not that any explanation would have sufficed. Before whatever dam was holding back her rage burst, Meduser stormed off. *Again, really?*

In the ensuing silence, I looked at the torn letter near my feet and dared not move.

"Back to work, everyone," said Talking Smiley.

Looking around, I was astonished at how many people had paused to witness the abuse. More eyes in more heads than I could count had taken time out of their day, not to help, but to gawk and feed Meduser's casual cruelty with their passive acceptance. To them, my continued humiliation was a sideshow, something to talk about over lunch.

Picking up the pieces of the letter, I felt numb and empty. Without bothering to read it, I flattened out the pieces, stacked them neatly on top of each other, and put them in my pocket, next to the lunch that I still carried. At my station, I buried myself in work.

Meduser's latest storming-off certainly caught me by surprise. The saga with the red tag storm-off I could kind of see coming, but this one was out of the blue. She was mature in years, but the way she snatched the letter, the sense of personal betrayal, throwing the letter and storming off—it was all so infantile. Such behavior from a grown woman seemed so surreal, an unfortunate segue into regression. I had to replay it over in my mind several times to be sure it was real.

If the strategy of handing out assessment letters was meant to inspire people, I don't think it worked. Somehow, management hadn't anticipated the potential for conflict. Maybe that was the whole point? Maybe management wanted people to argue and compete. If so, perhaps they'd got more than they'd bargained for. Was management demented, plain stupid, sadistic, or all the above? I felt some heated debate coming on at the next worker management meeting. Yet another meeting I had no interest in but was obligated to attend. The only meetings that had been of much use were my meetings with Mr. White Owl, and they'd become far fewer in recent times, much to my regret. I wanted to seek him out, just to say hello, share a smile, and ask him how he was doing, but I didn't want to make trouble, even if I could have found him.

Meduser didn't come back to the bench until just before finishing time. Who knew where she'd gone for most of the day. I wondered whether there would be any ramifications from her latest outburst. I was at least half wrong. Within forty-eight hours of her tantrum, she was no longer my supervisor. Talking Smiley pulled me into his "office" and told me henceforth, I'd be working with Olga. Naturally, I was happy, but Talking Smiley seemed annoyed at having to change anything. He'd told me all along he didn't want me changing the dynamic.

To some, my existence in the factory was upsetting or confronting or inconvenient or whatever. Whatever it was, it was impacting Meduser, and she, in her own manipulatively devious way, was reminding people, even if it meant having to put herself down. Her desperation meant everyone else had to see my unwanted success. As the outsider, it would always take less effort to blame me for any unpleasantness. Even if people could see I wasn't to blame, they'd still side with one of their own, especially if siding with me also put them in the moral and financial danger of being perceived as disloyal.

Just because I could see through Meduser's game didn't make it less effective. I'd changed the dynamic. I was breaking a ground rule set when I'd first arrived, impossible as it was to do otherwise. I couldn't expect people to be happy about it, even if they couldn't really say much to me about it.

Talking Smiley told me he'd directed Meduser to apologize to me and that I was to let him know if she didn't. I almost fell off my stool. To her credit, she approached me before she left for the day. She told me she'd been under a lot of stress lately, wasn't quite her normal self, and said she was sorry. She told me Olga would be a really good supervisor, and she wished me well working with Olga.

I didn't ask Meduser for any details about what exactly was causing her so much stress and didn't buy her apology, suspecting it had more to do with complying with an order rather than anything else. Perhaps there were repercussions for her after all?

Wanting to sound magnanimous, I thanked Meduser for being my supervisor and told her not to worry about what'd happened. I didn't find her convincing, just as I didn't find Talking Smiley convincing. She must have known giving me so many red tags was not only unfair and would cost me a big chunk of pay, but also put my job at risk. In Talking Smiley's case, I sensed he only stepped in because the attack on me had gotten too difficult to sweep under the carpet. He always seemed concerned with preserving his appearance of authority. If he had any concern for my welfare, he would have stepped in long before the red tags saga.

Turning to leave, Meduser made an off-the-cuff comment that immediately struck me as significant. "You know, Anja, factories like this can be lonely and dangerous places. If you give me your personal loyalty, I'll see to it that you're looked after."

I tried not to visibly balk at Meduser's offer. She'd barely finished apologizing, and not a few minutes later, she was threatening me all over again. My head was spinning, but not so much that I couldn't answer her. "Well, if I'm doing a good job in a decent workplace, that should be protection enough."

"Do you really think that's how life works?" she shot back, with a knowing smirk.

Meduser's response struck me as so instinctive as to be sincere. It was probably the most honest thing she'd ever said to me.

"Oh, really?" I asked rhetoricall. "Why don't you write me a letter describing how it really works, and I'll bring it to the next workers' meeting. Maybe we can discuss it there?"

Meduser snorted with bemused contempt. There'd be no reconciling with her, ever. We didn't talk much after that. She'd always remain an enemy, but at least she'd been brought to the point of having to speak to me as a peer, which is more than I'd ever expected of her.

Working with Olga quickly proved to be like a holiday compared to working directly for Meduser. Although fundamentally disinterested in me, Olga didn't actively appear to be plotting my downfall. Best of all, I was free to really focus on my work. All things considered, it was that blissful breather that gave me the strength to face an even greater challenge.

CHAPTER 21
SHADOW DANCE

Just when I'd stopped looking out for Janez, as I was heading for the bakery one day after finishing a madhouse shift, he suddenly reappeared, smiling, brimming with confidence. Dismounting my bicycle, I tried playing it cool. But I couldn't deny I was excited to see him. However, I was also upset with him for disappearing and for looking so happy. Truth be told, I was annoyed with myself at how happy I was to see him. I couldn't help it. In spite of our difficulties, we'd had so many exciting times dancing together and, if nothing else, I wanted more of that. I didn't want to scare him off, but neither did I want to give him the impression I was needy or easy.

"Friends of mine are putting on a barbeque dance in the forest this Sunday. When they invited me, the first person I thought of was you. I miss our dancing. I miss you. I know you have to go to work early on Monday, so I could pick you up and have you home before nine p.m. Would you come with me?" he asked, his eyes caressing mine tenderly.

The manly melody in his voice had me quietly swooning down to the soles of my boots. He sounded so sweet, and I adored hearing him say he'd missed me.

"I'd like to go dancing with you," I heard myself say before thinking about it, "but only if you let me pay for the petrol for your Vespa."

Janez laughed off my suggestion.

I'd never been to a dance in the forest before and couldn't understand the odd location until Janez revealed there'd be a lot of Western music and liquor. I couldn't afford to get in trouble, but Janez assured me it would be all right. Apparently, the events were a regular fixture for a select crowd. I'd have preferred if we'd simply gone back to dancing in his uncle's office, but I was worried if I protested or said no, I might not see him again, especially after the awkward way we'd parted last time. Convincing myself it would be all right, against my better judgment, I assured Janez I'd go. Janez left abruptly, happy I'd said yes, whereas I walked away from our meeting with a queasy feeling in my stomach. How would I explain it to Mum and Dad? Would they even let me go?

Later that evening over dinner, I told Mum and Dad I was planning to go to a dance on Sunday and that a friend from Sezana would be picking me up on his Vespa. To my shock, they hardly said anything, apart from suggesting I come home early. The path to excitement fully cleared only made me more nervous. Lina didn't need to ask the identity of my friend with the Vespa. Even if I wasn't entirely sure she believed nothing more than dancing had occurred thus far, her main priority was finding out if she could come to the next event.

It took an age for Sunday to arrive. I hadn't been able to think about much else for the whole week. At four p.m., all dressed up in my special Sunday clothes, and waiting in my room for Janez to arrive, I heard the sound of a Vespa pulling up outside. Lina and I raced to the window, and sure enough, there he was, dismounting his Vespa. We just about flew down the stairs to greet him. As quick as we were, by the time Lina and I raced downstairs, Janez was already seated at the kitchen table, chatting with Mum and Dad as Val looked on with sullen curiosity. The chit-chat was sparse. Mum looked displeased and Dad looked vacant. To my dismay, it was obvious they didn't approve of Janez. Brushing aside my concern, I introduced Janez to Lina.

To my relief, before long, Janez and I were on our way. I hadn't held Janez since the last time we danced together. It felt good to have my arms around him, clinging on while perched on the back of his Vespa.

About three quarters of the way to Sezana, we turned off the main road. Bouncing up and down on the Vespa, we slowly made our way up a winding dirt road until we came to a large clearing. There were quite a few cars, Vespas, bicycles, and—to my surprise—a few army trucks parked unevenly on one side of the clearing. Thinking we were going to be arrested, I tapped Janez on the shoulder, pointed to the trucks and asked if we were about to be rounded up. Janez laughed and told me not to worry.

The Vespa bounced its way to the other side of the clearing, stopping in front of a huge tent with a barbeque going just outside the entrance. People milling about turned to assess the latest arrivals. Comfortable we were partygoers rather than unwanted authorities, they got back to the business of socializing.

Traditional music emanated from the tent, competing with the noise from a large diesel generator perched on a nearby truck bed. Before venturing inside, Janez asked me to excuse him briefly and gestured for me to hang back. He approached a group of more mature-looking people, and there was a quick exchange of greetings. They looked slick, well-to-do, and held themselves with confidence; surely, they were from the city. Janez looked like a good-natured country boy but seemed very at ease in their company. Some of them stole glances at me, looked me up and down, and smirked. I'm sure they thought me a homely country girl, rather than one of the posh girls of substance from the city. I grew thankful Janez hadn't introduced me.

To my relief, Janez returned relatively quickly. "Sorry, Anja. They're a stuck-up bunch, but being family friends and my uncle's clients, best to stop and say hello. Let's go inside." It was so nice to feel the firm grip of his hand holding mine, I quickly forgave him.

Inside the tent, the tobacco-filled fog was so thick it obscured the top. Waving my hand, I tried making a breathable space out of the hot, filthy soup passing for air. I'd never seen a tent so big as to hold such a mass of people. Some fell about drunk, others sat at long trestle tables, eating, drinking, sweating, and shouting over the music from the folk band. I could hardly believe we hadn't heard the racket from the main road or that the whole thing hadn't caught fire. People chomped enthusiastically on their barbeque, washed down with rivers of beer.

The wooden dance floor was largely abandoned to those social stragglers who'd been squashed out of the main throng, forced to enjoy their own conversations with an unfashionably large amount of elbow room. I followed Janez closely as he approached a group seated at one of the crowded trestle tables. Janez slapped a man on the back, who turned as if ready for a fight. As I recoiled in fright, they exchanged hearty greetings, and people squeezed along, instantly making room for us.

Janez introduced me to a blur of strangers who indistinctly smeared themselves across my field of view. One by one, they spat out barely audible names, punctuated by the occasional handshake made greasy and wet from handling barbequed meat and cold beer. Their smiles, detached and no less greasy than the handshakes, emphasized the gulf between us. I didn't have a hope of retaining anything, not that it was a concern. They reminded me of the people I'd seen outside. Stylishly smug and attractive—these were the urbane elite. For them, eating with sticky fingers was a novelty. Their natural habitat was a world away from mine. Sniffing me out as not one of their own, they pretty much ignored me as the introductions passed. While they chatted with Janez, I did my best to look interested and couldn't have felt more invisible.

The snippets of conversational flotsam I caught made it clear they worked as professionals and were from families who'd raised them in comfort. They spoke as if socializing were a competitive sport and traded witticisms or anecdotes about their hired help or powerful friends like poker players throwing down winning hands. They droned on proudly about their latest purchases and family holidays along the Dalmatian coast, taking in the Bay of Kotor or staying in the Julian Alps. Communism was clearly no impediment to their class consciousness, at least not here, hidden in the forest where they could be themselves.

Hearing of their privileged world reminded me of Ivarn's description of his life before the state began his persecution. I doubted this lot would have impressed him, but he would have understood their desire to retreat into the woods to let their hair down. Ivarn had described how hired help, like plumbers or electricians, were often prized informers who'd use small cameras to surreptitiously take pictures of what was inside customers' flats and houses for the purposes of spying as they did their maintenance work. Pictures or personal letters, book collections, and the contents of medicine cabinets were favorite targets for prying open a window to people's thinking and weaknesses. All it took was a subversive turn of phrase in a letter or a suspect book languishing on a shelf to begin more intensive investigations. Rural living was hardly free of informers, but it was harder for them to hide in the hubbub of daily life.

Janez tried to rescue me by insisting I get my own fingers dirty with food and vino. I politely declined, which only seemed to be interpreted by his friends as defiance and an existential threat to the natural order of things. Suddenly, half the table was insisting I eat, mocking me and charming me in equal measure, as only the urbane rich do when offering crumbs to the rural poor. Janez, followed hotly by one of his female friends, left to fetch me something. Her desperate manner caught my eye. Janez's other friends went back to talking, their ignorance of me becoming more and more of a mercy.

Janez and his eager assistant eventually reappeared carrying jugs of vino and beer, and a platter of barbequed meat to share. After putting down the platter, Janez's friend ran a hand across his belly and kissed him on his cheek before returning to sit on the other side of the table. I stole several glances at her to help me gauge the significance of what I'd seen. The subtle tenderness and familiar intimacy in her touch and his attentiveness rang alarm bells. In my peripheral view, I noticed her glance darkly at me, and my gut told me to watch out. Doing my best not to provoke her, I looked away at the smoke from people's cigarettes wafting upward toward the electric lights hanging overhead. I couldn't help but contemplate how much putting on such a circus cost. Surely a king's ransom. These people looked like they could afford it.

With some trepidation and more than a little curiosity, I observed about half a dozen soldiers almost fall into the tent. They laughed as they juggled food and beer, while puffing away on cigarettes that hung so loosely from jabbering mouths, I was sure the ash they produced was becoming seasoning. I'd seen the army trucks outside so wasn't totally shocked at the sight of them, but it felt odd watching Communist soldiers mixing easily with the bourgeoisie. It made me think about how out of place I was. What was I doing here?

Janez suddenly again took an interest in me, turning and shifting closer. Under the table, the outside of his thigh pressed against mine. I leaned toward him slightly; the increasing pressure between our thighs felt nice. As he ate, his hypnotic eyes smiled at mine. Certain he could see my desire for him, I felt naked. Feeling a throbbing blush come on, I smiled and looked away. Putting his arm around me, he pulled me closer and whispered, "Soon that folk music will stop, the band will change instruments and start playing rockabilly. That will be our cue."

"I can hardly wait."

"I saw earlier you noticed the soldiers. They're friends. We supply them and their officers. Many are here out of uniform, with all the Western booze, cigarettes, food, and music they can handle for an evening, which is quite a lot, and they do all the logistics, setup, and tear-down. Setting up part of a field hospital and kitchen is a big job, but it makes for a fantastic night club, don't you think? With all the lights, bar, food, and people, you'd think we were in Hamburg on a Saturday night," he boasted.

To me, Hamburg was a universe away. I could only shrug and wait for the dancing to start. His revelations about his family importing booze, at scale, and ties to the military quietly rocked me. I instantly remembered how unimpressed Mum and Dad were with him and wondered if they knew. Before I had a chance to really take in these new facts, the band stopped, changing instruments to loud cheering from the crowd.

As the band started belting out Western rockabilly, people, including some drunken soldiers, wasted no time in filling the dance floor. Some did little more than jump around awkwardly while others had some idea how to swing and jive. It felt good seeing people enjoying themselves, even if they weren't my kind of people.

I didn't need much encouragement from Janez to get up and dance. I'd hardly spoken to anyone, and dancing was something I could sink my teeth into. Walking onto the dance floor, I could feel the sturdy wooden ply sheets flex under the giddy pounding of many happy feet. Janez and I joined hands, and in an instant, we too were stomping our way around the floor. Others soon figured out we were hot and got out of our way in a hurry as we swirled and twirled around.

Our bodies reveled in adlibbing from one crazy move to another as a gathering crowd let out excited yelps and shrieks. I was too busy to notice as Janez lifted me up high. In the groove, we gyrated, jumped, and spun and spun and spun as we cavorted around. Our moves, practiced in the small office, translated effortlessly. Setting those moves free on an open dancefloor was pure joy. Janez and I couldn't stop smiling at how liberating it was as we glanced cheekily into each other's wildly sparkling eyes. We zipped and zapped around, counterbalancing each other tightly while we swung around in bursts, one move effortlessly flowing into the next. Other dancers, along with many in the crowd, clapped us on. The appreciation made my heart soar. Song after song blended into each other. We just kept right on dancing, both of us perspiring profusely, his gorgeous skin glistening. As we kept on pounding away at that beautiful dance floor, we milked our freedom for all it was worth. The world beyond Janez and me was an inconsequential blur, as were all my worries.

The band transitioned into something slow, a lonely guitar ballad against lazy drums. Without skipping a beat, our bodies met. We held each other close and slinked around in a gentle rumba. My breathing deep and mellow, I melted against his firm chest and felt his pounding heart beating against mine. Pressing into his beautiful frame, I yearned for his firmness to know something of mine. Just as I was losing myself in the tenderness, Janez's movements became forceful, sending a frisson of anticipation through me as he telegraphed a change of pace. In an instant, he masterfully drove me into a cascade of aggressive tango moves. We sprang into a massive tango attack, invigorating every fiber of my being. Our frames like steel, our moves forceful, sharp, and angry, we slayed the floor with aggressive aplomb. Flourishes spent themselves naturally into something altogether calmer and soothing. Our white-water of dance resolved itself into sensual slides, welding the entire length of our torsos together in one long romantic con-summation of unbridled sensuality. We were in constant and utterly direct communication, our bodies flexing tightly together and our legs entwining rhythmically. It was incredibly arousing, and I relished that he knew he was driving me toward a blissful crisis. All too soon, the music stopped.

Coming back to earth, I lifted my head from Janez's chest and opened my eyes. Many dancers and a good part of the crowd looked in a kind of awe. There was wild applause, whistling, yelping, and cheering. It all erupted with such suddenness, I thought it might blow the roof clean off. Apart from singing, people had never looked at me like that before.

Janez said, "We've gone and done it now; we created something beautiful. You're beautiful and amazing," he said, as I desperately buried myself in his embrace.

Turning to the crowd, at the top of his lungs, Janez yelled, "And she can sing like an angel too!"

The crowd paused, again exploded with whistles and applause, and started chanting, "Sing! Sing! Sing!"

Janez fell to the floor laughing, taking me down with him. I just wanted to die!

I didn't know whether to laugh or cry at how ridiculous it was, but before I could complain, I was being lifted up high. Gasping for air, I screamed. Held aloft by a group of laughing soldiers, I was hoisted to a spot in front of the band. Dumbfounded, I gathered myself together as best I could as a microphone was brought out for me. Ignoring the mic, I tried to leave, but the crowd and the soldiers were having none of it.

With no easy escape, I straightened myself up. Singing without Lina wasn't something I was comfortable with, but I didn't want to come off a spoilsport. After a quick word with the band, I sang a couple of slow folk songs without putting too much into it. The crowd was very appreciative, and I did have a bit of fun. After a quick bow and thanking the band, I made my way off the stage only to have my path interrupted yet again. A couple of drunken soldiers got down on one knee and jokingly proposed marriage, much to the crowd's delight. Smiling politely, I sidestepped the proposal, well and truly glad to no longer be the center of attention.

At our table, glasses of wine appeared for Janez and me. Janez gulped and heartily slammed his empty glass down on the table while I sipped slowly. His friends hadn't really noticed me before, but their glances made it clear they were certainly aware of me now. Smiling and staring at me, partly suppressing surprise, partly impressed, but mainly judging. I smiled sweetly at Janez's eager assistant who was staring at me with even less generosity than before. Then I asked Janez the time. It was time to go.

Emerging into the fresh and dark evening air, we held hands tightly and headed away from the lights. Suddenly, someone called out, "Janez!"

I instantly recognized the silhouette as that of the girl, Janez's eager beer assistant. Asking me to wait, he doubled back. They exchanged words, and then she gently stroked his face, kissed him on the cheek, and walked back inside the tent.

"Sorry about that. Let's get you home."

I made a point of resisting temptation and not asking what was going on with her. On one level, it seemed obvious, but the last thing I wanted was to embarrass myself by jumping to conclusions and now didn't feel like the time to bring it up.

On his Vespa, we slowly rode back down the dirt road, the dim headlight barely lighting our way. All the way back to my house, I held onto Janez and couldn't stop thinking about how much fun I'd had but also about that girl. I'd wanted so much to kiss Janez tonight, and perhaps a little more. But after seeing that girl, I knew tonight wasn't the night and wondered whether any other night would be either. I wasn't sure whether to be angry at her, myself, Janez, or all of us.

The night air was fresh on the back of Janez's Vespa, but clinging tightly to him with my arms and squeezing him between my thighs made me warm. We pulled over just out of reach of the lights of home. I'd gotten so comfortable, getting off of his Vespa was difficult.

Resting my hands on Janez's broad shoulders, on tippy toes I kissed him twice on both cheeks, then promptly felt like kicking myself for not doing more. I didn't want to take my hands off his shoulders, which made us both laugh. Taking one of my hands in his, he kissed the back of my hand sweetly and smiled at me, a naughty look on his face. I thought he was about to move in for more but before I could respond, he said goodnight and made like he was about to ride off. It felt so awkward.

I stepped back to give him room, and he cranked up the Vespa and rode off into the night. I couldn't help wondering if he was heading back to the other girl. After I could no longer make out the lights of his Vespa, I walked home dejected and confused. From the way he'd held and kissed my hand and the way he'd smiled at me, I knew we'd see each other again. For the time being, I could live with that.

No one was up, so I went straight to my bedroom. Lina was sitting up in bed, pretending to read. I wanted to keep the depths of my desire for Janez and my concerns a secret. Fat chance of that. It hurt me to keep a secret from Lina, so I gave her an abridged version. She listened politely and told me to follow my heart and what I thought was best. I didn't want to hear it.

Some days later, one night while in bed, I woke in terrible fright at the sound of tapping on the bedroom window. Lina was still fast asleep, but I was transfixed at what looked like tiny stones bouncing off the window. Quietly I went to the window to see who or what was in our courtyard. The outline was unmistakably Janez. I waved at him, excitedly.

Janez motioned for me to come down. Turning to put on some clothes, Lina asked me what was going on. I apologized for waking her and told her not to worry.

"You're not seriously going down there?"

"I won't be long."

As I crept down the stairs, every tiny creak seemed as loud as an earthquake. Outside, I was so excited to see Janez I just about leaped into his arms. Rushing from the middle of the courtyard, we took refuge in the shadows.

"What are you doing coming here in the middle of the night?" I asked in a joyful whisper.

"I was out with friends and had an unstoppable urge to see you. You've stirred feelings of longing in me I never knew I could feel for another person." I listened as if to a revelation.

Coming in the middle of the night to profess his feelings was so bold it inspired in me the desire to be adventurous, but there was still a question burning inside of me.

"If you want to see me this badly, what feelings do you have for that girl at the dance?"

Janez looked confused for a moment. "Oh, you mean Stana," he said wearily. "Stana and I have known each other since we were little."

"And?"

"At one point, we started going together, but whatever feelings there were between us petered out long ago. She's a good person and a dear friend, but she has trouble letting go."

Unsatisfied, I retreated from his embrace. "Seeing how she was with you at the dance, it didn't look to me like her feelings were petering out."

Janez crouched a little, put his hands on my arms, and looked me straight in the eye. "You're the one I want to be with, Anja. Stana and I will always be friends, but it's you, Anja; you're the one, not Stana," he said firmly, as I searched his eyes, looking for truth in the dim light, craving authenticity as well as his touch. I wanted to ignore the feeling I wasn't getting either.

Janez pulled me into his warm embrace and kissed me passionately. Before I could figure out what to think next, I was overwhelmed. His kiss penetrated deep inside me, arousing me powerfully. My body tingled and oozed in his embrace, and Janez started to become ravenous. All thinking retreated as I returned his kiss forcefully.

Part of me wanted so much to turn him fully on so I could be totally devoured by his passion on the spot. Clawing at his body, Janez loosened the buckle on his trousers. Recalling where we were, I couldn't go on.

"Janez."

"It's all right, I know."

"I'm sorry."

"Don't be. You're right. We shouldn't here. I'm so happy now I know you want me as much as I want you. There's no need to rush."

We let go of each other and tidied ourselves up. To cement our mutual understanding, I pulled Janez toward me and kissed him sweetly on his lips.

"I'd better go, Anja, but I have an idea. If you leave a pebble in the corner of the windowsill of the bakery, I'll know you're free to meet me out here the same day, just after sundown," he said, reaching into his pocket and handing me one of the small stones he'd been throwing at the window.

"We can maybe go for a stroll in the moonlight and talk," he said in a devilish tone.

"Can't we do that at your uncle's office?"

"Things are a little too busy at the office, and besides, it'll be good for us to spend more time together rather than just hanging out at the bakery and dancing in my uncle's office. Once the busy period there is over, we can go back to dancing there as well."

It sounded wonderful if slightly strange. Nevertheless, I heartily agreed, excited we finally seemed to be on the right track. We kissed again before parting, and I watched him jog down the road into the night. Making my way inside, I heard the faint sound of a Vespa accelerate slowly as it went down the road. Upstairs, I crept into my bed.

Lina whispered, "That sure was a long drink of water."

"I was thirsty. Go back to sleep."

Getting as comfortable as I could in bed, I was still restless. I savored the taste of Janez still fresh in my mouth, my skin still tingling from his touch.

Over the next week, we met several times just outside my house after dark. I'd leave the little pebble in the corner of the bakery windowsill, and that evening, Janez would hand it back to me. At the bakery, I felt sure someone would notice what I was doing with the pebble, but no one ever said anything, and it seemed to work perfectly. For a while, that pebble became like my little talisman. At work, I'd put my hand in my pocket to feel the pebble and it would remind me of the times we'd already had together. Running the pebble between my fingers, I'd charge it up with hopes I didn't dare verbalize. That pebble became like a battery helping to power my dreams for the times yet to be for Janez and me. At night, Janez would ask me to hold out my hand. He'd place the warm pebble into my palm, then close my hand and tell me to make a wish before putting the pebble in my pocket. He never asked me what I wished for; I don't think he needed to. Then we'd chat as we'd go for a walk, and we'd kiss, just out of sight of the village. It was all so lovely, until one night.

As I'd done numerous times before, I snuck outside, delighted at seeing Janez in the woods nearby. I was looking forward to a quiet stroll and a warm embrace. As he approached, he looked eerily beautiful in the silvery moonlight. Butterflies furiously flapped about in my stomach at the sight of him. I'd been leaving the pebble out every few days but in truth, I wanted to see him every day. I thought about him a lot. Now here he was, so close, I could almost taste him as he came near.

We gazed into each other's eyes, and he handed me back the pebble as he'd done numerous times before. The sounds of the night were lively, as was the distant clanging of pots in the kitchen. Janez's eyes twinkled in the dim moonlight and the fringe of his hair hung down over his forehead as it was gently tossed about by a fresh breeze. We held hands, our fingers interlocking. It was magical. I wanted him to kiss me. I wanted him to touch me all over. I thought perhaps tonight would be the night for us to consummate our affections for one another, fully and without reservation.

As we turned toward the forest to begin what I thought would be a walk toward bliss, I was startled by the sound of someone walking briskly toward us. Dad's unmistakable figure rapidly loomed out of the darkness. I froze. Janez, also startled, took a step back. Dad had an incredibly nasty look on his face. He meant business, boy oh boy did he mean business. Dad glared at Janez like death himself was about to pounce. "Leave my daughter alone, you womanizer. I know what you are and why you're here. Get lost and don't ever come back, if you know what's good for you," said Dad, his eyes flashing like blazing disks of fury.

Dad didn't touch Janez, but it was clear he was ready for anything if anyone gave him any lip.

Janez was a strong lad, but even in the dim light, in the face of Dad's intensity, he stood stiff with fear. Janez, a rigid plank of pale whiteness, wasn't moving. I was shocked and horrified, frightened at what might happen.

An awful terror filled my chest as I turned to Dad. His eyes widened and with Janez not moving to leave, I felt like Dad was about to go over a tipping point. As Dad looked like he was about to leap onto Janez and mangle him, Janez collected himself and bounded off like a frightened animal. I couldn't blame Janez for running, but I was now so upset that I myself wasn't sure if I could contain my distress. Terror, shame, and the heartbreaking feeling I might never see Janez again swirled inside my head like a hurricane.

With Janez gone, Dad squared up to me. Feeling terrified and upset, I could hardly bring myself to look at him but could see his chest heaving with anger, his breathing heavy and forceful.

Dad held my arms, his hands gripping like strong talons, and shook me. "What do you think you're doing?" he demanded, restraining an intense rage.

I knew I wasn't supposed to be out here, about to get up to who knows what with a boy my parents hardly knew. It was all so terrible. I was already petrified, and Dad shook me again, this time harder.

"What do you think you were doing out here with that liar and selfish idiot?"

Limp in Dad's vise-like grip, all I could do was shake my head in fearful horror. Releasing one hand, he struck me on the face with an open palm, forcefully jerking my head to one side. As the stinging throbbing rose in my cheek and face, I came to the shocking realization Dad had slapped me. I knew he'd held back, but the violence of his strike was still plenty vehement; he wasn't mucking around. My body felt like it was turning to water from all the shame, hurt, and sorrow.

Dad was normally so calm. He'd never hit me before. It was my fault. My eyes welled up, and streams of tears ran down my numb face. I cried in heaving bursts of bitter sorrow, saliva running messily from my mouth, my tears running like a waterfall. I felt Dad's hands trembling, and he loosened his grip slightly.

I looked up at Dad in disbelief. He was on the verge of tears and looked as broken as I felt. He seemed so much smaller now. Instead of anger, all I could feel was love and anguish churning in my gut that I'd driven him to the end of his patience. Dad sobbed like he was tearing himself apart. He hung his head, and his hands shook. Pulling me into his chest, he put his arms around me, and we cried together. Dad leaned back, and we met each other's gaze.

"I'm sorry. I'm so sorry, my beautiful daughter. I don't know if you ever can, but please forgive me."

All I could think to do was gently stroke his cheek, wiping away as much of the wetness as I could. Dad searched the sky for understanding.

"Please don't cry, Daddy. I still love you."

"God, please forgive me. I'm so ashamed. I love you so much."

Squeezing Dad to me, I rested my head against his chest and yet more tears fell, this time softly and silently. As we clung tenderly to one another, the numbness in my cheek dissipated. It didn't hurt anywhere near as much as the sorrow in my heart. Dad took out a hanky and dabbed my face very gently, wiping the saliva from my chin.

Dad and I retreated into the house. Mum, Val, and Lina stood in the kitchen, their sad faces full of sympathy. Sitting at the table, Mum took some dried chamomile flowers from a jar and lit the stove to warm some water for tea. The making of tea signaled it was time for a debrief. Waiting for the water to boil, Mum regarded me with clear unhappiness.

"Did you not realize that idiot of a boy and his idiot friends had taken bets he was going to be the one to take your virginity?" she asked with incredulity.

"Not my Janez," I said, the words ringing hollow even as they came out of my mouth.

"Oh, really? Did you not realize he's got numerous girls on the go? I'm mortified you'd be among them," she said, venomously.

"But he's so nice."

"Until he gets what he wants. He's famous for womanizing, but not nearly famous enough, judging by your behavior," said Mum, anger turning to pity.

"But he told me he'd never felt about anyone the way he felt about me."

"My poor girl, you deserve better."

A penny began to drop. It was like I'd been tipped upside down. The shame I'd been taken for a ride, almost fully taken, stung harder than the slap from Dad. I fought the realization. Searching my mind for any memory of anything I'd done to justify him seeing me as something to use, I drew a blank.

"Do you not realize what kind of reputation you'd get, losing your virginity to a boy like that, outside in the street, in the night?" asked Mum, this time with more disappointed resignation than indignation.

I was utterly dejected that I'd almost driven my life into a ditch and so happily.

Putting the chamomile flowers into a large pot, Mum poured in the boiled water. The tea brewing, she got a mug for each of us and sliced up some lemon.

Mum sat at the table and said, "If he'd been able to have you, if you'd have given yourself to him, he'd have bragged to his friends, enlarged his own egotistical reputation at your expense, won his bets, and made you the object of ridicule. You'd have been branded a fool and a strumpet. Our family disgraced, your entire upbringing questioned, and no man with commitment on his mind would touch you. Defending whatever reputation you had left would be like trying to hold back the tide."

"I wasn't thinking."

"Don't for a minute think he would have committed to you. There's no way he'd give up the other women he's sleeping with, not after years and years of conquests, not with the habits he's acquired."

"How could I have been so silly?"

"You weren't the first, and you won't be the last. I understand; he's handsome and charming. His family is connected, and he's selfish. They see themselves as above people like us. To him, you would have been a bit of sport, wonderful fun memories maybe but still a plaything. Why ruin your future for someone so selfish? Just think if he'd gotten you pregnant. Count yourself lucky he didn't get you," she said, relieved, but still unhappy.

Mum put some lemon slices into each mug and then poured each of us some tea. After she poured tea, she put down the pot, kissed me on the top of my head, patted me gently on the back, and sighed as she sat at the table. I was still silent, still dejected.

"I can't believe I hit my own daughter," said Dad, burying his face in his hands.

"Never mind that; you saved her," said Mum. "She almost ruined herself tonight. Hopefully, it will help her remember her priorities and remember she shouldn't keep things like that a secret from her own family."

"How did you find out? If you knew what he was really like, why didn't you let me know before things got that far?" I asked, as sheepishly as I could.

Mum shot back, "Word gets around more than you might realize, young lady, especially about goings-on involving your womanizing friend."

Dad chimed in, "It was lucky he was bragging about you early on. A lot of people know about the only Triestini girl working at the radio factory. You both stick out, albeit for different reasons, so it wasn't hard to connect you. The only way you can learn to look after yourself is to do it. It's no good if we make all the decisions. We mostly didn't mind you dancing with him and guessed you'd keep things from going too far, eventually figuring him out for yourself. It was hard at times letting it continue. We didn't think he'd manage to start pulling you out of the house at night. That's when we really started to worry and watch things more closely. Even then, we still didn't want to interfere and risk driving you into his arms before you had a chance to figure out his intentions. We underestimated how far things would go. In a way, it's our fault for not confronting you earlier. Please understand we did what we did out of love for you," said Dad, through watery eyes.

"I'm sorry I let you down."

"You didn't let anyone down. We couldn't be prouder of you. All of us make mistakes, including Mum and me. Trust me, there'll be other dances and there are plenty of boys. Choose one that's right for you. If anything, I let you down by hitting you. I hope one day, maybe you can forgive me," said Dad, wiping his eyes.

"You should forgive yourself, Dad, because I sure do. I love you," I replied, giving him a hug. He cried, his chest heaving, both of us choking back tears.

Slurping our tea, somehow, we got to chatting about how much fun dancing was. I taught Val and Lina a few rock-and-roll steps, which they picked up quickly. Even Mum and Dad gave it a go, which made us all laugh.

CHAPTER 22

ROOM 105

The first snow of winter hit hard. That morning, opening the front door, lantern in hand, I was greeted by an overnight buildup to knee height. Filling the bucket with snow, I put it on the stove. After breakfast, it was quite a job getting the bike out of the barn. For the first kilometer to the factory, the snow was too thick to ride. I carried and dragged the bike as best I could. Stopping frequently to give my muscles a rest, I started freezing. There was little choice but to carry the pain as well as the bike. Luckily, it was a crisp, clear morning with no sleet. In the dark and through sparse clouds, the stars were still out in all their twinkling beauty. I imagined some were angels looking over me. No matter how often I'd seen them, I never failed to be awestruck at how thick they were in the sky. The wind, however, was not so beautiful—biting and sharp. My feet and hands froze while the rest of me sweated under heavy clothing.

Just when I thought I couldn't carry the bike anymore, the snow thinned out. The road was clear, apart from the occasional patch of black ice. As I mounted the bike, my arms and legs felt like jelly. Whenever I stopped to catch my breath, my feet and hands started burning like they were on fire. I had to keep moving.

I looked back down the road behind me, which quickly disappeared into blackness. But I could still see a pinpoint of light way off in the distance. It was moving about, as if being carried. Someone else was on the road, which was unusual at this time in this weather. Every so often, I stopped and looked over my shoulder. The light was there, keeping the same distance.

As daylight came, I turned to get a good look. It was another person on a bike, but as I'd stopped, so had they. When I stopped twice more in the morning light, twice more the other rider also stopped. There was no denying it—I was being followed. Perhaps I was hallucinating. I became frightened but wasn't sure what to do. The experience dogged me all day at work, always in the back of my mind.

The next morning, I was hypervigilant as I headed out on the road. No snow this time, but sure enough, after about a kilometer from home, I turned and there it was, the light. It didn't matter whether I pedaled harder or slower, the light was always the same distance away. Too far away to make out any details but close enough to keep up and observe. The next morning was the same routine. And again, the morning after that.

Whoever it was, was letting me know they were following. It was intimidating, but to what end? I was only an ordinary worker; it made no sense. I wondered whether it might somehow be related to Janez's party but couldn't imagine why.

For weeks, the routine continued, the only variation being the amount of snow. I often thought about it but didn't dare tell my parents lest they make me quit. Fear, frustration, and anger at being followed were frequent riding companions. I thought about confronting the mystery rider but wasn't sure how dangerous that might be. I'd even taken to carrying a small knife with me, just in case, even though I wasn't quite sure whether I'd actually have the strength to use it. As long as they kept their distance, I rationalized it was better not to escalate things.

There was no point explaining to my shadow rider I was just a simple farmer's daughter. Whatever innocence there was in this world once had long since died. After a while, my shadow rider became a part of the scenery. I was determined to not let whomever it was get in the way of me living my life and made a point of not changing my routine. I still needed to go to work, regardless of whatever mind games someone wanted to play. After a time, I stopped looking out for my shadow altogether. The deeper into winter it got, the more threatened I felt by the weather rather than some stranger. Some mornings, the snow outside our house in the morning was at chest height and there was no going anywhere. Even government agents and informers had to stay indoors if they wanted to avoid being frozen.

*

It'd been a while since I'd seen Mr. White Owl, until one day at the factory I saw him watching from a distance. As soon as he caught my gaze he disappeared into another part of the factory. After work, I hung back, expecting he'd show up after everyone else left. Sure enough, at my bench working, I felt a presence. Looking up, there he was.

"You're not leaving for the day?"

"I was just finishing up. It's nice to see a friendly face. How have you been keeping?"

As I smiled at him, he smiled back, and I felt he was genuinely happy to see me.

"Let me see your work. I'm curious to see how you've progressed."

Instinctively, I looked around to see if anyone was watching.

"Don't look around," he whispered, barely moving his lips, "you're being watched, more closely than usual. It's a test. I know you'll pass with flying colors."

"That's nice."

"Not really. You'll be offered a promotion. It'll sound good, but the new crowd will make your current workmates seem angelic. I came to warn you. Turn the promotion down, and you'll come under intense suspicion, but at least you can go back to the farm. Accept and you'll probably regret it. You've already achieved so much but think carefully about staying. All things considered, it may be safer for you to quit."

My eyes lost their focus and my jaw dropped as Mr. White Owl lovingly poured poison into my ears, after all he'd done to encourage and support me.

Holding up the partially assembled radio as if holding up a trophy, he proclaimed, "Very good, Anja. You've come a long way. If we had a factory full of workers like you, there'd be no end to what we could accomplish for our country. Keep up the good work!"

Gently placing the radio onto the workbench, Mr. White Owl equally gently placed a hand on the back of my shoulder. He'd never touched me before, and I felt the significance of it. He patted my shoulder, acknowledging the pain his tender warning was causing.

I wanted to hug Mr. White Owl, out of gratitude for the risk he'd taken in visiting me, out of sorrow at the prospect of losing my job, and at the thought I might never see him again. I dared not look at him directly. If I did, I was sure I'd want to embrace him and let my tears out.

"In all my years here, I've never been so proud to work with anyone as I am to have worked with you, Anja. By the way, it was a good thing you listened to your parents about that Janez lad. Good dancer but terribly self-centered. You can do better. Take care of yourself, kid," he said, letting his hand gently fall from my shoulder as he left. I was all alone, yet again.

Despite the realization my private life wasn't so private and that I might be in some danger, I did my best to remain composed. Clumsily, I gathered my things. As I rode home, the light of my shadow rider in the distant dark sent a shiver up my spine.

At home, more than ever, I made a point of not doing anything out of the ordinary. If I gave anything away, my parents would demand I resign immediately, which would have been understandable. I didn't want anyone demanding I do anything before I'd had a chance to think for myself.

The next day, I rode to work as usual, still unsure what to do, my shadow rider in tow. It was getting colder, but at least it didn't snow every day. I was still getting in quite early when barely anyone else was around. At my workstation, pulling out my stool, there was a note on the seat. I didn't like notes. With a furrowed brow, I reluctantly read it. Vultre wanted me to come to his office as soon as I got in. I put the note in my pocket, Mr. White Owl's advice screaming in my head as I made my way to Vultre's office.

Apart from my first morning at the factory, which now seemed so long ago, I hadn't spent much time in the senior executive offices. At this time of morning, going through the big metal door, past the pictures, and down the hall felt creepy, just like the first time. There was nothing to suggest anyone was there, except the light I could see coming from Vultre's office. The place felt like it was full of ghosts and skeletons, none of which I really wanted to see.

As soon as I stood in the doorway to Vultre's office, he looked up and smiled. Vultre wasted no time asking me to come in and sit down. Checking the hallway, he shut the door, as if our meeting was meant to be a secret.

"Anja, we haven't got much time before others arrive. We're setting up a taskforce spearheading a new miniaturization effort for certain national applications. You'll be part of a small team assembling prototype transformers for telecommunications equipment. Your goal will be to produce approximately fifty transformers each day. Staying within production tolerances will see you paid a base rate of eight thousand dinar per month, however, a bonus rate will apply to any transformers you're able to produce to the required standards above the target of fifty per day. The taskforce will probably last a few months, long enough to finalize process, unit, and management design, and roll out production at scale. If you do well, I might get you to participate in a trade fair later on and train supervisor types in assembly techniques so they can supervise mainstream production teams. You'd start right away, meaning you'd collect all your things and report to room 105 after this conversation. What do you say?" he said, smiling. If he'd had a tail, it would have been wagging.

"I quit."

Vultre's face went blank, all joy draining out of it.

"What are you talking about?" he asked, defensive at my

impertinence.

"I want to leave."

Vultre paused, trying to understand.

"If this is about money, the rates are fixed, no negotiation," he said, annoyed.

"It's not about the money."

Vultre's annoyance mixed with frustration. Perhaps he thought I might still be playing him.

"What do you mean, you want to leave? I'm offering you an incredible opportunity. You're not making sense," he said, swallowing his anger.

"I know I'm not welcome here. I've had enough," I said uneasily, sensing my response might only inflame him.

Vultre lifted a hand and slammed the palm down hard on his desk. The sharp cracking filled the little office like a massive clap of thunder. The sound startled and shook me even though I saw it coming. As if concerned his outburst might draw unwanted attention, he immediately regained his composure and held up his hands, signaling for me to remain calm despite his momentary lapse of control. The cogs in his head visibly turning, Vultre seemed to remember what I was referring to.

"Yes, ah, look, I'm aware of the troubles you've had since coming here. Believe me, quitting is not the right response, morally speaking, nor is it the profitable response. You're braver than that and smarter than that," he said, a hint of accusation in his tone.

"There's only so much a person can take," I said, sensing his frustration.

"Stop talking like that," he responded, in a more conciliatory but still insistent tone. "Look, I understand. You're not one of them. You know that. I know that. Everyone knows that. Triestinis have a hard time. I'll grant you that. Outwardly, some here may be nice to you. But instinctively, you'll always be thinking they hate you, and you might be right."

"They can afford to make mistakes and act like idiots, but I can't afford to do either."

"You're right, Anja. It's prejudice that goes right to the bone. It's no good anyone pretending it can change quickly."

"Or at all, ever."

"It takes trailblazers that keep coming back to set the example because they're tough enough to do it. Change takes generations, if it happens at all. The fact is, we're here now, and we all have to learn to make it work in whatever imperfect way we can. If you weren't so resilient, you wouldn't have made it this far. We still have a factory to run. I can't watch over every little thing and make everyone play nice all the time."

"I never asked anyone to baby me, but it's like I said, everyone has their limit."

"Look, taking this opportunity will be a lot like quitting, in ways that matter, but also a lot like staying in ways that matter. You'll enjoy better conditions, better pay, and better colleagues."

Vultre sensed I remained unconvinced.

"Can't you see you've already won? You beat them all. You've proven yourself, and now it's time for something better. You've earned it."

"How do I know what you're offering isn't worse?"

"Look, since coming here, you've impressed much more than anyone expected, and I don't mind saying I've stuck my neck out for you. Not just by giving you a job, but also in nominating you for this taskforce. I understand many have not been kind to you here, and it's understandable anyone in such circumstances may be tempted to leave. But this is not the time to give into temptation and reward others' prejudice and jealousy. This is not the time to undermine your achievement and negate your future prospects by leaving."

"Easy to say."

"I understand; you want to be the one to decide. I respect that. Okay, here's what we'll do. If at the end of the taskforce, you still want to leave, so be it. But for now, I want you to forget this feeling sorry for yourself nonsense. Gather your things, and report to room 105. Is that clear?" he asked, sounding both compassionate and annoyed. The feeling in his voice was more convincing than his arguments.

I wasn't sure why he was so desperate to have me on the taskforce. But I liked the idea of rising above my circumstances, like I could do more, be more, and get more for my family. Vultre stared at me intently, impatient for an answer.

"Okay," I said, vanquished, somewhat dazed, and still harboring mixed feelings.

"Right, off you go then," he said, with a mixture of relief and irritation. I went to leave and realized I had no idea where room 105 was, so I turned back to him to ask.

Vultre interjected, "It's in the sterile zone. Go to reception, ask whoever is there for room 105. One of the girls will show you. There's no need to say anything to Giuseppe or anyone else if they've already arrived this morning. Leave anything you're working on there in situ. Take whatever personal things you've left at your bench and go."

I hadn't even left Vultre's office before he was already reabsorbed by his paperwork, shaking his head like an exasperated parent.

CHAPTER 23

SECRETS AND CIGARETTES

When I arrived at my workstation, to my relief, no one else in my now ex-team was around. Not leaving behind any of my things, as Vultre had instructed, was as easy as picking up my overcoat, and I chided myself for even leaving that while I'd gone to see him. For all my mixed feelings, my feet skipped at the prospect of going to a new, higher-paying job, away from these people. Pressing Mr. White Owl's advice to the back of my mind, rationalizing it as an overblown concern, I made my way to reception.

"I've been told to report to room 105. Would you point me in the right direction, please?"

I'd be lying if I said I didn't feel just a little pleasure as the receptionist, the one who'd sworn at me, dropped her paperwork. Springing into action, she asked me to follow her. As she led me down an unfamiliar hallway, it felt like we were walking between walls around the outside of the main factory. Descending a long concrete staircase, we entered another hallway. Dimly lit, the floor, walls, and ceiling all looked roughly finished. The air was cold and damp. Moving through the concrete maze didn't give me a sense of moving up in the world.

At the end of the winding hallway was a most unassuming but very sturdy looking metal door. Instead of walking up to it, the receptionist stopped at a shallow groove in the floor, a few meters away from the door. She stood motionless. Unsure what to do, I finally asked if we were going to go through the door.

"This is as far as I go," she said before turning and walking briskly back up the hall from whence we'd come. After waiting a few moments, I gripped the cold metal doorknob and turned it slowly. On the other side was yet another hallway. At the end of the short straight hallway was a man, a soldier type sitting at a desk with a lamp and a telephone on it. He stared intently at me. Feeling like an idiot who didn't belong, I slowly closed the door behind me and gingerly made my way toward him.

A strange feeling tugged on the edges of my awareness. It wasn't just the odd situation or the guard; there was something else, something weird, something I'd not felt this strongly before. It was like there was an invisible someone—or something—in the hallway with us.

The guard—an older but rather thickset gentleman—fingered a gun on his hip while regarding me coldly. Desperately swallowing my cottonmouth, I told him I'd been told to report to room 105. Opening a desk drawer, he took out two thick paper cards and handed them to me. One of the cards was laminated in clear plastic and had a large length of looped string attached to it. There was a photo of me on it, my name, and a number written neatly underneath the photo. Rubbing the shiny plastic between my fingers, I wondered how they'd gotten my identity photo but thought it better not to ask. The other card had my name and another number on it but no photo.

The guard handed me two blank sheets of paper and told me to write my name neatly near the bottom and sign both sheets.

"Make sure to wear your photo identification at all times whenever you are in the sterile zone and hand it back to me whenever leaving."

The guard pointed to a thin wooden rack mounted on the wall next to where I was standing. I'd been so nervous, I hadn't even noticed it. The rack was full of little slits, most of which held cards that looked like mine. On one side, it had IN at the top and on the other side, it had OUT at the top.

"When you arrive, take your card from the OUT side and put it in the IN side. Find the empty slit with your number above it, and put the card into that slit, and wait for me to note the time before attempting to enter the sterile zone. The same for leaving. Got it?"

"Yes, sir."

"Wait while I telephone for someone to collect you."

Within moments, the door to the side of the guard's desk opened, and who should emerge but Mr. White Owl! My heart lifted immediately. Mr. White Owl spoke briefly to the guard, signed a ledger, and motioned for me to approach. It was only a few steps, but I just about leaped over to Mr. White Owl, doing my best to conceal my impatience to say hello. Smiling knowingly, he motioned for me to follow him.

"Hold on! I haven't finished the security briefing."

Both Mr. White Owl and I stopped in our tracks. Looking down his nose, the guard rose out of his chair to reveal he was at least six-and-a-half feet tall. I'd never seen an Italian-looking fellow who was taller. His mother must have mated with a giant.

In a stern voice sounding like it came from the bottom of a cave, he said, "Never take off your identification while you're in here. Anyone without identification clearly visible isn't far from getting shot. When you're not here, you don't talk about what you see, do, say, or hear in here. That includes your family, your friends, or your boyfriend. As far as outside people are concerned, your work hasn't changed, so there's no need for you to tell them anything's changed. If anyone starts asking questions, keep your mouth shut and report it to me. Take nothing out of here, and don't bring anything in you know shouldn't be here. Only do the work given to you. Only talk to your supervisor about the work given to you. Don't ask anyone any questions, and don't have any discussions unless your supervisor directs you to. It's against the rules for anyone to do or know anything that isn't directly related to the specific thing they're working on. If you see or hear anything that goes against the rules, you have to report it straight away. If you don't, we'll treat you as if you're the one breaking the rules. Stop carrying your lunch around in your pockets. I don't like seeing anyone around here with bulging pockets. Same goes for bags. Any personal items you don't need that day cannot come in. I can look in pockets, bags, or inside anything or anywhere else I want, any time I want, for any reason I want. Remember, you are never alone in here. If you break the rules, we'll find out. Just because you're young and pretty doesn't mean I won't shoot you if I catch you doing something wrong. Remember the papers you signed today. Got it?"

"Yes, sir."

"Good!"

His job done, the guard sat and swiveled his chair, turning his back on us. Mr. White Owl, seemingly oblivious to how shellshocked I was from the torrent of rules and easy threats, beckoned me round a ninety-degree bend into yet another hallway.

"Don't mind Mario; he's like that to all the new people. He's really quite nice once he gets used to you. Don't overly worry about the rules. We mostly stick to them. If you keep to yourself and come to me for anything you need, that should keep you out of trouble. Similar approach to the one you used to survive topside, so it shouldn't be too much of a stretch."

If Mr. White Owl was trying to lighten my mood a little, it wasn't working. As we continued walking, the weird feeling I'd felt after crossing that first doorway was getting stronger.

The guard, Mario, had mentioned the lunch I'd been carrying in my pockets and my so-called boyfriend. If he was referring to Janez, he certainly was not my boyfriend. I recalled the mysterious escort I'd collected on the way to and from work. I didn't exactly have anything to hide, but just how many others knew about my private life? The obligation to report or be reported—and being subjected to violence if I didn't—didn't fill me with warmth. Had I done the right thing in coming here?

"I thought we had an understanding that you leaving was for the best," ventured Mr. White Owl, snapping me gently back into the moment.

"Vultre rejected my resignation."

"Hmm, you obviously weren't forceful enough," said Mr. White

Owl, shrugging and giving me an understanding smile.

"What is this place?" I asked, as we rounded another ninety-degree bend to see another guard seated at another desk at the end.

"Whatever it ultimately is for you, you've already signed for it along with everything that comes with it."

It wasn't the kind of answer I was hoping for. The phone on the guard's desk rang twice, but she made no attempt to answer and waved us through. Even seated, the Teutonic blonde looked tall with her tightly-plaited hair. I imagined she and Mario had to be an item. Walking past, I noted the pistol on her hip and a hefty-looking, long gun leaning against the wall behind her desk, no doubt handy for killing a lot of people in a hurry. I'd seen too many guns in my life, especially that kind. Mr. White Owl opened another metal door to the side of the guard's desk, and we entered yet another hallway.

"The work will not be completely alien to you. Unlike topside, you'll see more foreign types. The focus here is on the work rather than ethnic or dare I say it, Party purity. But loyalty is still everything."

I was well acquainted with the meaning of my ethnicity but wondered how far the expectation of loyalty went. Signing blank papers and lots of guns suggested expectations went pretty far. The weird feeling from before yet again reasserted itself, only this time I could tell a little more about it, even if what I was feeling wasn't making any sense. There was something odd in this place, like a disembodied presence that somehow knew I was here. It was the strangest thing I think I'd ever felt.

"Since you didn't quit, we might as well make the best of things. If you're able to thread the needle, this could actually work out for you. More money, more interesting work, a modicum of acceptance, and even a bit of status. All things hungry, poor outsiders crave, especially talented ones. Admittedly, we don't often get singers in here."

"You're not going to ask me to sing, are you?"

"I won't, but I can't vouch for others," he said, laughing. "Between you and me, there was a bit of discussion about whether your propensity to perform indicated a craving for notoriety, but in your case, the risk seemed negligible. Besides, you've got what I sense is a special mindset."

"What mindset?"

"An ability to connect, with people mostly."

"Don't we all?"

"It could be an asset if developed."

For the first time, Mr. White Owl said something that irked me. I took it as an omen the rules here might involve me being used in some way I wouldn't be comfortable with but might find it hard to get out of. His reference to a special mindset was just plain silly, and I wasn't sure what connection he was on about. Did he really think I gave a shit about status?

Rounding another corner, we entered a big room. It looked like the basement of another factory. The floor area seemed slightly smaller than that of the previous factory but all underground, which amazed me.

"We're in the basement of a different building. You'll notice there's no propaganda on the walls. It should suit someone unconcerned with status."

Was he reading my mind?

Production sights and sounds still abounded, workbenches and people milled about, unrecognizable things were being assembled, but it was less frenetic and much quieter.

"Forget the frying pan, welcome to the fire, Anja," said Mr. White Owl, leaning in with a tinge of amusement.

Later that morning, I was assembling transformers at my new workbench in what felt like a parallel universe, strangely familiar yet also a world away. The transformers were tiny in comparison to what I'd been making before but much harder to put together well.

Within days, I was up to combining seventy-two individual parts for each transformer to produce a total of about seventy transformers each day. Working six days a week, the fifty transformers got me the base rate of eight thousand dinars per month. With the extra transformers at the bonus rate, I was making between twelve thousand to thirteen thousand dinars a month. It was more money than I'd ever earned before and more than a lot of people like me could hope to earn. However, I had no illusions about getting rich and said as much to another worker who'd engaged me in polite chit-chat about pay as we happened to walk into 105 together. However, something Mr. White Owl said later that day reminded me how the whole arrangement was too precarious for idle conversation.

"Is your Dad enjoying his new quality tobacco?" asked Mr. White Owl.

"How did you know about that?"

"I know a lot of things. Like how your Dad's tobacco and Rakia habits, his only real vices, are poisoning him slowly, but he enjoys them so much. I can understand how painful it must be for you, yet at the same time, you're enabling it. But to answer your question, the more personal or secret a thing is, the more intense the feelings about it, the more attention it attracts."

"I don't know what you're getting at."

"In time you will."

"Should I be offended, you know a thing like that?"

"I hope you're not. I know you love and are proud of your Dad more than anything. You have good reason to be. In fact, the whole village is proud of your Dad. Even before his work for the Italians and Americans, I know he'd saved a neighbor who'd suffered a heart attack. Your Dad was able to identify the man's condition, calm him, make him as comfortable as possible, give some aspirin, and send for a doctor. Simple, critical things that saved a life. When the Communists took over and came through your village, they made a point of assessing your Dad's influence among villagers. After everything your Dad has been through, it seems criminal to deny him his simple pleasures. Ironic a man who'd nursed so many to health, is slowly but surely killing himself through drinking and smoking."

"Why are you telling me this now?"

"I can see you've settled in nicely. But don't get too comfortable. Be wary of who you talk to, especially in here. Not everyone who engages you in small talk is doing it just because they're happy with the money. There're a lot of eyes on everyone in here and as this world is new to you, you need to keep your wits about you," he said.

I immediately twigged he was referring to the unnecessary conversation I'd had walking in. I couldn't quite tell if he was warning me or threatening me. Whichever, his advice had the desired effect, but I couldn't deny I was enjoying 105 much more than the regular factory.

Mr. White Owl's comments reminded me of the first time I handed Dad a generously sized pouch of quality tobacco I'd bought for him from money I'd earned at the factory.

"Why are you crying?" I asked Dad.

Holding the pouch of tobacco tightly, he finally admitted he was struggling to find the words to say *thank you*. I thought he was being sweet, but he told me he'd been keeping a secret from me about Grandma. She'd always told him off for how much he drank and smoked, but her concern didn't always seem to come from a loving place. It was like she wanted to control him. He told me he was crying because his own Mum didn't understand him half as well as his daughter. He was desperate to make sure I didn't feel controlled and smothered in the same way his mother had made him feel. He wanted me to make my own decisions in life, regardless of what he or Mum thought. Me buying him tobacco somehow proved to him I'd learned to do the right thing, even if it wasn't necessarily a good thing.

"This is the first time in my life anyone has ever bought me tobacco. I'm so lucky to have such a wonderful daughter, but there's something I have to tell you," he said to me, looking at the pouch in his hand.

I was so happy to hear him say the words; then he hit me with it.

"For years, Grandma needled me that you hadn't been fathered by me, but by my own father, your grandpa. I knew it was a lie, but it still cut me."

I couldn't put into words the shock and hurt.

If nothing else, Dad's admission put into context Grandma's treatment of me as a youngster. Now for the first time, I understood how far her meddling went. I'm not sure I'll ever understand the why of it but in a strange way, it felt good knowing.

It had taken Dad years to come to grips with Grandma's meddling, and in the end, he even refused to see her. It wasn't that he hated her, quite the opposite. It was his love for Grandma that she'd used to hurt him. Dad was always polite to her and respected her, but her behavior was too difficult to deal with. For all her poisonous machinations, she'd only succeeded in poisoning the one relationship most important to her. It was such a waste. And now, the daughter whose entrance into the world Dad had been encouraged to think was illegitimate and to feel shame over was the one earning to keep the family afloat and him in tobacco.

"We didn't see Grandma much, but I remember she was sharp as a pin and a wonderful woman, when she wanted to be," I said.

"Unfortunately, your Grandma drove everyone away."

"I still loved her. It was your forbearance as her son that taught me the importance of that. As she became old and frail and facing death, I was so glad to be by her side."

"My lovely Anja, you were the only one."

"As hard as it was to see her suffering, I was so grateful for the opportunity to be with her because in those latter times, I learned to see past her mistakes. It was only then she finally and truly became my Grandma. I remember holding her in my arms as she passed peacefully, the two of us alone in the same bedroom where she'd been born. Her passing broke my heart."

It's funny how the good and bad can flow into one another. Even though I'd been told off for having a simple chat over pay with a colleague, it almost seemed worthwhile for making me remember what was really important in life.

*

Not long after joining the taskforce, I had a strange and extraordinarily vivid dream. Walking, I looked at my hands and feet. They shimmered, and I knew I was dreaming. Even so, it seemed dreaming was more real than waking. At a serene pebble beach, I looked out toward the deep ocean. Out of the water came a dazzling sight: a unicorn ridden by a fairy. The unicorn and the fairy were also shimmering and sparkling in the light of the full moon, looking regal and resplendent. They looked at me briefly and rode off and up, across the night sky. Looking at my feet on the pebbles of the beach, there was a single glowing pebble. Picking it up, I woke.

Pondering my dream, I wrote it off as a poor farm girl's whimsy, but it was vivid and strange enough to stick with me into the day. Its enduring gift was the feeling something strange was about to happen.

The following day at work, a very strange thing did indeed happen. From the time I arrived, that weird feeling of the place itself knowing I was there was very strong. Mr. White Owl came to find me late morning.

"Want to see something very few people get to see?"

"Sure."

After having chided me for breaking the rules, I got the feeling Mr. White Owl was about to break some rules of his own. Leading me down a secluded hallway into a meeting room, he unlocked one of many filing cabinets, took a small wooden box, and put it on a small table in the middle of the room. Putting his hand into the box, he carefully lifted out a little black thing that fit into the palm of his hand. It was like a shiny piece of licorice, except it was somewhat translucent. The instant I saw it I knew it was something outside normal experience and sensed it was related to that weird feeling I often got while there. However, I felt whatever this thing was, it was just the tip of something much larger.

"What is it?"

"We think it's some kind of very powerful transformer. We're aiming to eventually produce something that is as close to it as possible," he said, amused at the audacity of his own suggestion.

"You 'think'. . .You mean you're not sure what it is?" I asked, surprised.

"We're still testing. So far, *transformer* is our best bet," he said, modestly.

"Where'd it come from?" I asked.

"Well, it's definitely from someplace and belonged to someone," he answered, seemingly unaware of how comical he sounded.

I wasn't sure if he wasn't allowed to tell me or couldn't tell me; it was difficult to tell. With Mr. White Owl, there was always a sense of things submerged.

"How long have you had it?"

Mr. White Owl immediately surprised with an admission. "A few years, I guess. The people who gave it to us weren't really sure what to make of it and were kind of relieved to get rid of it."

"What are you going to do with it?"

"Well, it's quite simple really. When we get stuff like this, specialists look at it, write up findings, and forget about it. When we can, we feed the findings into factories like the one attached to 105, to help with improvements."

Shockingly, he suggested I hold the item. Hesitant at first, I relented at his continued gentle encouragement, trepidation quickly replaced with a feeling of privilege. The object slipped easily into the palm of my hand, almost too easily, as if eager to feel my touch. Like nothing I'd ever felt before, it felt deep somehow, was hard, but also unusually light. Most bizarrely of all, I wasn't sure whether I was holding something made, grown, or alive, or that was once alive, or. . .I didn't know what. I couldn't place it. Yes, it was like this thing had been part of something that was alive at one point. It might be sleeping. It made no sense, but I felt an immense sense of responsibility in holding it. That weird feeling about the place itself knowing me in some way was all over me. After a time, I felt uncomfortable and handed the thing back to Mr. White Owl. To my relief, Mr. White Owl put the object back in the box and into the filing cabinet.

"Anja, I want you to share with me any ideas that come to mind, regardless of how unusual they seem, especially if they reoccur."

Laughing out loud at the suggestion a farm girl from Zana would have any ideas relevant to such work or any notion at all of how to produce such a thing, I could only shrug.

"Sometimes, the best ideas come from those whose minds haven't been ruined by the conformities of education."

The only idea coming to mind was that there was no way what we were doing was even close to making anything like that, but I didn't want to tell Mr. White Owl that, nor did I want to tell him about my other feelings of weirdness. Increasingly, I felt in danger at him having shown it to me. Even so, when I thought about how hard it was pounding away to combine parts together to make the transformers and how carefully it had to be done in order to make them durable and reliable, the little thing I'd just held in my hand struck me as simply amazing. It was so sleek and compact yet gave off a sense of depth and power. I could hardly begin to imagine how it had been crafted or come into being. I quietly marveled at how far ahead of us whomever made it must be. It was then my heart pounded with fear. I wondered again if it was a good idea for me to have ever seen it, and I was filled with a sense of impending doom.

Just when I thought things couldn't get any stranger, they did. There was a knock at the door, and a moment later, Mr. White Owl greeted a man, a priest—at least, he was dressed like a priest. Walking toward me, the priest smiled in recognition at my surprise at seeing such a person so deep inside a Communist facility.

Shaking my hand, in perfect Italian, the priest said, "Hello, I'm Father Passer. It's a pleasure to meet you. Tell me, where were you born?"

"Zana."

"Only the jug, not the wine. All were born before time," he responded, making no sense. Profound confusion mixed with that weird feeling bouncing away in my brain like a runaway ball. Again, I sensed this individual was somehow related to the feeling of a presence in this place but that he was only the tip of an unknown iceberg.

"Err, okay," I said, sensing correcting his nonsensical statement was pointless. It was the only thing I could think of saying.

In perfect Slovenian, he continued, "Congratulations on your promotion. Now you're walking a path here, you should consider yourself part of my flock. Call on me anytime you feel the need."

Noticing I was doing my best to stay composed, Mr. White Owl explained that in this place, people of faith were encouraged to stay close to their faith and that Father Passer was here to support me spiritually in any way I required. I listened, gob smacked, as the priest assured me I could talk to him at any time about anything. Handing me a small box, Father Passer suggested I open it.

Inside the box was a set of black rosary beads. "Those are for you," said Father Passer.

Concerned, I politely declined his gift, but it was no good. Father Passer politely kept insisting I accept, only relenting when I took the beads in hand. With that, Father Passer excused himself and left. Looking at the beads, I wondered if I understood what'd happened.

CHAPTER 24

TRUST THE PROCESS

For all the high-tech strangeness of my beginning in 105, the novelty wore off surprisingly quickly. What grew was the satisfaction. I got more income to spend on my family, developed my skills without interference, and worked more closely with Mr. White Owl, who'd already taught me so much. The rosary beads I'd been gifted felt foreign, so they stayed carefully hidden in a wardrobe in a downstairs guest room. I already had a set from Mum, which I rarely used but felt more like me. There was something about the rosary beads Father Passer had given me, beyond the circumstances in which I received them, that felt unusual, a faint echo of the artifact I'd held briefly.

One day, about an hour before the end of the workday, a bunch of guard types, led by Mario, came into 105 and fanned out around the perimeter until those of us working were all surrounded. Extra guards congregated at the entrances and exits. People instantly stopped work, stunned, as was I.

The guards were imposing enough in their stature and demeanor, but judging by the looks on people's faces, it was the number of pistols, rifles, long knives, machine guns, and grenades they carried that particularly focused everyone's attention. These soldiers looked hardened and tooled up for a fight. Much to everyone's chagrin, their attention was focused on us, the workers. 105 was a sizable place, but the number of armed soldiers in our underground location instantly shrank the space and induced a highly claustrophobic atmosphere. Bone-shaking fear quickly replaced initial surprise. Mr. White Owl was right; I should have run away while I'd had the chance. Now it was too late.

It wasn't looking good. Mario piped up, "Ladies and gentlemen, please excuse the interruption, and give me your full attention."

Mario was being way too modest, since a bunch of armed goons standing around a room was always going to get everyone's attention. He seemed to be enjoying himself a little too much.

"This operation is to be packed up, immediately. Down tools, visit the bathroom if needed, and quickly and thoroughly pack up everything you have been working on into crates that you see my colleagues are now bringing in."

His tone became stern as he ordered us to be meticulous in our packing, not talk unnecessarily, and to be quick about it.

105 was normally incredibly clean and tidy anyway, since we were not allowed to leave anything on benchtops at the end of each day. While we were opening up drawers and emptying shelves into the crates and boxes, the smell of vinegar and bleach filled the air. Some workers poured bottles of vinegar and crushed-up lemons into buckets. Others were pouring what smelled like bleach. Areas that had already been packed and cleared were being wiped down from top to bottom, and people were prevented from going back by armed guards.

"Those of you not moving with the project are to return to your previous locations and positions tomorrow and are not to speak of this place to anyone, at all, ever."

And that was it: a few words from Mario wound up everything just like that. Some people packed up, slowly, still not quite sure about whether we'd make it out of 105 alive, while others feverishly packed as quickly as they could. I was somewhere in between. Melancholy gripped me, not just because I figured my pay would go back down. 105 was much more enjoyable than my previous circumstances. The taskforce was being wound up just as I was getting started.

After a few brief months assembling transformers, attending meetings to discuss how to optimize production processes, and after getting used to much more independence, not to mention no longer having to carry my lunch around in my pockets, it was all over. I'd miss freely giving my opinions to people who seemed genuinely interested. I'd worked harder in 105 than at any other time before in the factory, and from the way others behaved, I imagined the same was true for most. Banging away at transformer parts, getting them in the right configuration, quickly, precisely, securing them in place, and then repeating the process all over again, was hard, repetitive, not to mention sweaty work. But getting into the rhythm of it, muscle memory would take over and thoughts quickly turned on how to improve things. It had a lot in common with harvesting crops once you got into the swing of it.

In 105, trying different things was encouraged. Collaborating, experimenting, and tinkering reminded me of what Dad constantly did to try to improve the farm. Nobody tried to tolerate or celebrate my ethnicity. We all addressed each other as professionals and simply focused on the work. There was a lot to like and miss about that. I was glad Mr. White Owl's initial concerns all seemed misplaced, but not wanting to jinx things, I never told him as much. The prospect of going back to my old area was not a welcome one.

While I was packing, Mr. White Owl came over and whispered in my ear, "Hang around once you've finished. We'll go to Vultre's office together."

"Am I in trouble?"

"Depends on your definition of trouble, but asking means you're starting to understand." *Not the reassurance I was after.*

It didn't take long for me to finish packing. Looking on as others finished packing and headed for the exit, handing in their passes as they left, I speculated about the reason for being kept behind. Perhaps Mr. White Owl showing me the strange artifact had gotten us into trouble.

My whole time at the factory I'd been doing my best to live by Dad's advice. Focusing on the work, I was polite and respectful, including to those who'd tried to bury me—not much fun at the time, but it felt better on the inside after the initial sting of the insults passed. I didn't bother responding to abuse unless it was absolutely necessary, spoke as little as possible, and constantly told myself it was only a temporary purgatory. Taking solace in survival against the odds was a huge victory, but 105 had taught me to be impatient for more. Dad had told me the best revenge was getting into a position where you no longer felt the need for it. If he'd been able to think like that after everything he'd been through, maybe I could as well. Dad's advice was good but putting it into practice wasn't easy.

Harder to bear than anything was the notion I'd never be able to talk to my family about 105. A lot of things, like being followed, I just couldn't burden them with. Anything done to me, they'd feel as least as much. Mum would only use it to verbally bludgeon me into quitting. Nobody was perfect, certainly not me. However, I thought I'd done my best at sticking to Dad's advice, especially after all the crap. At least I could share those paydays, and I didn't want to jeopardize that. The feeling of cash flowing through our home was glorious. The long bike rides were wearing and bitterly cold this time of year, but I was used to harshness. Perhaps in the future, I might even be able to afford a radio. How nice it would be to give Mum and Dad a radio so we could dance to the music. First, we needed electricity. Running water would also be nice. With Communists in charge, who knew when those things might happen?

Finally, 105 was almost empty, leaving only Mr. White Owl, Mario, some goons, and little old me, in vinegary and bleached silence. In that surreal moment, Mr. White Owl turned to me. "Are you curious to see where the crates have all disappeared to?"

"Sure, why not?" I was flabbergasted at my overly confident curiosity.

Mr. White Owl smiled approvingly as he motioned for me to follow him. We tagged behind Mario and his remaining goons as they moved, guns at the ready, toward the service entrance. I could have sworn they were expecting WWIII.

Moving through a large exit door and rounding a corner, we came upon a goods lift big enough to fit a small truck. Ascending toward fresher air, we emerged onto the ground floor of another warehouse. It was a hive of activity, busy soldiers loading crates onto trucks, yet more soldiers positioned near blacked-out windows. Mario and Mr. White Owl made their way toward the main entrance. I followed, terrified of getting left behind.

A soldier jogged up to Mario and Mr. White Owl. After a brief exchange, Mario gave a whistle and waved his hand about as if he were conducting an orchestra. There followed an intense burst of activity: men jumped onto trucks, truck doors and trays slammed shut, and engines fired up.

A soldier wearing a radio on his back suddenly emerged from a side entrance, spoke briefly with Mario, and then disappeared outside again. The big warehouse doors opened, colder outside air and the quickly waning afternoon light flooding in and mingling with the sickening smell of diesel as the trucks pulled out. The radioman reappeared and shadowed Mario along with several other guards as they moved to a smaller truck and piled in. Before long, they too disappeared into the fading afternoon as Mr. White Owl looked on. It was quite something to see so many dangerous men working with such rapid and well-rehearsed purpose.

Suddenly, men in workers' overalls appeared out of nowhere and headed for me. Thinking I was finished, I braced myself. Instead of grabbing me, they gently moved me aside and began shifting chairs, shelving, filing cabinets, portable workbenches, and everything else stacked against the wall near where we were standing. I was astonished there was so much furniture which, in all the excitement, I hadn't noticed even though I'd been standing right next to it. Many removalists' hands made light work of emptying out the remaining furniture. Without saying a word, the removalists closed up and locked the large doors. The last removalist to leave through the side entrance shut and locked the side door on his way out. Mr. White Owl smirked at my apparent disorientation at the commotion.

"Enjoy the show?"

"It all happened so quickly."

"Let's go." Our footsteps echoed as we made our way back the way we'd came. Mr. White Owl switched off lights as we went.

Back in 105, it now looked like a big empty room with a few sticks of lonely-looking furniture and a discarded newspaper that had somehow escaped the move or been left on purpose. The aroma of lemon vinegar and bleach was still fresh.

Mr. White Owl held out his hand. "You can give that to me now," he said, looking at the pass still dangling around my neck. Somewhat reluctantly, I handed it to him. He closed and locked the big double doors to the service entrance, and we walked back down the hallway that had been my regular entrance to 105. The guard desks were gone, even the big wooden wall-mounted cardholders were gone, only the cold foreboding dampness remained.

When we arrived at Vultre's office, the door was open. Vultre was hunched over his papers, the linoleum on the floor still falling apart. Mr. White Owl knocked lightly. Vultre looked up with a frown deeply chiseled into his face, annoyed at the disturbance. He quickly broke into a smile and motioned for us to come in.

"Anja, I've been looking forward to this," Vultre said, putting his glasses down. I looked at Mr. White Owl for reassurance, but he was watching Vultre as the man congratulated me. It made me suspicious.

"You've contributed to the achievement of taskforce goals. Your considered advice has helped us identify ways to reduce component breakage, use of consumables, and save assembly time. Your assemblies are consistently by far the most reliable. You're on time, rarely take sick days and, amazingly for a woman, don't gossip. It's fair to say you're one of the best—if not the best—radio assembler we've ever had in the history of this facility. Recognizing your high achieving is becoming a habit, of which I'm very glad. While it's not always possible to recognize good work overtly, I wanted to call you in to personally convey my thanks."

To me, Vultre's gushing only suggested things must be pretty bad.

"I agree entirely with Vultre's assessment," said Mr. White Owl, a massive grin on his face, a fact so disconcerting I did a double take. I was used to seeing Mr. White Owl smirk at me in frequent suggestions that I amused him but seeing him smile so much was unusual.

Reluctantly, I felt compelled to open my mouth without really knowing what might fall out of it, but before I could speak, Vultre continued, "There's a trade show in Zagreb next month. Diplomatic interlocuters and technical advisors, along with important Hungarian and East German wholesale clients will be there. Our delegation will only be staffed by our best. I want you on it."

"I don't quite know what to say."

"Once word of your participation spreads in the factory, you'll be envied and respected."

"But what could I possibly contribute?"

"You will demonstrate assembly to our valued partners and may have to field questions. Naturally, we'll also be there. In the meantime, you'd return to your previous team."

"Oh."

"No need for concern. Your duties would be to train others in the new production techniques we've sketched out. Even though you'd technically still be a junior, in reality you'd be the one giving the instructions. Who knows, do well at the trade fair and the training assignment, we might set you up as a quality controller. A lot of independence in that role," he said, dangling an undeniably welcome carrot.

It finally dawned on me what he was talking about, recalling some months ago he'd mentioned that I might be needed at a trade fair.

"Is attending a trade fair something you think you'd be able to handle?" asked Vultre.

"I'll do my best, but I don't speak German or Hungarian," I uttered, in a backhanded attempt to seem keen.

"Never mind. They'll bring interpreters. Is anything bothering you?" he asked from behind his bushy eyebrows.

"No," I said, sensing I should simply shut up.

"Excellent. Are we all good then?" he asked.

"Ah, fine," I said faintly, underwhelming even myself with the light reassurance of my answer. Vultre smiled a little smile of resignation, and I sensed his expectations being lowered. He continued showing his determination to remain optimistic. "Excellent. . ." Before he could finish the thought, there was a knock at the door.

Vultre promptly got up and opened the door. Swallowing a gasp, I immediately recognized the distinguished-looking man entering. It was the Party official who'd given the big propaganda speech at White Sunday. I hoped to God he didn't remember me, but as soon as he clapped eyes on me, he smiled like he'd just been given an early Christmas present. Presumably he didn't care for Christmas. Up close, the stylish, understated finery of his attire contrasted with the weather-beaten wrinkles on his face. He looked around Dad's age and appeared in good shape, like a man who'd known hard work, once upon a time.

The distinguished propagandist looked into my eyes with effortless, playful confidence and just enough intensity to communicate he was intrigued, but not so much as to suggest I was in danger, at least not immediately. He was already clearly probing with his eyes in an effort to entice me into a flirtatious exchange. His boldness and directness sat easily alongside the memory of his showmanship at White Sunday. This man was aware of his power and experienced in using it for his own enjoyment. However, he was not someone I wanted to know, which, from the eager introductions, didn't seem to matter to anyone present. I found myself reluctantly shaking hands with a man who introduced himself as Dragon.

Dragon seamlessly transitioned into a charming shark routine. "Vultre!" he shouted, "How long have you been hiding this vision of loveliness from me? How dare you! If I'd known the most beautiful woman with the most beautiful singing voice in Slovenia was working here, I'd have returned from the Belgrade Party congress sooner." The powerful man was being effusive but confirmation he'd remembered my singing was painfully embarrassing.

While Dragon's self-deprecating flirtations were flattering, I reminded myself I wasn't attracted. One of the downsides of singing was that, even if people enjoyed it, some thought of performers as little more than prostitutes. I didn't consider myself easy or a performer. Nevertheless, seeing a person of his stature effortlessly play the regal fool was almost endearing. I could appreciate he had real charisma and imagined many women would have gladly given themselves as a willing conquest.

I made the mistake of smirking at Dragon's comical performance, and he pounced. "There, you see, Vultre? She almost laughed. There's hope for an old man yet," he said, breaking into laughter while putting me on notice. As I blushed, Vultre and Mr. White Owl laughed.

To my relief, before long, I was ushered out of Vultre's office by Mr. White Owl. The next day, I arrived early back at my old workstation to be met by Mr. White Owl.

"Walk with me," he suggested. It soon became clear we were heading back to 105.

Mr. White Owl signaled for me to be quiet as he led me back up through the service entrance of 105. Once inside, he led me to a far wall away from any windows or doors.

"Many parts of the factory might as well have eyes and ears," he whispered.

Reaching inside his overcoat, he pulled out a folded-up newspaper and handed it to me.

"You should read it when you get home."

To my surprise, there was no further conversation. He simply suggested I make my own way back while he stayed and that it would be preferable to not let anyone see me emerging from the entrance hall to 105 if I could manage it. For the rest of the day, the newspaper burned a hole in my pocket.

Alone in my bedroom, I opened the newspaper to find a pale green envelope held to the inside by a large paperclip. Inside was nothing but four postcards with place names, some dinars, and a train timetable.

Looking at the timetable, I noted two entries on the same Sunday were underlined, the first train from Železniška postaja Sežana to Ljubljana and the last train back. The pictures were of the Tivolski grad and Cenkinov grad in Tivoli Park, the Grad Fužine, and the Glorieta Football stadium. The picture of the stadium had an entry ticket taped on the back. I didn't care much for sightseeing and hid the gift with the rosary beads.

On Sunday, I woke up early, telling myself I was looking forward to farm work, but I couldn't stop thinking about the postcards. Who was I kidding?

Getting changed, I made it just in time to catch the early train. For the whole trip, I told myself off for giving in to temptation.

Arriving in Ljubljana, I began taking in the sights on the postcards, wondering what, if anything, was supposed to happen. Despite the cold, I was constantly wondering what Mr. White Owl was playing at. My last stop was the stadium, which was abuzz with football fanatics.

As I took a seat inside among all the jostling people, someone immediately squeezed in next to me. Even under a heavy coat, scarf, and hat, I recognized it was Mr. White Owl in his stylish version of leisure wear. I was relieved but also apprehensive about what it was that necessitated meeting like this.

"Stay calm," he said.

My face leaked a wry smile at the suggestion.

"Have you enjoyed your sightseeing?"

"I'd be enjoying it more if I knew what was going on."

Chit-chat frustrated me at the best of times.

"It's relatively safer to chat here, as long as we keep our voices down."

It was quite noisy already, so I didn't think there was much chance of us being overheard.

Mr. White Owl relayed how Dragon's factory visit was no accident and that the taskforce had been moved to avoid him finding it. Apparently, Dragon's informants had tipped him off about the taskforce's location, leading him to stage the unannounced visit.

"So far, my own informants have been giving better tip-offs, which, not for the first time, afforded us a brief opportunity to move everything."

"If all you comrades are on the same side, why bother moving anything?"

"The Party faction to which Dragon belongs must be kept away from the taskforce."

"But why?"

"It has to do with the deeper purpose of the taskforce. You're better off not knowing."

"Haven't I already been through enough to be told?"

"What I can tell you is that administrative and bureaucratic fiefdoms, military, and other security organs are too often compromised. The ground on which taskforces operate moves like quicksand, so we often move them. Taskforces piggyback manufacturing, medical, or economic organizations. In this way, deeper parts remain hidden from the wrong people."

At the time, I was so fixated on what he wasn't telling me I couldn't really grasp the enormity of what he was telling me. I'll admit, I felt a little testy.

"So the tribal elders, their hands on all the levers, screw up the country while lining their pockets because they don't know how to share. Then it's left to outcasts, working in the dark, getting paid a relative pittance, to fix things. And if any good comes out of it, the profit and credit go to the same higher-ups who have been screwing things up, as if it was their idea all along. Now they're fighting over who's going to control it all. Is that what you're saying?"

"Interesting way to put it," said Mr. White Owl, "but yeah, that's about the size of it. I always knew you were smart. You've moved to a deeper layer of the onion, but you can't be part of this relocation because Dragon has taken too much of an interest in you already."

"What kind of interest?"

"You must understand, Dragon is dangerous. His ilk gets into bed with anyone. Trading hardware, data, favors, influence, pleasure, and whatever else takes their fancy. In his world, it's all on sale. As irredeemable social climbers, they might say they serve a higher purpose, but what they really want is power. Dragon is many things, but whatever he is, he can't be ignored. Taskforces survive, in part, because of the dirt they manage to get on people like Dragon. Hiding is the main game, dirt is the insurance. Dragon is constantly trying to infiltrate our network, get information to trade, and neutralize our insurance," said Mr. White Owl.

"But I'm just a girl on the shop floor; how does any of that involve me?"

"Like I said, he's taken an interest in you."

"Oh," I said, struggling to take in what Mr. White Owl was telling me. I began to understand why he'd insisted on meeting in such a peculiar way.

"How many taskforces are there?" I asked, trying to distract myself from the realization Dragon wanted me in some way I wasn't ready to imagine.

"Even if I knew, I couldn't tell you."

"How have you managed to survive?"

"By mixing truth and deception. We work out what people like Dragon want to believe, and we help them believe it while doing something different. When he suspected the factory, we left some crumbs pointing in the wrong direction while the real action gets sent elsewhere."

"If Dragon's so dangerous, why am I being left at the factory?"

"A lot of effort goes into security. Around us today is a team of people that made sure it was safe before I came to sit next to you. Don't bother looking; you won't see them. Having Dragon on your tail means moving you is too risky—for you and the taskforce."

For the first time, I wasn't finding Mr. White Owl convincing.

"Am I some kind of sacrificial offering while you all go elsewhere leaving him to do God knows what to me? I thought we were friends?"

I asked, feeling the ground collapsing.

Mr. White Owl seemed to express genuine, if limited, sympathy. "I understand your concern. I did suggest you quit while you still could."

"But I didn't listen."

"I understand giving up an income is hard. On the surface, you see a factory. You see radios. You see paperwork and people working. You see the job you do, the help you provide your family, and all the tribulations you've endured. All that is important, but there is also so much more going on. There are forces at work I cannot in good conscience tell you about."

"But if I'm to really understand what I'm dealing with, I need to know."

"Mistakes are too easy and too costly for me to reveal too much at this time."

Unsatisfied, I observed, "I know there's much you keep from me. I would've been happy on the farm, but thanks to the nationalization, farming isn't enough anymore." Hearing myself, I wondered whether the factory had changed me in ways that meant I couldn't be happy with farming anymore.

"I could see how hungry you were and how much you wanted to succeed, but with all the hostility, even with my help, you weren't going to make it where you were."

"If you helped me out of pity, I don't need it."

"It's got nothing to do with pity."

"Then what?"

"I was like you once, an outsider in need of a chance. In many ways, I always will be. I've noticed how skeptical you are whenever anyone recognizes your talent, and I can't blame you, but the fact is we can use people like you. So we made you part of 105's outer layer."

"You may call it the outer layer, but to me, it feels more like I'm bait."

"We thought you could contribute, and you have, admirably. It was all going so well. But alas, we can't control everything. We try to distract and influence Dragon, but we can't control him. His meeting you was not our design. With Dragon taking an interest, moving you is not worth the risk."

"But he knows nothing about me; how interested can he be?"

Mr. White Owl laughed. "Since when do men need to know anything beyond what they can see in order to be interested?"

"This is no time for jokes."

"I'd wager Dragon already knows you're not a Communist, that you're a good girl, and hopefully, he'll conclude you're not cut out for his interests. Still, he'll want to work out how you came to be working in the factory. If you suddenly turn up in some other place that will only make him chase more, possibly leading him to the taskforce."

"I don't want things escalating."

"You'll return to the factory and in time, you can quietly quit if they don't trump up some excuse to fire you first, or you can plow on as you were doing before. If Dragon decides you're no threat, he might even let you stay."

"So much for wanting to work."

"If you're interested, there may be other taskforces. I'd look forward to tapping you again if you'd like. You've already begun learning how to deal with what we do. We can always use another good operator we can trust."

"I like working, but I don't want to get involved in some kind of war I know nothing about. If you really want me to understand, you need to give me all the information, up front. Trust runs both ways. Just how dangerous is it that I'm being followed? Is that Dragon or you?"

"If it bothers you, I can look into it. They could be putting you on notice to be careful, or they could be hoping you'll panic and reveal something, or they could be working up to questioning or recruiting you. If they wanted to attack, you probably wouldn't see it coming, and it probably would have happened by now."

"That's not great comfort."

"Consider it part of the native fauna in the landscape you now inhabit. In our work, going too deep, too fast, is not the way. Best not to rush your learning process. All the more reason not to take unnecessary risks."

"I didn't ask for any of this when I applied for a job at the factory."

"I understand. Unfortunately, we're all dealing with things we didn't ask for."

"I'm just someone wanting to help support their family."

"And you're doing a fine job at it. Luckily for you, you have an aptitude, including today," he said encouragingly.

"I'm not convinced, and having to come all the way here to have a more open conversation doesn't inspire me with confidence."

"Your concern helps keep you sharp, and that brings us to the other reason I brought you here. Moving forward, it might be useful for us to communicate without having to go to today's level of inconvenience."

Mr. White Owl reached into his overcoat and pulled out a scrunched-up piece of paper. Leaning forward, he dropped the paper near my feet. His suggestion I pick up the litter after I'd tied my shoelaces struck me as ridiculous. The look on his face suggested he wasn't kidding. Doing as he asked, I could feel the ball of paper had something heavy and hard in it.

"A little awkward, but well done for your first time. You'd be surprised how tricky it can be doing simple things when the pressure is on."

I opened the paper. In the middle was an old-looking bolt.

"The top screws off in the opposite direction to the main thread to reveal a hollow, perfect for passing notes." I was back to getting notes. I didn't like notes.

"If, at work, you see a green coffee mug on the far-right side of the top shelf of the kitchenette nearest your workbench, go to the supply room, look for the shelf containing nuts and bolts and in the far-right corner, in the rear-most container of nuts, you'll find a bolt like the one I've given you. If you want to leave a message, leave it in the rear-most box of nuts on the far-left corner of the same shelf, and after using any cup to have a drink of water, leave the cup next to you on the workbench."

"What should do if all I want is to have a drink of water?"

Mr. White Owl raised his eyebrows. "Use a glass instead."

Apparently, once I'd mastered that process, he intended teaching me more secure variations. When I wasn't using the bolt, I had to keep it well-hidden. My collection of illicit items was growing.

Mr. White Owl then posed a question that caught me off guard. "Have you been practicing with the rosary beads?" he asked, with a skepticism suggesting he already knew the answer.

"Why does it matter?" I asked, defensively.

Mr. White Owl regarded me with exasperation. "You're Catholic. Use the beads."

"You're not Catholic, what do you care?"

"How do you know I'm not Catholic?"

"Are you?"

"What does it matter?"

"If you're so keen on those particular beads, you use them."

"But the beads were given to you. They're yours. Why are you so reluctant to use them?"

"They feel strange."

"How so?"

"When I hold them, they give off some kind of. . .I don't know."

"Say it. I won't laugh."

"It feels like electricity. But it makes no sense. Like that thing you gave me to hold out of the filing cabinet; it's weird."

"You'll get used to it. They'll help focus your prayers," suggested Mr. White Owl, cryptically. "Electromagnetic crystalline frequency amplification," he said, as if verbally hitting me over the head.

I had no idea what he was on about. From the factory, I had a vague understanding of frequencies and the like, but I couldn't understand how those things related to rosary beads.

He tried clarifying. "We all resonate with something. The beads help with resonance reception, storage, and transmission. They intensify quantum entanglement within the morphic potentiality field, opti-mizing interdimensional bridges between local manifestations and the infinitely numinous," he explained, making perfect sense to himself but precious little to me.

Realizing Mr. White Owl was serious, I wondered which of us was crazier, him for involving me in a murky bizarre world, or me for letting him.

"The beads are similar, but more basic than the thing you held in your hand. The design means gratitude, love, and devotion will power, tune, and target the device, the bridge, and your trajectory. The beads are no panacea, but they'll help get you started, like an alarm clock. The idea is to eventually not need them in your process of waking up."

"What do you mean?"

"Wake up to where you come from. When you sleep and dream, you're partially awake. It's normal waking life that's the dream."

"I don't understand."

"If we had more time, I might prescribe Ayahuasca to help you understand, but without appropriate support that may lead to transitory believing instead of knowing. For you, nutmeg might be better," he said, speculating to himself. I shook my head.

Sensing my disbelief, he became insistent. "Have you been recording your dreams?"

"No more than usual. They're so strange. How can I understand anything?"

"There's limited time. The physioeconomic oppression you rail against now is increasingly likely to modulate into more dangerous bureaucratically-invisible systems of consciousness manipulation. Defense requires deeper individuated connection with the divine and greater resonance with manifest liberty on the human dimension."

He was confusing me totally.

Giving up, he said, "Don't worry, you're Catholic; just use the beads like you know how. Focus on your faith to get you through. I hope you make it," he said, smiling reassuringly.

If only I could have shared Mr. White Owl's optimism. I at least appreciated his patience in talking to someone who didn't seem to get what he was on about.

The match over, the crowd began leaving. Nearing the entrance, Mr. White Owl leaned in. "Don't be too hard on yourself. It won't necessarily all come at once, or it might. You did good today; trust the process."

Before I could thank him, he'd disappeared into the crowd.

CHAPTER 25

VICTORY DANCE

Now that I was working in the regular factory again, the old fear of being hunted was back. But Vultre was right: people behaved differently toward me, even if I still got the impression most didn't particularly care for having a Triestini around. Perhaps I was different. I worked more thoughtfully but with less effort. In some ways, it reminded me of using the scythe on the farm. But while that environment was full of companionship and love, the factory reminded me of how alone I was there.

Vultre and Mr. White Owl had helped me beyond what I could have expected of people in their positions. But doubts lingered about their selflessness. 105 taught me to admit, at least to myself, that my motivations were also mixed. I wondered if I'd become overly attached to the satisfaction, independence, and money. To be sure, I was helping support my family, but time with family had been stolen, and that made me poorer. My attachment to work was increasing my tolerance for risk in ways that made my future less, rather than more, certain. At least I could now leave my lunch bag unattended. Perhaps that was progress of a kind. And for that I was grateful.

Those who had hated me before still gave me hateful looks, but there seemed to be, dare I say it, a certain respect. I enjoyed the responsibility of teaching others in the new production processes, and for a change, I was in charge. Daily, I found myself standing in front of a room full of colleagues, and all were required to listen. Some visibly chafed, but they knew the quickest way through was to learn and quietly endure.

Their suffering held no particular attraction. On the contrary, teaching felt like helping and helping felt good. It civilized and nourished all involved. In an environment full of stupidity, teaching from my own little corner, for the good, was a small oasis of sanity. For the first time, it was like I wasn't swallowing water while swimming against the tide. Unbeknownst to me, the rip was still there, I was just too naive to realize it was hidden in deeper interpersonal waters.

Talking Smiley, in spite of my best efforts, insisted on doing things his way, meaning the wrong way. He had a need to know how things should be done in order to supervise others, even if he wasn't going to be doing it himself. I didn't mind him challenging my views in class, but I did mind his not wanting to see reason. He fought me on everything.

Mr. White Owl suggested I talk to Vultre about Talking Smiley's opposition. Vultre's plan was for me to challenge Talking Smiley to a competition. Talking Smiley and his team could do the assembly his way while everyone else in the production area used the new approach. After a month, we'd see whose output generated more complaints from quality control and customers. If Talking Smiley's way worked out better, Vultre would authorize a reversion to old production methods.

Vultre left it to me to propose the competition to Talking Smiley at the next teaching session. He readily agreed, egged on by many. However, his condition for agreeing was my departure if he turned out to be right. I didn't bother arguing, with the lack of any expectation he'd resign if I turned out to be right. Unsurprisingly, Meduser as usual loudly aligned herself limpet-like with Talking Smiley.

Before agreeing to Talking Smiley's terms, I should have taken into account the probability of his team cheating. I needn't have been concerned, as Vultre had already re-engaged his management consultant colleagues to make sure there was no hanky-panky. A part of me wanted to believe Vultre had my back, but I suspected Vultre's own prestige was also on the line.

Thankfully, the contest was an anti-climax and over long before the month was out, a fact which particularly amused Mr. White Owl.

Matching product batch and serial numbers to finished units returned showed Talking Smiley's method was associated with the overwhelming majority of inferior units. I didn't rub anyone's nose in the result. Part of me wished I could have taken glee in victory, but the whole episode seemed an embarrassing waste. I'm not sure the validation counted for much. If anything, I was more hated than before. For once, my interests had coincided with senior management's. For me, the best thing coming out of the contest was Talking Smiley and Meduser avoiding me, even to the point of avoiding eye contact. Sweet treats indeed.

When I was buying bread at the bakery, Janez frequently crossed my mind. Both his behavior and his absence still hurt. The smell of warm loaves reminded me of why I was working, and I made a point of not letting what he'd tried to do to me get in my way. Part of me was warming to the promise of more permanent independence at work, even if it seemed too good to be true. Truth be told, part of me wanted to endure at the factory because I could. I now felt I had that power. Perhaps my ego was clouding my risk appreciation.

Proving I'd not been totally seduced, as the trade fair loomed, my aversion to it grew. I'd overheard other employees talking about the event in the kitchenette, at the lockers, in the bathroom. While they debated who'd be chosen for the delegation and cast bets accordingly, I looked for excuses that could keep me out of it. A high-profile role on a trade delegation didn't seem compatible with keeping under the radar or, more specifically, keeping under Dragon's radar. There was no overt indication Dragon was remotely interested in the event, but with foreign nationals involved, the potential was there for Dragon to be sniffing around.

In a moment of weakness, one night over dinner at home, I spilled the beans about the trade fair and the prospects of promotion should it go well. I was desperate for any ideas about how to get out of participating without losing my job. Amazingly, Mum was almost supportive.

"Of course, the big bosses like you. You're hardworking. You care about doing a good job. You're not a lazy Communist. But you should still leave. I bet most of the women who get promoted are bitches who mostly work with their mouths or on their backs. You're too good for that place and those people," she said, pounding the table with a determined fist, dinner fork in hand.

Dad gave me his compassionate look, as he often did when I talked about work, like he knew I was almost continuously in trouble I didn't want to talk about.

"How do you feel about it?" he asked.

"Uneasy. If I want to keep my job, I don't think I really have a choice."

"I'd bet you're one of the best workers they've had. You're young and thanks to Mother, you're also pretty. It figures they want to use you. Bosses use people; they're Communists, it's what they do. It's natural, like breathing. The higher the stakes, the more underhanded they are. If your bosses get scared you might take their job or that you'll look smarter than them, they'll hurt you. If you're promoted, you'll probably have to become a Communist, even if in name only."

"What do you think I should do?"

"If you want to stay at the factory, you're probably right about not having a choice about being on the trade delegation. But it's up to you, nobody else. You can always come back to the farm or you can look for work elsewhere. We love you. Whatever you want to do is all right with us."

"But we need the money, Dad."

"Don't worry about money. I know you like to help because you love us, but our love for each other is not based on money. We can survive. We always do," said Dad, kissing me on my forehead. I always felt so nourished by his affection.

The rest of the family was so happy at Dad's response, they applauded. I was frustrated at Dad's ability to put me at ease without answering my question.

"I'm going outside for a smoke," announced Dad, casually retrieving tobacco from the pantry. Both the tobacco and the pantry I helped keep stocked from pay I earned at the factory. Seeing him rifle through a full pantry was all the answer I needed.

With Dad outside, I asked Lina and Val, "So what do you think I should do?"

"I'm so proud of you," said Lina. "I miss you around the farm. We all do. It's not the same without you. Even so, it's amazing you're working in such a high position and whatever you decide to do, I'm completely in your corner."

"Are you kidding, Lina?" asked Val incredulously. "Anja should absolutely go to the trade fair. Anja, I think if you go, you'll be great. You'll be so great, I bet they'll write about you in one of those Communist workers' magazines. Sure, you'll mix with dirty, lazy scumbag Communists, but you'll get more respect."

"Okay, that's enough. It's time for bed," interjected Mum.

That night, in bed, unable to sleep, I turned things over in my mind endlessly. In the morning, I woke disturbed and drained. I couldn't shake the feeling I'd been running all night, like I'd been chased by something. Reassuring myself it was only the remnant of a bad dream, as I was in the bathroom washing my face, it came to me. I'd been chased by a dark figure. He was on foot but moved so fast. No matter how hard I pushed the pedals on my bike, he kept gaining. Somehow, he got in front, pulled a gun, and shot me in the chest. On my back, I felt warmth spread throughout my body as it lay against the cold snow. Looking up, I admired the beauty of snowflakes gently drifting downward and thought, *this is what it feels like to die.* There was no pain, except for a dull ache in my right hand. Lifting my hand, I noticed my index finger had almost been severed. A shiver of dread ran up my spine. My dreams had become so crazy since starting at the factory and that weird feeling from 105 was a frequent visitor.

Looking back at myself in the bathroom mirror, I had a minor epiphany. As I paid attention to my dreams, as I really looked at them, they looked back at me. My dreams were presenting my waking self with deeper information from a parallel existence, an existence more intimately connected with reality, but not as I thought I knew it.

I felt powerless to resist the feeling something was looming. In the dream, the threat felt like it was coming from outside, and I thought if I just pedaled hard enough, I might outrun it. But now I was awake, the threat felt like it was coming from deep inside, and I knew there was no way I could outrun my own feelings. I suddenly felt vulnerable. The dream was telling me I'd have to face whatever it was. It was just a matter of time. There was nothing for it but to keep pedaling. Digging the rosary beads out of hiding, I held them as I prayed. I knew I had to keep going to work, so that's what I did.

One Monday, just before lunch, Vultre came alongside my workbench and made polite small talk. As he droned on, a sinking feeling pounded my gut, and dream fragments blasted their way through my mind. The smell of gunpowder filled my nostrils, and my index finger ached. Feeling the threat catching up with me, I wanted to throw the half-finished radio I was working onto the floor, grab my bicycle, and disappear.

Vultre mentioned the trade fair was on Wednesday and made a point of loudly proclaiming I was being presented as the factory's star employee. I was sure others overhead and knew his support would quickly spread as gossip. No doubt, hateful minds would quickly incorporate salacious undertones, regardless of how baseless. When he finally finished gushing, I only said, "I'll do my best."

That afternoon, still on shift, a couple of colleagues walking past my bench congratulated me and wished me luck, which was out of character. I wasn't sure if they were making fun of me. I felt Talking Smiley's eyes on me, and looking over at him sitting at his desk, he dripped in insufferable self-satisfaction, as if he was in on something. The madhouse abounded with such petty moments. Colleagues emoting and talking around corners, not interested in—perhaps not even capable of—truth and being proud of it. So juvenile. Here, bullies didn't just rule the playground, they ran the school.

Being volunteered into the trade fair got me thinking about how far I'd come. I remained grateful to Vultre for the start, but part of me resented the pleasure he took in making unilateral decisions about me. It might be fun for bosses whose prerogative it is to pour perfumed poison into workers' ears, but we of the great unwashed had to suffer the consequences. In reality, bosses didn't care for quality if it didn't come with lightning speed. For them, speed with poor quality was only a problem if a customer was able to pin resulting faults on the factory. Even then, speed-obsessed management didn't wear the blame. It was the hapless worker, whose only sin was trying to keep up with insane demands.

For all the restrictions of 105, I'd been free to be as good at my job as I could be. In the rest of the madhouse, being good could be worse than being not good enough. It only took a hint of independent thinking from a worker for bosses to feel threatened. Independent thinking in underlings was dangerous because it made the boss look like they weren't in control. If the underling's thinking was good, it was intolerable because it made the boss look inferior as well as not in control. Good thinking from an underling who was also an outsider. Well, in the Communist system, that could be a death sentence.

Meduser's chief skill was the monotonous and repetitious application of cruelty so as to funnel downward production pressures while funneling up credit. Anytime I overheard her complain about pressure made me want to both laugh and puke. The dirty work of covering up bad decisions lay with workers. We were the ones who had no real control, despite all the meetings and workers' councils, and we were also the most vulnerable to abuse or to getting the boot. The pain of any adjustment was always pushed down so amoral sycophants like Meduser could be kept pleasantly pickled in beauty cream, hair spray, and other assorted bundles of cotton wool. The only real pressure of middle management seemed to be ensuring they were sucking up to seniors at least as much as the others. If nothing else, enhancing my independence and avoiding falling within Meduser and Talking Smiley's orbit again was motivation enough to give the trade fair my best shot.

Notwithstanding Vultre's description, I had no sense of what to expect at the trade fair. Just thinking about it made my stomach barrel roll. All I could think about was not wanting to stuff up and wanting it to be over as quickly as possible.

At home on the Tuesday night before the trade fair, nobody really talked much. We all pretended to busy ourselves with a kind of mundane chatter. I sought refuge in sitting by the fire, poking logs occasionally with a metal rod as if prodding my own thoughts to see if something less foreboding than dread of the trade fair would fall out.

As Mum darned shirts, Lina and Val played Briscola. The sense of Dad sitting intimately near seeped through my consciousness like a soothing balm. Breathing heavily through his hands as he rubbed the day's tiredness from his face, he said, "I'm off to bed. It'll be all right. But no matter what, to me, you're already a success. I'm proud of you."

Rubbing my back in gentle circles, he drew the tension right out of me. Too soon, he kissed me on the top of my head, and left for bed. In that moment, knowing I had his love, affection, and respect, I wasn't afraid of or needing to prove anything. It was effortless magic he had. Even when exhausted, he could conjure up a mix of tenderness and toughness that shone like the beacon of an immovable lighthouse on the edge of a vast, rolling sea of foreboding uncertainty engulfing me.

Before bed, I gave the rosary beads a workover, praying, thanking God for my wonderful family, promising I'd do my best to honor my parents, and that if any good came from the trade fair, I'd give all the glory of it to God and my parents.

*

In the pitch black of morning, even earlier than usual, I set off for the factory-madhouse. I wanted to give myself plenty of time to get ready and, more importantly, get a good look at how the cast of assorted monsters came together for their big carnival.

Every so often, I looked behind to see if anyone was following but saw no one. Winter was supposed to be easing, but this wind felt like it came straight from the Arctic. The super-chilled air tore at every inch of my flesh, like icy fangs ripping through the thickest layers of clothing covering my chattering bones. The further away I drew from Dad, the more acutely I felt intensifying chills of anxiety from which there was even less protection.

Something was not right.

During the night, I'd dreamed of being introduced to a man by a group of people who looked like strangers to me but who I felt somehow knew all about me. The man shook my hand and smiled at me, presenting himself a friend. When I looked at his shirt and trousers, they disappeared. Rather than a naked body, underneath was the uniform of a police officer. I suppose I should have felt safe. Suddenly feeling under an intense microscope, I smiled, hiding that I felt betrayed, spied upon, and like I wanted to run. I couldn't imagine how such a dream could be relevant to me this morning. Were dreams ever happy? *Keep pedaling.*

Suddenly, a sound like distant firecrackers filled the still, morning air. It'd been so long since I'd heard anything like it, I couldn't quite believe it. A second burst stopped me cold, even if it didn't seem aimed at me. A third put it beyond doubt. Automatic gunfire.

It was coming from way out in front, somewhere between me and my destination. Who knew what that was all about, but I didn't want to find out.

I could turn back and risk missing work or keep moving forward and risk gunfire, but it was too cold to stay still. As I looked over my shoulder, way off in the distance, a spec of light was visible. Straight away, I felt it was my shadow cyclist. This time, I sensed whomever it was wasn't keeping their distance but pedaling hard toward me. If they'd had any sense, they'd be pedaling in the opposite direction.

Out of nowhere, the sound of an engine revving hard boomed over me. Grabbing my bike, I legged it to get off the road in time. A van, lights off, sped past, narrowly missing me, seemingly fleeing the source of gunfire. The van suddenly screeched to a halt. A young man got out of the driver's side. Running to the back of the van, he flung open one of the rear doors and gestured for me to get in.

"They're shooting anything that moves," he said, the sound of another engine revving hard in the distance and getting louder.

"Who's shooting?" I asked, looking up the road at the headlights of the other distant vehicle getting brighter. Were they chasing or fleeing?

"Soldiers, who else?" he shot back.

"Who are you?" I asked of him, as a young girl appeared from the other side of the van. Even in the chaos, I could tell straight away they were farmers' kids, not at all unlike me. How did they get their hands on a van?

"They killed everyone. . ." screamed the girl, trembling. Running to her side, I managed to catch her just as she fell, falling apart.

"Are you coming or not?" asked the young man, insistent.

My bike and I slid helplessly all over the back of the van as it sped off, veering from one side of the road to the other, the young man struggling to operate the controls with anything approaching competence.

"The cowards came in the middle of the night to force us off the farm, told us they were taking us somewhere safe. What would they know about safe? They flashed some bullshit paperwork and Dad, along with a few workers, went for the pitchforks. They managed to give one of the bastards a good solid poke in the guts. Not long after, the shooting started. They just mowed everyone and everything down. . .Mum, Dad, Grandpa, Grandma, even the livestock," blurted out the young man, jerking at the wheel and crunching his way through gears and angry tears.

"Oh, my God. . .I'm so sorry," I said, horrified, both at the impossible terror they'd just experienced, and the realization that I'd made a grave mistake.

"Somehow, my sister here and I, we got to their van," he replied, strangely vacant.

"What are you going to do now?"

"We're heading for the border. Trieste is not far. If we're quick, we'll make it," said the girl, with near-hysterical optimism.

"We better let you out somewhere. At least you might be able to make a run for it," he said, looking at me in the rear-view to his sister's obvious disappointment.

"If we stop, they'll catch us. Besides, if need be, we'll use her to bargain our way across," she screeched, waving her hands frantically, one of which I could see now shakily held a pistol. My heart sank. She obviously didn't understand border guards. They'd have little hesitation in shooting all of us, and whomever was giving chase would have no hesitation lumping me in with whatever horror story had gone on before.

Just as they began to argue, the young man grabbed the gun. My heart sank even deeper. With both her hands, she tried to wrest the gun from her brother's grip. One hand on the wheel, the other frantically trying to control the gun, he struggled to keep control as the van swerved from one side of the road to the other. The gun swung wildly in their tussle. I wanted to jump out, but we were going too fast. Diving under the tarp, I held onto my bike as if that might offer some protection. I cried and prayed for a quick end to the madness, a miracle to get us across the border if it came to that, and Mum's forgiveness if I never saw her again. In an instant, a shot rang out. The van stopped swerving and everything went quiet, except for the road noise.

When I came out from underneath the tarp, the girl was slumped against the passenger window. I'm not ashamed to say I screamed at the sight of her in a mess.

The young man slammed a clenched fist against the wheel, choking back tears, desperate to cling onto a modicum of dignity but finding none.

"I'll let you out just before the border post comes into view. You should be able to make a run for it from there. I'm sorry we picked you up," he said, blankly.

"Please stop here," I asked, feeling sick at the smell of shooting and fresh blood.

"I can't."

"Someone's on the road!" I yelled, catching a glimpse of a cyclist.

Slamming on the brakes, the young man brought the van to a stop, wailing as he grabbed his sister's body and held her tenderly to his chest.

"You in the van, hands up!" came a disembodied order from outside.

Afforded no time for grieving, the young man yelled out in a mixture of frustration and sorrow as he thrust the pistol into view of whomever was barking orders, half-heartedly taking aim. It felt more like he wanted to provoke whomever it was into putting him out of his misery.

In a split second, multiple shots tore through the windscreen, relieving the young man of his anguish. The only sound now was that of my teeth chattering in my trembling body, all of which felt like jelly.

"Anja! Are you all right? Come out of the van," yelled a strangely familiar, shadowy figure visible through the cracked windshield. How did he know my name?

Holding my hands up as I moved to the rear of the van, I fumbled open a door and slid out, unsure if my wobbly legs still had the strength to hold me up. Outside was a man, casually holding onto a bicycle with one hand, a pistol pointed at me in the other. Even though I'd only ever observed him from a distance, I knew straight away his outline was that of the fellow who'd followed me so many times as I'd ridden to or from work.

"Don't shoot," I pleaded, struggling to get the words past my dry throat.

"You best be on your way; you're running late for work," came the nonsensical, somewhat parental reply, as he casually retrieved the tarp from the van and spread it out on the road like a picnic blanket before disappearing back into the van. Work? Work was the farthest thing from my mind.

My jaw slackened at the easy efficiency with which the killer dragged the young man's lifeless body from the van, laying it out on the tarp. As the killer emerged from the van with the young woman's body, I heard the thud of distant flapping. The flapping got louder very quickly until it became like a deep thumping I could feel in my chest. Whatever it was, it was closing in fast. In no time at all, I sensed whatever it was would hit me. I wanted to run but an urge I can't explain kept me rooted to the spot. I was about to scream when something brushed my shoulder. The contact only lasted a split second, yet it was a like a caress, a caress conveying massive strength behind the lightest touch. The image of a pinecone flashed across my mind. *Why?*

I ducked instinctively, and a huge owl whizzed past me to then swoop at the killer. Just as he was depositing the young woman's body onto the tarp, he saw the owl and ducked to avoid talons extended in a display of fearless dominance. Tracing a lazy arc upward, the silvery white owl came to rest on the high branch of a nearby tree. I was transfixed by the sight of it, seemingly coming out of nowhere. Looking at the killer, he appeared equal parts enthralled and taken aback at the interruption. All was silent, all was motionless, and time itself seemed to stop. The great owl just sat there watching us, dinner-plate eyes twinkling, its large, powerful body shimmering in the dim light. In contrast to us, our feathered friend seemed clothed in an air of effortless quiet majesty.

I looked down at the bodies on the tarp, pressed against each other in the gray moonlight. The girl lay on her side, her head resting on her brother's shoulder and her arm draped over his torso. In death, they looked at rest and in peace together, as if shedding their clothes of flesh had come as a sweet relief. Bloodstains aside, I could have sworn there was a kind of tenderness about them. If I hadn't known they were brother and sister, they could have looked like lovers. Their final moments had been filled with terror, no one to comfort, console, or help them.

While they were free of earthly struggles, I was not. It could easily have been me lying there. I still had a family. Where was their family now? Who would remember them, grieve for them? They'd been ruthlessly cut down in their prime for no good reason I could discern, and it angered me. For all their apparent recklessness, they'd deserved better. I wanted to look away, but I couldn't. I wanted to say a prayer, but I couldn't. I wanted to scream, but I couldn't. I wanted to do something but didn't know what. My stomach rolled and twisted itself into knots as I noticed the killer retrieve the pistol from the van.

"Who are you?" I asked, wondering if I was next.

"You look shaken up. Are you all right?" he asked, in a comforting tone, as if I had nothing to fear.

In seconds, a retinue of shouting soldiers arrived, guns drawn. My cyclist savior flashed some identification, and after a brief conversation with an officer, he came to me and smiled.

"If you can get those legs of yours pedaling, you can still make the trade fair."

As I looked at the carnage to which he seemed insensitive, my blood boiled and my legs stiffened, along with the rest of me.

"Thank you for saving my life, or sparing my life, but what are you going to do about them?" I said, breathlessly pointing at the bodies on the tarp.

"Those two are nothing, certainly nothing to you. Forget you ever met them. Forget you ever met me. Forget this little commotion. Get on your bike, and hurry along."

"But I can't unknow what just happened. They told me what was done to their family," I said, angrily pointing at the two so-called nothings on the tarp.

"They were enemies of the state. Their whole family were enemies of the state. They refused to vacate their land when ordered to do so, and they seriously wounded a state official who dutifully came to enforce the law."

"I may be a simple farmer's daughter, but I didn't come down in the last shower. When their family refused to let their land be stolen from them, these goons came for them in the middle of the night and set about slaughtering them, and those two kids, who you refer to as nothing, made a run for it. And now they're dead," I replied, shaking with incredulity.

"You remind me of my daughter when she gets angry—all feelings and forever jumping to conclusions. So those two spun you a story, so what. Were you there? What do you know, I mean, really?"

"I know some things. I know you follow me, and now you appear spraying bullets and flashing some kind of badge, and murder seems perfectly all right with you. You must be one of them. This is all bullshit. I don't care who you are. I can't go through what I've just been through and keep quiet. I'm going to talk about what happened to them, to their family, and about you. If you have a daughter, perhaps you're human. But I'm sorry, whatever kind of human you are, your daughter should be ashamed to have someone like you as a father," I said, pointing at him.

"Anja, disrespect, ingratitude, and talking wouldn't be healthy choices," he said, slapping me hard across my face.

I was frozen and still in shock as he pushed me onto the tarp and then pushed me down next to the lifeless bodies. Eyes wide with sheer terror, I struggled as best I could. In an instant he wrapped the tarp around my arms and legs tighter than a spider wrapping its web around its hapless prey. He took the pistol he'd retrieved from the van and gently pressed the tip of the barrel against my temple, "I don't want you to commit suicide, Anja. But that's exactly what you'd be doing if you merely keep talking about talking."

In that moment, I stopped struggling and could feel the tears running from my closed eyes as I said a prayer for myself and for the family I was sure I'd never see again.

"I'm going to let you get up, but you've got to get a grip."

As I came out from under the tarp, he helped me up as if he were a gentleman. Dusting myself off, I tried not to tremble at the fear and rage still coursing through my body.

"Who are you to talk to me about disrespect and ingratitude? Who is the state to talk to me about anything? I've met men like you before. You can shoot me if you want, but when you look at your daughter, perhaps it's my bloodied face you'll be seeing," I said, as calmly as possible, clutching at a straw of dignity and defiance through clenched teeth. He snorted at me with pity and disdain.

"Wake up! You might sleep there, but you're not really a farm girl anymore, so don't push your luck. Think of your future. Think of your family's future."

Something in his tone left me in no doubt he was threatening my family. I snapped. Lunging at him, I rained down blows upon him with all my might. "Leave my family alone! They've done nothing wrong!"

Waving away my fists as if they were flies, he grabbed my throat with one hand and squeezed. I looked, wide-eyed, for anything that might help me, but all I could see were his angry lips and glistening teeth that in that moment looked like the fangs of a ravenous bear. I clawed frantically at his arms and face as he spun me around and put a hold on me like nothing I'd ever experienced before.

"If you want to go before your time, I can make that happen for you, right here," he said, hissing into my ear through his clenched jaw and pressing the gun barrel hard against my temple. As I choked and squirmed in his grip, unable to breathe, my strength began leaving me, and I could feel a fog enveloping me. I began sobbing at the realization there was no justice, none for me, and not for anybody. Perhaps death wouldn't be so bad if it meant the pain and struggle could end. In the few moments I had left, all I could think about was how much I loved my family and how every moment with them on the farm was the most precious thing life had ever afforded me. Had I really given up my life on the farm? Was it that obvious? The farm was part of who I was. Had life pushed me away from myself, as surely as this man was now pushing the life out of my body? If I somehow survived this ordeal, could I go back to the farm, even if I wanted?

My soon-to-be-extinguished path seemed inexorably different from that of the rest of my family, but it didn't diminish my love for them. If anything, the differences only increased my appreciation of how much they meant to me. Did we really choose anything in this life? It felt like we were all just little cogs in someone else's clock, clicking away, never even knowing the time, our time.

Releasing my throat from his grip, he pushed me away. My body hungrily gulped air only to cough it out again in great convulsing spasms. Rubbing my throat as I steadied myself, slowly regaining my composure, I noticed all the goons had stopped what they'd been doing to watch the spectacle.

"It's been quite an evening, or in your case, morning. . .either way you'll stop shaking soon enough. It's just the adrenaline working its way through your system. Keep breathing, easy, steady breaths. In a little while, it'll be like nothing ever happened."

"You're far too modest. I can assure you I'll never forget. . ."

"Oh, I'm counting on it, and so best you," he said, pointing the pistol at me to emphasize his point. "Watching you, I've learned quite a bit about how your mind works, and I admire your spirit. I just hope you work out how this world works fast enough so you can find some way of staying in it."

"How caring of you."

Feeling my body still trembling, the realization of how close to death I'd come and how seemingly easy it was for someone to kill another human being hit me like a gut punch, just like it had during the war. That feeling of helplessness was all over me again. *Please God help me.*

"Don't cry, Anja. It's not personal. Like you, I'm just someone with a job to do," he said, slowly taking a step back and lowering the pistol. Seeing defeat in me, the goons dutifully went back to cleaning up.

"If you won't tell me who you are, at least tell me why you've been following me," I spluttered.

"Someone higher up obviously cares about you and wants to keep you around. Against the odds, you're still alive and still have a chance in life. Be happy with that and get on with what you need to do. You'd better be on your way."

You mean, cares about me, not for me.

"Can you at least give me your name?"

"Nobody, I'm just nobody," he said, an exasperated sigh casually escaping from behind his studied professionalism.

"Am I asking too many questions?"

He smothered a laugh, a glimmer of begrudging respect flashing across his face.

"Is this what we've become to those with authority over us? To have everything we work for taken away, the very life squeezed out of us, only to then be disposed of. All of us perfectly wrapped in the demands of our respective roles. No real choices and no good answers to simple questions."

"You've got more to say than most. I'll give you that much," he said with despondent thoughtfulness.

Was it unhappiness at his station in life? Did he really have a daughter? Was he displeased he was human enough to feel some response to me was warranted, even if lies were all someone in his line of work could offer in return? Or was he relieved his anonymity and ability to kill with impunity would shield him from having to face what he was?

I recoiled as he took out a switchblade which flashed and glistened in the dim moonlight. Grabbing one corner of the tarp, he plunged the knife into the material, cut out a small portion, and offered it to me.

"Here. Keep this as a memento, a reminder of how dark, lonely, and potentially short life can be. Serve power as it is, not as you expect it to be, and life will be easy, clear, and long. You might even enjoy a modicum of status."

"If all we do is serve power as it is, how will things ever change or improve for ordinary people?"

"Nobody with real power serves ordinary people, nor should they."

"All the guns in the world can't justify that statement."

"Ordinary people will always be ordinary. Rather than wasting resources on them, as much needs to be extracted from them as is possible."

"So everyone should just give up, is that it?"

"That's just how life is. Taking any other path only leads to pain. Look, hiding in the back of a van hurtling to nowhere quick or shivering under a tarp waiting for the end to come is no place for someone like you. But if you should find yourself there again, you'll only end up as worm food like those two, and you'll only have yourself to blame. Don't be afraid; go on, take it," he said, again offering me the cut bit of tarp.

Perhaps it was his way of telling me I wasn't going to talk my way around him. When I refused to accept his gift, he draped the material over my shoulder as one of the goons brought my bike to me.

As I pedaled away from the carnage as quickly as I could, the bit of tarp flew off my shoulder. When I looked back, I saw Nobody smiling at me, waving fondly. A chill ran up my spine. In that moment, I knew nothing and nobody would change, at least not easily, willingly, or happily. Life wasn't like that. We were all playing our roles, whether we liked it or not, buying time while we all tried to work something out before it was too late. Whether he realized it or not, Nobody had that in common with the rest of us. We were all in this mess, and things would just play themselves out regardless of what anyone said or thought they believed.

Part of me expected not to get more than a short distance before being shot myself. Just another loose end to be tidied up, my body to be picked over and dumped somewhere by vultures dressed in uniform. As if by their own accord, my legs and feet kept pedaling, faster and harder as I realized I'd been spared, for now, for some reason. Perhaps Nobody wasn't a total liar after all. I was broken but alive to fight another day. I was sure Nobody didn't know the whole story, and I wondered if anyone really knew what was going on anywhere. From Fascist occupation to Communist takeover. Different names. Different faces. Different books. Different war. But all the same lies. Same theft. Same starving masses, and all the same senseless mayhem. Perhaps only God knew, and will ever know, why. Even without the why, I wasn't ready to give up.

To me, the world was all wrong, but Nobody had one thing right. If I pedaled fast enough, at least I could make the trade fair. For now, at least, I'd have to be content with searching for a better life in the new world, rather than dying under a tarp in the old one.

www.ingramcontent.com/pod-product-compliance
Lightning Source LLC
Chambersburg PA
CBHW061657190726
48289CB00006B/1913